FORGET YOU EVER KNEW ME

FORGET YOU EVER KNEW ME

JUDY DAILEY

FIVE STAR

A part of Gale, Cengage Learning

GALE
CENGAGE Learning®

Farmington Hills, Mich • San Francisco • New York • Waterville, Maine
Meriden, Conn • Mason, Ohio • Chicago

GALE
CENGAGE Learning®

LIBRARY OF CONGRESS CATALOGING-IN-PUBLICATION DATA

Dailey, Judy.
    Forget you ever knew me / Judy Dailey. — First edition.
      pages ; cm
    ISBN 978-1-4328-2948-3 (hardcover) — ISBN 1-4328-2948-3 (hardcover)
    — ISBN 978-1-4328-2945-2 (ebook) — ISBN 1-4328-2945-9 (ebook)
    1. Physicians—Fiction. 2. Life change events—Fiction. I. Title.
PS3604.A3468F67 2014
813'.6—dc23   2014025069

First Edition. First Printing: November 2014
Find us on Facebook– https://www.facebook.com/FiveStarCengage
Visit our website– http://www.gale.cengage.com/fivestar/
Contact Five Star™ Publishing at FiveStar@cengage.com

ACKNOWLEDGMENTS

This book is a work of fiction. To the best of my ability, the events in this book accurately reflect the time periods in which it is set. Because parts of it occur during the Presidential elections of 1952 and 1992, there are occasional references to real people and to political parties active at the time. In every case, the quotes and actions attributed to those individuals and political parties are fictional. Readers interested in the history of health care in the United States may want to read *Health Care for Some: Rights and Rationing in the United States since 1930* by Beatrix Rebecca Hoffman, University of Chicago Press, Chicago, 2012. Any errors, of course, are mine.

Many people have contributed to this book. In particular, I would like to thank my parents, Beulah and Clarence M. Cobb, M.D., the librarians at the University of Washington, Clara Brown, Mary Buckham, Cathy Cobb, Mary Ellen Dennis, Judy Egner, Anna Fahey, Waverly Fitzgerald, Marie Friedericks, Dr. D. P. Lyle, Janet Reid, and the Tuesday Night Critique Group past and present: Keri Clark, Chris Danforth, Catherine Hendricks, Mike Munro, Mary Margaret Palmer, and Joe Stowitschek. This book would not have been possible without the support of my husband, Tom, and our writing dog, Gunner.

CHAPTER ONE:
ELLIE

I discovered only one suspicious death in Zillah, Indiana, in October 1952, that of Luther Pierce, a twenty-two-year-old veteran of the Korean War and janitor at the elementary school. Joe McCarthy was running for a second term that fall, and newspaper photos showed "I Like Ike" signs hanging from every silo and barn.

According to the *Zillah Courier,* Luther's body was found by the high school football coach on the two-lane road in front of the coach's farm. I never met Luther, but I do remember Coach Whittaker, a big, blond man with a weathered face and narrow eyes. He was revered in Zillah for a certain focused ruthlessness. The year I graduated, he led the football team to a series of lopsided victories: 35 to 3, 42 to 7, and a memorable 51 to 0. Whittaker wasn't content with a win. He had to grind his opponents into dust.

He was the kind of teacher who smacked a yardstick on your desk if you stared out the window and made kissing noises if you smiled at a boy. He tormented the slow kids and mocked the smart ones. Thirty years later, I can't think of him without a chill running along my bones.

On the morning of Luther's death, Whittaker pulled out of his driveway at seven and headed for the high school. Besides being a teacher, Whittaker was a conscientious farmer. I know he would have already milked his small herd of Jersey cows and opened the gate to their pasture. The chickens were fed, the hogs were slopped, and his wife had hung the first load of laundry on the clothesline in the backyard.

Whittaker stopped his pickup next to Luther's body, which lay in the middle of the road. He climbed out and studied the crumpled form of a young Negro man whose left arm ended in a healed stump above his elbow. Luther's neck was bent at an awkward angle. The side of his head was crushed. Blood stained his khaki work shirt. Tire tracks crisscrossed his jeans. A deep, black furrow ran from his groin to his thorax and obscured any other wounds.

Whittaker would have stepped back, satisfied. It looked like a clear case of hit and run. He heaved himself into the truck and angled it across the road to shield the body from further damage. Then he walked home to telephone the sheriff.

I imagine a morning sky, clear and shining blue, marred only by wisps of high cirrus clouds, angel wings that signaled a change in the weather. From his driveway, Whittaker could see for miles in every direction, across acres of stubble where corn had been harvested, past barns and orchards and outhouses. A line of willow trees traced the creek that meandered through his fields and flowed past the clock tower of Community Memorial Hospital. The hospital tower, taller than the surrounding church steeples, marked the outskirts of Zillah.

As he ambled to his house, Whittaker may have snagged a Gravenstein from the apple trees that lined his driveway, taken a few bites, and thrown the core into the bushes. He telephoned the sheriff, who in turn called my father, Bennett Kendall, the county coroner. That post, largely ceremonial, paid ninety-eight dollars a month.

By the time my father arrived at the scene, sheriff's deputies were stationed at each intersection. He parked his car parallel to Whittaker's pickup, bracketing the crumpled body between the two vehicles.

Already the temperature was climbing. It was going to be one of those Indian summer days when the sun softened the asphalt underfoot and mirages shimmered above the road.

I can picture my father squatting next to Luther's body and examining it from all angles. He would have probed the gash and sniffed for alcohol before talking to the sheriff. He may have said the wound was consistent with the victim being struck by a flatbed truck. He may have commented on the surprising lack of blood. I don't know. It's not in the official report.

My father did pronounce Luther dead. He confirmed his identity—Luther Pierce was the only one-armed black man in the county after all—and supervised transferring the remains to the hospital morgue.

According to the sheriff's notes, Luther's body was moved less than thirty minutes after Whittaker found it. The coach missed breakfast with the football booster club, but he was sitting at his desk in the biology lab before the start of second period.

Years later, I found the newspaper account of Luther's death hidden in my father's attic. Someone—my father?—had crossed out the words "struck and killed by a vehicle." But my father never openly disputed the official story of Luther's death.

A silent, self-contained man, my father spent long hours alone, locked in his study. I grew up thinking he hated me, hated his wife, hated living in Zillah. Following his death, I understood my father's ruling passion for what it was—a deep, bone-wrenching grief—but by then it was too late to love him.

I don't know if my father stayed at the scene of Luther's death after the sheriff left. He may have followed the trail of dried blood to the field where the cows grazed, or he may have rubbed out the footprints in the dirt lane between the pasture and the road.

I don't know if he found the bullet lodged in Luther's heart

9

either, but I suspect he did. For all his faults, my father was a competent physician. But not as good as my mother.

Chapter Two:
Maggie

Chicago, Illinois. August 15, 1952

First, do no harm.

Maggie Kendall climbed the tenement's narrow stairs to the third-floor apartment. It was close to sunset. The day's heat and humidity hung in the stairwell like a flannel blanket, holding in the smell of fatback and boiled greens.

Straightening her shirtwaist dress, Maggie knocked briskly on the Johnsons' door. Behind her, Nurse Franklin toiled up the last few steps, her breath a harsh rumble.

Maggie wished a different nurse had been on call when Mr. Johnson telephoned the clinic, someone younger and more flexible. Gwendolyn Franklin proclaimed herself a nurse "of the old school," by which she meant male doctors, anesthesia at the first sign of labor, and payment in full before the coloreds took their babies home.

The bare pine boards on the landing groaned as the nurse paused to wipe her cheeks and adjust her starched cap. Maggie repressed a sigh. The older woman was welcome to her opinions as long as they didn't interfere with her work. But why in the world had she taken a job at the Maxwell Street Clinic? And for her to assist at this delivery! If anything went wrong, it would provide more fodder for Nurse Franklin's campaign to make the clinic "fit for respectable people." Her words, not Maggie's.

As Maggie lifted her hand to knock again, a tall black man in denim overalls opened the door. His shoulders and arms

11

glistened with sweat. He smelled strong and hard, as if he had been working in the stockyards all day.

"Good evening, Mr. Johnson." Maggie saw her own concern reflected in his tight jaw and lined brow. During his wife's last examination at the clinic, Maggie discovered the baby was in a breech position. It had stayed there despite her best efforts to turn it. This delivery would be long and difficult, especially for a first-time mother.

"Dr. Kendall, please hurry!" Mr. Johnson drew her into the apartment. Maggie heard a woman moan and a rush of soft voices.

"Let me see her." Maggie followed Mr. Johnson through the hallway, conscious of the blood singing through her veins. This is what she was born to do. For a moment, she was five years old again and listening to the minister eulogize her parents, who had passed on during a flu epidemic in '27. They had refused to send for a doctor they couldn't afford to pay.

Maggie squared her shoulders. She wasn't going to lose Mrs. Johnson or her baby.

She followed Mr. Johnson into the back bedroom. It was small and neat, with only a narrow path between iron bedstead and flimsy dresser. Two teenage girls stood wedged against the wall at the head of the bed, their eyes bright with excitement. Mr. Johnson introduced them as his sisters. Nurse Franklin hovered in the hallway, gilded by the rays of the setting sun through the window behind her.

Maggie nodded at the girls. She set her bag next to the worn Bible on the wooden chair and studied her patient.

Mrs. Johnson's hair was matted, her face strained, her eyes soft and unfocused. Maggie felt her pulse, which thumped in her thin wrist.

During Mrs. Johnson's appointment a week ago, Maggie had positioned a stethoscope below Mrs. Johnson's sternum and given her the earpieces. As Mrs. Johnson listened to her baby's heartbeat, elation danced across her delicate face.

"How much longer, Doctor?"

Maggie stuck the stethoscope in the pocket of her lab coat. "Any day now."

"Will you deliver my baby?" Mrs. Johnson's fingers tightened on Maggie's hand. "I don't want nobody else."

"Of course." Maggie grinned. "Make sure your husband has a nickel for the phone."

Mrs. Johnson had smiled as she struggled to sit up on the examination table. She clasped her hands over her abdomen. "Will it be a boy or girl, Doctor?"

"I don't know." Maggie hated this question. She refused to parrot her obstetrics professor who advised, "Always tell the parents the baby's going to be a girl. Half the time you'll be right, and the other half, they'll be so happy it won't matter."

Mrs. Johnson smiled sheepishly. "My mama sent me a necklace to hold over my stomach. She said if the pendant swings back and forth, I'll have a boy."

"That's as good a method as any."

Now Maggie counted Mrs. Johnson's heartbeats as another contraction rippled across her abdomen. *Still in the first stage. Plenty of time.*

"Keep breathing." Maggie patted Mrs. Johnson's hand. "In through your nose. Out through your mouth." She turned to Mr. Johnson. "Where's the kitchen?"

He nodded to the left. Maggie hurried from the bedroom. She dropped her wedding ring into the pocket of her dress and soaped up at the small porcelain sink, paying particular attention to her close-clipped fingernails. Back in the bedroom, Nurse Franklin helped Maggie into a lab coat and handed the girls white caps and gowns from her bag.

As instructed, Mr. Johnson had been saving unopened news-

13

papers for the past month, and a foot-high stack stood next to the bathroom door. Nurse Franklin helped him spread the papers on the dining room table to create a clean birthing area. They covered an end table with newspapers, too, and Nurse Franklin laid out Maggie's instruments. Mr. Johnson emptied the kitchen garbage pail, lined it with newspapers, and stuck it next to the end table. He washed his hands and put on a cap and gown.

While they worked, Maggie timed the contractions, which were coming every two or three minutes. She talked quietly to Mrs. Johnson as she measured her cervix. Eight centimeters. Maggie gently inserted her gloved hand into Mrs. Johnson's vagina and felt the baby's buttocks still lodged against the mother's pelvis. *Damn!*

Nurse Franklin wedged herself in the doorway, uniform bunched above her hips. "We're ready in the dining room." She must have sensed Maggie's uneasiness because she added, "Unless you want me to call an ambulance."

"An ambulance?" Mr. Johnson questioned Maggie over Nurse Franklin's shoulder. "What's wrong, Doc?"

"Nothing, Mr. Johnson." Maggie glared at the nurse. "We're doing fine."

Nurse Franklin sniffed, but she stepped back. Maggie wiped her hands on a clean cloth and took Mrs. Johnson's arm. "Time for a walk."

"Oh, Lordy, Lord, Lord," Mrs. Johnson muttered. But with her husband steadying her from one side of the bed and Maggie on the other, she managed to stand. Clutching the sheet around her bulging abdomen, she tottered into the dining room. The girls helped her climb onto a chair and stretch out on the table.

Nurse Franklin opened the windows. The sun had set. Despite the brick wall of the building next door, a cool breeze snaked into the apartment. It lifted the edges of the newspapers

Nurse Franklin checked her watch again. "Three forty-one." Moses Kendall Johnson hung from his mother like a ripe fruit: shining, perfect, beautiful.

"Come on, little one," Maggie whispered.

Another contraction and she saw the hair at the back of his neck, straight and dark against the tight curls of his mother's pubis. Maggie drew him toward her, flexing the soft bones of his skull.

"Three forty-three," Nurse Franklin said.

"Don't push," Maggie ordered the mother. She lifted the baby's feet over Mrs. Johnson's pubic bone and slowly, slowly, with a soft sigh, his face emerged.

Mr. Johnson cried, "Thank you, Lord, thank you."

"Three forty-five. Right on the button." Nurse Franklin's voice held a note of triumph. Maggie grinned. Maybe she'd convert the old battle axe after all.

Moses Kendall Johnson, dusky pink and healthy, wailed as Maggie cut the cord. Nurse Franklin wiped and wrapped the baby before placing him on his mother's chest.

"Do you want him circumcised?" Maggie asked as she examined the episiotomy for signs of tearing.

Mr. Johnson mumbled "No" and bent over his wife and child.

Maggie stretched her back, relieved. After a difficult birth, she hated to do a circumcision with fingers as swollen as sausages and just as clumsy.

The younger girl dropped Mrs. Johnson's leg and reached for the child. "I wanna hold baby Moses."

Mrs. Johnson yelped as her knee hit the table.

Her husband growled, "Watch what you're doing."

At the same time, Maggie snapped, "Come back here. We're not finished."

In a few minutes, Mrs. Johnson expelled the placenta. The girls covered their eyes while Nurse Franklin examined it to be

on the table and carried the sour smell of rotting garbage. Nurse Franklin fanned her face with a folded paper and drew the sheer curtains for privacy. Two streets over, the El clattered and roared.

Maggie asked Mr. Johnson to turn on the overhead light. It glowed warmly, draping Mrs. Johnson's neck and face with shadows. "Nurse," she called. "We're ready."

Now that the delivery had started, Nurse Franklin settled into her routine. No more clicks of disapproval, no more arguments. She pulled Mrs. Johnson's hips forward until they were at the edge of the table. Maggie showed the girls how to hold Mrs. Johnson's knees, one on each side of the table, so the opening of her vulva was exposed. Blushes rose under the girls' soft chocolate skin, and they turned their heads aside.

"Shall I shave her now, Doctor?" Nurse Franklin held up a straight razor.

"No, Nurse. That won't be necessary. Clean her with swabs."

With a noncommittal grunt, Nurse Franklin stowed the razor in her bag and pulled out a bag of sterile cotton balls.

Mrs. Johnson groaned, and a heavy trickle of blood and mucus flowed from the birth canal. One of the girls cried out. The other winced and fixed her eyes on the wall.

"You two need to stand still," Maggie said as she moved into position between Mrs. Johnson's open legs.

"Has the baby started?" Mrs. Johnson gasped. "I feel something."

"Everything's fine." Maggie handed a damp cloth to Mr. Johnson, who hovered near his wife's face. "Wipe her forehead, please. And talk to her. Help her relax."

Nurse Franklin dipped cotton balls into a basin of disinfectant and swabbed Mrs. Johnson's pelvic area. With her foot, she slid the garbage pail close to the table and dropped the used cotton into it.

The contractions grew stronger as the cervix continued to dilate. With her right hand, Maggie eased the tiny buttocks deeper into the uterus. With her left hand, she found the baby's head and slowly pushed it toward the baby's buttocks, trying to flex the trunk and turn it. The baby kicked and settled back down into the pelvis, buttocks first.

Maggie withdrew her hands with a twinge of anxiety. If the baby was in distress, she'd have to send Mrs. Johnson to Cook County Hospital after all, a place where the crowded wards stripped poor mothers of their dignity and their husbands were treated like criminals. Sending Mrs. Johnson to Cook County would mean she'd failed her patient.

She listened to the baby's heartbeat. It stuttered for a second and then rebounded. There was no sign of fresh bleeding. Good. Everything was under control.

Maggie stroked the mother's exposed abdomen. "Your baby is determined to be born bottom first, Mrs. Johnson. The delivery will take a little longer than we expected." Maggie stared into her patient's muddy eyes. "You'll need to be strong. And you'll have to do exactly what I say."

Mrs. Johnson nodded. She held her husband's hand so tightly her knuckles whitened.

"Good. Keep breathing. Don't bear down until I tell you to." Maggie glanced at Nurse Franklin. "I'm going to do an episiotomy."

The nurse handed Maggie a syringe of anesthetic. Maggie injected Mrs. Johnson, waited a minute, then used a scalpel to make a quick incision. Mrs. Johnson didn't seem to notice. Maggie checked the opening to the cervix again. It was fully dilated. "Time to lift her legs."

Nurse Franklin stepped in front of Maggie. She raised Mrs. Johnson's ankles and knees so her calves were parallel to the floor and about twenty-four inches above the tabletop. As the

nurse lifted, she exposed patches of sweat under her arms and between her breasts. "Keep her legs right there," she told the girls. "Don't let them move."

The nurse stepped out of the way so Maggie could check Mrs. Johnson's perineum. The baby's buttocks were visible. She took a deep breath. *First, do no harm.* Maggie placed her hand on Mrs. Johnson's abdomen and felt a contraction. "Bear down," she said quietly. "Bear down."

Two hours later came the hardest part of a breech delivery—patience. Mrs. Johnson pushed with each contraction, slowly expelling the baby's body. Supported by Maggie's hands, the baby hung from its mother over the edge of the dining room table. Gravity urged the rest of its body to follow.

Maggie couldn't hurry the delivery. Too much pressure and the membranes that attached the baby's brain to its skull could tear and cause an intracranial hemorrhage—or death. But she couldn't relax either. A breech baby moving too slowly through the birth canal could pinch its umbilical cord against the mother's pelvic bones and suffocate.

"Three thirty-five," Nurse Franklin announced. "We've got ten minutes."

Ten minutes before the baby had to be breathing on its own.

A swollen scrotum emerged. Maggie glanced at Mr. Johnson. "It's a boy."

He smiled back, his eyes blurred. "We're going to name him after you, Doc. Moses Kendall Johnson."

"I'm honored, Mr. Johnson."

Nurse Franklin harrumphed, and Maggie turned her attention to her patient. The umbilicus slid past Maggie's fingers. She untangled the baby's legs and pulled free a loop of pulsing cord. It came easily. His oxygen supply wasn't impaired. His shoulder blades emerged, and Maggie breathed a sigh of relief. Now for his neck and head.

sure it was complete. Then she wrapped it in newspapers and dropped it into the garbage pail.

Maggie covered Mrs. Johnson's legs and dismissed the girls, who collapsed on the sofa, giggling nervously until Mr. Johnson banished them to the kitchen.

Maggie's arms throbbed. She stretched her fingers and flexed her wrists. She watched Moses nurse in Mrs. Johnson's arms. As she remembered the soft weight of her own daughter, Maggie's nipples tingled. She wanted to go home and hold Ellie, to sit quietly in the rocking chair and sing her child to sleep. But not yet. She'd stay with the Johnsons for another three or four hours to make sure there were no postpartum complications and little Moses was feeding well.

She repaired the episiotomy. Then Mr. Johnson helped his wife slide down from the table. She clasped her son to her breast and tottered back to bed. The magic left the room.

Nurse Franklin stomped between the kitchen and the dining room, washing Maggie's instruments and repacking her bag, while Maggie sat at the dining room table and completed Moses Kendall Johnson's birth certificate. As the nurse worked, she muttered under her breath. "We were lucky this time, dear God, so lucky. Thank you, Jesus. It was touch and go. We should have sent her to Cook County, that's what we should have done. Should have called us an ambulance and sent her along." Nurse Franklin crossed herself. "Sweet Mary and Jesus, what a night." Finally, she bustled through the door and banged down the stairs.

The blasted woman was as bad as Maggie's husband. Nurse Franklin wanted to close the clinic, and Bennett wanted to leave Chicago. She shook her head and sighed. She didn't want to go home to another fight with Bennett. Not after a delivery as hard as this one.

At five a.m. mother and baby were doing well. Maggie left

the apartment and walked to the El. She left the El at LaSalle Street, picking her way down the clanging metal steps. A breeze from Lake Michigan ruffled the stack of *Chicago Tribune*s next to the newsboy on the sidewalk. Overhead, a seagull cried like a hungry child.

At the bottom of the stairs, Maggie crossed the street blindly, seeing again Moses in his mother's arms. Despite the breech presentation, the delivery had been textbook perfect. She wanted to leap into the air, tap-dance her way down State Street, and shout alleluias. She grinned so broadly that the passersby smiled back, and an elderly man tipped his hat. What a beautiful day to be alive.

Half an hour later, Maggie sat beside her husband on the unmade bed in their basement apartment. She spoke to him softly, trying to not wake the child who dozed on a cot six feet away. "I told you yesterday. I don't want to leave the clinic. Not yet."

Bennett's body stiffened.

"Don't you want Ellie to have a better home than this?" His harsh whisper grated against the cinderblock walls. "Think about it! Doc's medical practice is ready for me to take over." He took her hands. "Please, sweetheart."

Maggie forced a smile. She remembered the cocky grin he had worn the day he marched off the troop ship and pushed his way through the crowd to her. He hugged her so tight the medals on his uniform had bruised her breasts.

She had known he wanted to move back home someday to step into his father's shoes. Someday, but not today. Not when little Mrs. Rodriguez was almost ready to deliver and Mrs. Brown and—

Maggie pictured the clinic's crowded waiting room. She pulled her hands free and stood. She put on an apron, tied the bow at her waist, and smoothed the flowered rayon over her dress. Clean diapers hung from the water pipes that ran across the ceiling. She fingered one. It wasn't dry yet. No matter how high the temperature outside, the basement was always cool and damp. She turned around.

Bennett leaned against the wall, arms folded across his chest. The collar and cuffs of his blue, long-sleeved shirt were crisp, his khaki pants had a knife-edge crease, and his shoes were spit polished. He always carried a clean handkerchief in his back pocket. It, too, had been starched and ironed. The Army had trained him well.

"I know you want to go back to Zillah, Bennett. But, but . . ." Maggie's mouth dried as she searched for the right words. "I can't abandon these women."

"Nonsense, sweetheart." Bennett's voice turned business-like as he added, "Surely Dr. Samuelson can dig up another physician for the clinic. What about that little colored girl in the class behind you? She seems pretty gung-ho."

"Charlotte? She'd jump at the chance."

"Okay, so what's the problem?" Bennett waited for her to acquiesce.

"You have to choose, Maggie," he said at last, when she refused to answer. "What comes first? Your family or your job?"

"The clinic is not just a job." This discussion was pointless. Bennett had gone to medical school because he wanted to follow in his father's footsteps, not because he was driven, not because he was harried and chased by the specter of death.

"What is the clinic, then, if it's not a job? A calling? A ministry? Did you turn into a Holy Roller overnight?"

"No, of course not." Maggie shut her eyes for a second.

"And you get paid, right?"

Her hands clenched. "Yes, I do get paid."

"Then it's a job. Case closed. So why is your job more important than Ellie and me?"

Maggie's tired eyes burned. She would never tell him about Mrs. Johnson's delivery because he would never ask. "I want to have both. A family and my practice."

He stepped away and stared out the basement window, his eyes level with the sidewalk. "Okay, you can have both. But in Zillah." He turned to face her. "We're moving back home at the end of the week. I've already paid Mrs. Woods our last month's rent and given notice at the VA. We're ready to roll." He held out his hand to her.

Recognition surged through Maggie, as if she had put on reading glasses and a blurred page had jumped into sharp focus. If she wanted to keep her family together, it would be on his terms, not hers. It was as simple as that.

Here was the real marriage. Not the moment of saying "I do" in a candlelit church, surrounded by her family, dressed in satin and lace, holding gardenias and phlox on a white leather Bible, but now, in this cramped basement, in her wrinkled dress, without hat or gloves, speaking softly while their child napped.

Now was the moment when they stayed together or fell apart.

She whispered, "Yes, I'll come." She reached out to Bennett, let herself be drawn into his arms, let him kiss her hair, let him run his hands down her body and cup her buttocks, and heard him breathe a sigh of relief and longing.

Over his shoulder, she watched her daughter sleep.

Chapter Three:
Maggie

September 6, 1952

Dear Aunt Vessie,

We made it! We're safe and sound in Zillah, the promised land. We arrived yesterday, our boxes and suitcases packed into a small trailer that Bennett bought for five dollars on Maxwell Street. He hooked the trailer to the back of my Studebaker, and it creaked along behind us like a gypsy wagon. Not at all what the good citizens of Zillah expected of their new doctors, I'm sure, but everyone honked and waved as we drove through town.

Bennett's mother, of course, was not amused, and hustled us inside her house as if we were criminals. Louisa wants him to step into Doc's shoes, take over Doc's practice, and head up the Burlington County medical society. I guess the gypsy wagon didn't fit with her idea of what "Doc Junior" should be.

Tomorrow Bennett meets with the hospital administrator to sign the papers so he will be admitted to medical and surgical privileges at Community Memorial Hospital (such a drab name, don't you think?). It's only a formality. I'll make sure Ellie is settled (Louisa, fortunately, is besotted with her), and then sign a contract with the hospital myself.

I told Bennett I'd like to start a practice like the one I had in Chicago. He said he probably could dig up some poverty-stricken families for me to help. He was making a joke, but that's exactly what I plan to do.

Tuesday the hospital trustees host a reception to welcome us to Zillah. I'm already nervous. These farmer folk may have read about "lady doctors" in *Life*, but are they ready to encounter one in the flesh? We shall see.

Your loving niece, Maggie

CHAPTER FOUR:
1992

Zillah Courier. *Wednesday, September 2, 1992. Newsmakers.*

Indiana State Attorney General and former Governor Peter Grandheim, 63, acknowledged yesterday that he is being considered by President Bush for a judicial appointment to the 7th Circuit of the U.S. Court of Appeals, the most prestigious federal court in our region.

Grandheim returned home to northern Indiana last night from a weekend retreat at President Bush's compound in Kennebunkport, Maine. He is a longtime friend and supporter of Vice President Dan Quayle, who suggested his name to the president. It is widely rumored that the Appeals Court position may be a stepping-stone to the Supreme Court if a vacancy arises during Mr. Bush's second term.

Grandheim declined to comment on the nomination. "Nothing has been decided," he said. "President Bush is anxious to hit the ground running when he begins his second term in the White House. He wants to have all the right people in place to move forward with his vision for America. I'm honored to be considered for this important position."

Speaking about the nomination, Sheila Roske, chair of the Indiana State Democratic Party, claimed that Grandheim's business partner, George Whittaker, has raised more than $10 million in PAC contributions from Midwest donors for the Bush-Quayle campaign. In addition, Ms. Roske noted that their company, G&W Construction, headquartered in Grandheim's hometown of Zillah, recently won two lucrative contracts to build military housing in Indiana.

"Indiana Democrats believe federal judgeships should not be sold to the highest bidder," said Roske. Grandheim's name could go to the Senate Judicial Committee for consideration as early as tomorrow.

CHAPTER FIVE:
BRADY SZLOVAK

Noon, Saturday, September 5, 1992

Three minutes after he took the call from dispatch, Lt. Brady Szlovak of the Zillah PD drove into the gravel parking lot on the west side of the Twilite Motel.

A patrol car waited in front of Unit 14, and a Medic One ambulance idled next to the motel office. Brady pulled next to the blue-and-white and turned off his engine. Relief washed over the face of the uniformed patrolman, who paced outside the barrier of yellow tape. His name was Jeswine, if Brady remembered right. No beer, jes' wine.

Brady stepped from his car and motioned for Jeswine to wait while he scoped out the scene. The Twilite had been built half a century ago when Highway 25 was the main north-south route between Chicago and Indianapolis, and Zillah a convenient stopping point. The motel units, constructed of faded-blue cement blocks, stood like abandoned toys in an arc around a courtyard where sorrel and milkweed grew between the paving stones and the water fountain had long since dried up. A crow poked at an overflowing garbage can outside the manager's office.

Brady shook his head. Slovenliness offended him. So times were tough in the motel business. So what? Was that any reason to stop picking up the trash? Or to let the weeds take over? How much would a can of paint cost? Brady's dad had spent his life servicing John Deere farm machinery. There had been plenty of lean times, but even when the cupboard held nothing but cereal and canned soup, the house had been clean, inside and out.

He scanned the immediate vicinity. A tavern abutted the north side of the Twilite Motel, a restaurant and a wrecking yard lay to the south. To the west, across four lanes of traffic, the Sugar Shack offered adult video and private booths. Brady knew this strip of the highway well. He had worked a couple of homicides here, but never one at the Twilite itself.

Two more patrol cars pulled into the parking lot. Brady told the officers to secure the perimeter of the motel and fend off gawkers. Already cars were slowing down as they passed on the highway. Outside the tavern, a trio of bleary-eyed men stood spitting and smoking as they watched him approach the patrolman.

"Officer Jeswine?"

The uniformed officer snapped to attention. "Yes, sir."

Jeswine had freckled, sunburned skin, bleached blond hair, and farm boy muscles that stretched his blues over his biceps and thighs.

Brady suppressed a smile at the kid's shiny eagerness. "Can you tell me what happened here, Officer?"

"Yes, sir, Lieutenant Szlovak." Jeswine flushed as he stumbled over Brady's name.

"Slo-vak," Brady said. "Ignore the Z."

"Yes, sir. This appears to be a homicide." Jeswine opened a three-by-five notebook and frowned at it.

Brady studied the crime scene as he waited for Jeswine's report. Yellow tape crisscrossed the door to Room 14 and extended over the gravel parking lot until it was even with the front bumper of Jeswine's patrol car. A female officer sat in the driver's seat, yakking on the radio. She laughed loudly, caught Brady's eye, and hung up. He felt a twitch of satisfaction.

A housekeeper's cart lay on its side within the yellow-tape boundary. Small bars of soap spilled across the sidewalk. One or two had been ground into the gravel, and a sweet floral smell hung in the humid air.

"My partner and I got the call at ten-oh-three," Jeswine said. "The motel manager, a Mr. Harry Gill, reported that one of his housekeepers, a Graciela Hernandez, had found the body of the other housekeeper, a Carmen Torres, in Unit 14. Dispatch had already called an ambulance. We arrived at the scene at ten-oh-eight. The medics drove in right behind us."

Jeswine glanced at the ambulance next to the yellow tape. Brady nodded to the two figures inside it. Jeswine studied his notebook again.

"When we arrived, the motel manager, his wife, and Ms. Hernandez were standing outside Unit 14. The door to the unit was closed. My partner told them to move into the motel office and wait for further instructions. I opened the door, checked that no one else was in the room, and let in the medics. They determined the victim could not be resuscitated and left the unit. I told dispatch to call the coroner's office. Someone's on their way." Jeswine looked up as if he expected to see the ME's van pull in.

"I then proceeded to tell the medics to wait in their vehicle." Jeswine glanced at Brady.

"Do you know anything about the person staying in Unit 14, Officer?" Brady asked.

"Very little, sir. According to my partner, the name on the motel register is Margaret Mueller Kendall. She checked in three days ago and was supposed to stay another week. She paid for the room in cash. The manager did not request any identification. She came in a cab, so he didn't get a license plate number."

"Did he describe Ms. Kendall?"

"Yes, sir." Jeswine flipped a page. "She's between fifty-five and sixty-five years old, about five-foot-three, slender build, with shoulder-length brown and gray hair. She has a large red mark on her left cheek and very short fingernails. The manager said she sounded well-educated."

"Clothing?"

"Jeans, leather jacket, shirt. Nothing special there."

"No."

Jeswine closed his notebook. "One other thing, sir."

"Yes, Officer?"

"There was a dog in the motel room, sir. Alive and injured. He had dragged himself to the door. I took a clean sheet from the housekeeper's cart, wrapped him up, and put him in the patrol car. The medics checked him out. He appears to have been hit in the head with a blunt object. I'd like permission to transport him to the vet." Jeswine flushed again. "Sir."

"You can't remove evidence from a crime scene." Brady heard the irritation in his own voice. "That's a violation of department rules."

"Yes, sir. I know, sir." Jeswine stepped to his patrol car and peered through the back window. Brady followed suit. The dog lay motionless on the back seat, its body shrouded in a blood-stained sheet. It was impossible to tell what kind of dog it was. A black ear poked out at the farthest end of the sheet and twitched.

Brady nodded to Jeswine's partner, Officer Smallwood, a wiry, dark-haired woman in her thirties who sat in the front seat. He opened the back door, and the dog's ear twitched again. The patrol car smelled bad, but no worse than when a drunk puked, which happened often enough. The molded plastic was made to be hosed off.

Brady sighed. He was a firm believer in following the rule-book, in perspiration, not inspiration. But the animal had already been moved. He turned to Jeswine. "Did you chalk around the dog's body at the scene?"

"Yes, sir."

"Okay. Officer Smallwood will take it to the vet. You'll stay here with me."

Brady motioned for Officer Smallwood to roll down her window. "Call dispatch and find out which vet the K-9 unit uses. You're taking the dog."

"Yes, sir." Smallwood stuck the key in the ignition.

"Wait a second."

"Sir?"

"Write this down."

"Yes, sir." Smallwood pulled out a notebook identical to Jeswine's. She opened it, propped it on the steering wheel and flicked her ballpoint pen.

"Tell the vet that we need a complete forensic examination of the dog. And you stay with the dog to make sure it happens. Tell the vet to clip the dog's toenails and collect them in an evidence bag, comb the fur for fibers, and check the teeth with a magnifying glass. If there's dried blood on the fur, clip it and save it. If the dog is wearing a collar, check it for fibers, too. Check the dog tags, scan for a microchip, and get the owner's identification."

Brady glanced up at the motel office. "It probably belongs to our mysterious Margaret Kendall. We need an address and phone number for her. And tell the vet to collect the dog's stool for the next twenty-four hours, if he survives that long. If the dog dies, I want an autopsy so we can check the stomach contents. And save the bed sheet. It'll have to go to the lab. Got it?"

Smallwood scribbled rapidly. "Yes, sir."

"Call me if there's any problem."

Smallwood cranked the engine and left in an unnecessary

blur of sirens and lights. Brady walked over to Unit 14 and ducked under the crime-scene tape. Jeswine had put up enough yellow ribbon to block off a feedlot.

The door to the motel unit was unlatched. Brady pulled a mechanical pencil from his shirt pocket and used the eraser to push the door partially open. Jeswine stood in the doorway beside him.

The smell hit Brady first: dog shit and blood, sweat and fear, stale cigarette smoke and disinfectant. He stuck a couple of pieces of Dentyne gum in his mouth and chewed rapidly.

He looked at the bed. His stomach clenched. Brady wasn't a religious man, hadn't been religious since he quit being an altar boy at St. Stanislaus and took up girls instead. But the old parish priest had gotten one thing right. Murder was a sin, if only because the victim died before she had a chance to make her peace with God. And if you didn't believe in God, then substitute parents, husband, children. This woman was killed before she could say good-bye to those she loved. Her death would leave wounds behind, wounds that would never heal. The City of Zillah might pay his salary, but he worked for the victims' families. They deserved the very best investigation he could muster.

Brady turned to Jeswine. "Okay, Officer. Let's review what we've got here."

He pointed to the double bed where the maid lay face up. Her head and shoulders dangled over the side closest to him. The wound to the side of her head gaped like an open mouth. Blood had soaked the sheets and pooled on the bare linoleum floor. A trail of blood and feces showed where the dog had dragged himself to the door, and a chalk mark indicated where Jeswine had found him.

"Did you move the victim's body, Jeswine?"

"No, sir." Jeswine gulped. "I did touch her head to see . . . to see if—" Jeswine's face turned green. He clenched his hands.

"Keep breathing, Officer."

Brady studied the room, giving Jeswine a chance to regain his composure and remember how a cop behaved.

A table lamp lay next to the body, the base covered in blood. Probably the murder weapon. She wore a blue polyester skirt and a white polyester blouse that looked vaguely like a uniform. Her skirt was pushed up around her thighs. Her thick brown pantyhose appeared intact, and the buttons on her blouse were still fastened. Brady ruled out sexual assault. Unless the ME said different. She wore white ankle socks over her pantyhose. Her tennis shoes were stained with dirt.

Brady glanced at Jeswine, who seemed to be breathing normally. He pointed to the body. "Did you see any other damage, Officer?"

"No, sir. Just the head."

Brady nodded. Despite her ruined face and skull, he could see the woman had combed her hair and applied makeup sometime before she died. A tiny gold cross twinkled in one earlobe, the other was bare. "Did you pick up an earring?"

"No, sir."

The motel room was about twenty feet square with a cement block partition that extended halfway into the room from the left-hand wall. Brady pointed to the partition with his pencil. "Bathroom?"

"Yes, sir. According to the manager, there's a shower, toilet, and sink."

"And cockroaches."

"Yeah." Jeswine made a strangled sound, like a choked-back chuckle.

"Any windows?"

"One. Too small and high for a normal-sized prowler. At least that's what the manager thinks."

Brady nodded again. Okay, he'd stop worrying about marauding midgets. At least for now. He pushed the door with his pencil so it swung open another couple of inches. From the position of the body, he guessed the attacker had stood behind the door and hit the maid as soon as she walked into the room.

He turned to Jeswine and thought out loud. "If we're dealing with a robbery, why did he kill her?"

"He, sir? Have you ruled out the woman who rented the room?"

"For now. She wouldn't have torn her own room apart."

"So was he high? On PCP or meth?"

"It's possible, but I don't think so. Someone tossed this room, but they didn't destroy it. It doesn't say out-of-control druggie to me."

Jeswine stepped closer to the threshold and studied the scene. "I see what you mean, sir," he said, but his voice held a question.

"Look at that." Brady pointed to the drawer of the nightstand. It had been pulled out and overturned on the bed, dumping a Gideon Bible on the corpse's stomach. "After our perp bludgeoned her, he kept on searching."

Jeswine gulped. Clearly he wouldn't have stayed in that room a second more than he had to. "What does that mean, sir?"

"I'm not sure. But it suggests that he was looking for something pretty specific. And that he was highly motivated to find it."

"Drugs? Money?"

"Could be. But, according to the manager, the woman who rented the room appeared to be middle-aged. It doesn't seem likely she'd be dealing drugs." Even in a backwater like Zillah, the median age of a drug dealer was eighteen or nineteen. After twenty-five, they were incarcerated or dead.

Brady studied the bed again. The sheets and white chenille

bedspread were threadbare and slightly yellow. It made his skin crawl to think about sleeping on them. He saw two pillows, neither inviting. Tucked between the far pillow and the headboard was a roll of brown fur, maybe the arm of a stuffed Teddy bear. He studied the bedclothes and saw another piece of the stuffed animal, possibly an ear, caught in the folds of the covers. Damn. He didn't want to think a kid was part of this.

"Did you ask the manager whether he saw any toys in the room, Jeswine?"

"Toys?" Jeswine said, startled. "No, sir."

Brady checked his watch again. Ten twenty-eight. Still no sign of the crime-scene team. "Stay here and guard the door. I'll talk with the manager."

He spent a few minutes with the medics first. They confirmed Jeswine's report. The victim was a Hispanic woman between twenty-five and thirty-five. They had tried to resuscitate her, but the wound was obviously fatal. "That's unofficial," the driver added.

The ME's office jealously guarded its prerogative of pro-nouncing death, which was fine with Brady. "Who checked out the dog?"

"I did," the driver answered. "He had the same kind of dam-age as the woman. A blow to the head. He might have gone after the killer."

"It'd be nice if we found a big piece of butt in the dog's teeth." Brady glanced into the side-view mirror of the ambu-lance, keeping an eye on the manager's office.

The driver laughed. "Sorry, Lieutenant, no dice. I checked the dog's mouth before Jeswine wrapped him in the sheet."

"Good." Brady stared at the side-view mirror again. Had he seen a flash of light from the office?

He hurried across the parking lot to the office. The door opened as he approached. "Are you a cop?" a man asked. He stood in the doorway, tall and emaciated. His long, bony fingers worked the door knob. Behind him, a stocky peroxide blonde with a chest as wide as Montana leaned against the counter, chewing gum. Jack Sprat and wife?

Brady flashed his ID. "I'm Lieutenant Szlovak. Are you in charge?"

"Managers and owners. I'm Harry Gill and this here's my wife, Priscilla."

"May I come in?"

"Sure." The man stepped back as if reluctant to release the door knob, then abruptly turned and dropped into the chair behind the low desk. The office reeked of smoke and Lysol. The magazines on the corner table were as yellow and dusty as the pillows in the motel room, but the giant television next to it gleamed.

The manager's wife smiled and enveloped Brady's hand with plump palms as hot and damp as a summer night. He itched to pull away.

"Thank you for coming." She released Brady's hand and touched her eyes with a delicately extended finger, smearing blue mascara into her crow's feet. He didn't detect any sign of tears.

"Listen, Lieutenant," Gill said. "Like I told that other officer, we don't want no trouble here. This place can't take it. You know what I mean?"

"No," Brady said, deliberately obtuse. "I'm afraid I don't."

"Look around you, for God's sake. Does this seem like any kind of going concern?" The manager's hands flapped impatiently. "But it's all we've got. All we're living on." He slumped back in his seat. "What I'm saying is, have a heart. Don't put us out of business, man."

Brady sighed. "Mr. Gill, the best thing I can do is find out what happened, nail the guy who did it, and get out of your life. Okay?"

"Do I got a choice?" Gill flipped a pencil across the desk. It rolled to the floor. No one picked it up.

"Where's Ms. Hernandez, the woman who found the body?" Brady scanned the office and noticed a mirrored door hidden in the corner. Was it the source of the flash he had seen from the parking lot?

Without waiting for an answer, he pushed past Mrs. Gill, crossed the room, and yanked the door open. It led to the manager's quarters. On the other side of the living room, a sliding glass door opened onto a dirt alley. He didn't need to ask what had happened. Graciela Hernandez had fled. Nine times out of ten, flight meant undocumented. It fit. Bottom-of-the barrel wages, no benefits, no loyalty. Too bad, Gill, he thought. You and the missus should have tried scrubbing toilets yourself.

Brady marched back into the manager's office and dusted off a chair. Before he sat down, he took out a pencil and paper and a plasticized Miranda card so they'd know he was serious.

"Now, Mr. and Mrs. Gill, you get to tell me everything you know or guess about the woman who rented Unit 14. Then you're going to talk about Ms. Hernandez and Ms. Torres. We can do it the easy way, sitting right here, or we can do it the hard way, down at the station. Your choice."

Brady hated to use clichés, but it was the only way to get through to some people. And sure enough, Gill responded like the hounded innocents he had seen on television a thousand times. "I'm not saying nothing without my attorney."

CHAPTER SIX:
MAGGIE

1 p.m., Saturday, September 5, 1992

The Yellow Cab pulled off Highway 25 and bounced in the rutted driveway that led to the Twilite Motel. Maggie thought she remembered the motel from forty years ago, but she wasn't sure. She hadn't lived here very long. The only thing in Zillah that seemed familiar, ironically enough, was the new medical center—and only because it looked like all the other hospitals she'd worked in over the years.

The cab slowed. Maggie fumbled in her purse and pulled out three twenties. The cab wasn't metered, but whatever the fare, she planned to tip the driver heavily. He was an olive-skinned man with a hawk-bill nose, a full black beard, and a clean white turban wrapped around his head. Despite his fierce appearance, he had been very patient, driving her around town while she tried to find out where Janet and Bennett were living now.

Bennett, her ex-husband, and Janet, his second wife. No matter how hard she'd tried over the years, Maggie had never been able to imagine them in the same room together, let alone in the same bed. But, of course, they hadn't needed permission.

Bennett's address in the Zillah telephone book was a rural route number which encompassed half of Burlington County. Finally, she'd stopped at the hospital and asked Bennett's secretary who, assuming she was in town for Bennett's funeral, had been small-town helpful.

His funeral. Maggie drew in a deep breath. She had been

totally unprepared to learn Bennett was dead. She'd pictured him happily retired, puttering around on his farm—growing prize-winning kohlrabi or rutabagas and laying down the law at the hospital board meetings. But not dead.

She felt limp and restless, as if some small but essential part of her body had been cut away. Something like a gyroscope or a stabilizer. Something that had kept her focused all these years. And now he was dead.

Well, she couldn't barge in on Janet today. She'd have to wait until after the funeral tomorrow. Poor Janet. The last thing she needed was a ghost showing up on her doorstep.

But I need the knife.

The cab stopped. Without glancing up, Maggie wiped her eyes. "How much do I owe you?"

"Madam, are you sure you wish to proceed?"

Maggie looked through the window of the cab. Five or six blue-and-white police cars blocked the entrance to the motel. A uniformed officer leaned against the trunk of the nearest tree, studying the traffic, arms folded, studiously indifferent to the flashing lights behind him. Yellow tape crisscrossed the door to Room 14, her room, and three men in suits conferred near the cement block wall.

Fear arced through her chest.

"Madam?" The cab driver said, courteously insistent. "What is your desire?"

Maggie tensed. Whatever had happened here, she couldn't rush into it unprepared.

"There is a restaurant next door." The driver's voice held no hint of impatience. "Perhaps you would care to wait there until the policemen are gone." His soft singsong made Maggie feel like a child protected by a polite and well-bred nanny, like the little girl with her ayah in *The Secret Garden.*

"Okay."

The driver started the taxi and backed up slowly, parallel to the highway. He stopped at the front door of the restaurant. He stepped out and helped her from the back seat, his wiry body surprisingly strong under his shapeless white tunic.

There was a word for his clothing, Maggie knew. What was it? She tossed the question back and forth in her mind as he opened the door to the restaurant and led her to a corner booth by the window. She glanced at him, surprised. The location was perfect. She could watch her motel room without being seen.

"Thank you," she said.

He bowed, serene. Only his cocked eyebrow asked if the ruckus was connected to her. Maggie held out the money, but he waved it away with a light touch on her arm.

"It is not necessary," he said. "Once a day I transport an older person without charge for the good of my soul. You have blessed me." With a deep bow, he was gone.

"Now isn't that something?" The scratchy voice belonged to a waitress with scraggly blonde hair who bustled up to the table. Her apron was limp with grease spots, and her fingers yellow from nicotine. She held the stub of a pencil above a pad of check slips. "Imagine that A-rab presuming to put his grubby hands on an American woman."

Her voice rose at the end of every breath, making each sentence into a question. "Who does he think he is? Go back to where you came from. That's what I say. Go back if you can't keep your hands off of decent women."

"He was helping an older person," Maggie said. "May I have a cup of coffee with milk and without your opinion?"

"Well, you're no better than he is!" the waitress retorted and flounced away. Her thin hair flew around her shoulders; her red elbows jabbed the air.

"Yes, ma'am. That's the point." Maggie smiled as she propped her arms on the table and tried to imagine herself as an older person.

A different waitress, short and plump, deposited a cup and a pot of coffee on the table. "You look tired." She smiled as she moved the milk and sugar closer to Maggie's hand. "Would you like some help?"

"Yes, please. A little milk, one sugar."

The coffee tasted terrible, but no worse than she had expected. Maybe she should have ordered soup. Maggie wasn't sure she could keep the coffee down, so she sipped it slowly, adding milk until only a white froth lay at the bottom of her cup. After the last swallow, she set the cup on the table, too tired to search for the saucer. The heavy china clattered against the Formica surface.

Maggie put her hand into her purse, found her red calico bandanna and tied it around her hair, pulling it low on her forehead. As she closed her purse, her fingers brushed the folded newspaper inside. She didn't need to open it. The words had burned into her brain three days ago. She had been at the dentist, idly flipping through *The Chicago Tribune,* when she read, "Former Indiana governor and leading conservative Peter Grandheim in line for the Supreme Court?"

Peter Grandheim, a judge? Impossible. He belonged behind bars.

She had rushed from the dentist's office and used the pay phone in the hallway to track Peter down, feeding it quarters, then dimes and nickels until her change ran out.

He had been in Zillah, at the headquarters of G&W Construction. As soon as he recognized Maggie's voice, he had become the same old Peter: charming, self-assured, flirtatious. Like the past forty years had never happened. When she demanded that he withdraw his name from consideration on the Federal Appeals court, he hadn't skipped a beat.

"Give me a couple of days to come up with a reasonable excuse," he said. And Maggie had agreed.

Mistake number one.

Next door, the ambulance left the motel parking lot. Maggie studied the men and women working near her motel room. Judging from the number of officers, something bad had happened there, something very bad indeed.

But please, not to Freckles, not to her dear old dog.

The bell over the door to the restaurant chimed. Maggie wrenched her gaze away from the window. A policeman stood at the counter, talking to the friendly waitress behind the cash register. Maggie rested her scarred cheek on her hand and pretended to study the menu as she watched them. With her graying hair covered, she knew she could pass for a woman decades younger.

The waitress beamed at the officer, showing a dimple in her left cheek. She disappeared into the kitchen, and he slowly scanned the dining room. His gaze passed over Maggie, came back, dismissed her. The waitress returned with a coffee urn and a stack of paper cups. He thanked her and walked out. Maggie's chest ached as if it had been squeezed by giant pincers. She closed her eyes and blew out to expel the pain.

"Would you like to order now?"

Maggie looked up. The friendly waitress was back, her pencil poised.

"No, thank you." Maggie glanced out the window. It had started to rain, a gentle mist that grayed the sky. It blurred the neon sign of the strip club across the highway and turned the harsh red and blue lights into a fragment of Impressionist art. "Could you call me a cab?"

"Yes, ma'am. I'll be glad to. Don't you worry none. I'll come get you when it arrives."

Maggie breathed her thanks. She found a five-dollar bill in

her wallet and tucked it under the empty saucer. She stared out the window at the quiet hum of activity around the entrance to her motel room and tried to think.

Could Peter have sent someone to hunt for her already?

She had refused to tell Peter anything about herself over the phone. Not where she lived, not where she worked. And she had taken cabs instead of renting a car at the Indianapolis airport so she wouldn't leave a paper trail.

She had told him that she still had the knife, the one that could tie him to Luther's death. That was a lie.

Mistake number two.

Maggie stared at the table top. Her short, square-cut fingernails tapped against the saucer.

She couldn't go to the police. Peter was probably counting on that. If the police discovered—

Her thoughts skittered away from the memory of that rain-drenched and bloody night.

A television van pulled into the parking lot, and a young woman leaped out. Maggie scooted away from the window. That settled it. She couldn't deal with reporters and cops. Not yet. She had to get her hands on the knife. Surely Janet had kept faith with her.

She'd find another motel. Register. Sleep. Shower. Use a pay phone across town if she needed to call Peter again.

And Freckles. In a day or two, when she had the knife, she'd search the animal shelters. Surely, they wouldn't put him to sleep right away, not a sweet-tempered old dog like Freckles.

"I'm sorry," she whispered and heard how hopelessly inadequate the words were. "I shouldn't have left you."

She couldn't let herself think about Ellie right now. She just couldn't.

CHAPTER SEVEN:
MAGGIE

7 p.m., Saturday, September 5, 1992

Maggie pushed open the door to the Dew Drop Inn. She had slept eight hours in a new motel under a made-up name, eaten a handful of dry Saltines, drunk a pint of skim milk, and watched the reporters on television gleam with excitement as they reported the murder of a housekeeper at the Twilite Motel.

"Brutal," they said. "Bloody. No apparent motive. The woman who occupied the room is being sought for questioning, but the police have not released her name."

Maggie shivered. She had been the intended victim. She needed food, warmth, human company. She needed protection. She needed a gun. She hugged herself and rubbed her cold arms. If Peter had sent someone after her, she couldn't wait three days for a background check. She had to find a gun tonight.

She unzipped her jacket and shook the raindrops from her hair as she scanned the room. Cigarette smoke drifted over the bar. The sound on the television was turned off. The nearest tables were crowded with men in work clothes. Each of them checked her out as she walked past. The younger guys went back to talking. An older man kept glancing at her, interested. But he didn't look like Peter. That was the important thing.

In the corner farthest from the door, a middle-aged black man sat alone, not smoking, a *Zillah Courier* spread in front of

44

him, a glass of beer at his elbow. Maggie squeezed between the chairs.

She stopped next to his table and studied the pictures in the paper. The headline read, "After Almost Four Decades, Justice?"

"I was there," Maggie said, too desperate to be subtle.

"What?" He looked up. His face was smooth and purposefully blank, but his eyes, hazel-brown and almond shaped, drew her in. He wore a white shirt and a patterned maroon tie. The collar of his shirt was open at his neck, his tie loose. A suit jacket hung over the chair to his left. His nails shone as if freshly manicured, and Maggie saw a pale line across the fourth finger of his left hand, a memory of a long-worn ring. "You were where, exactly?"

"In Birmingham. After the church was bombed." Maggie dropped her jacket on the empty seat, pulled over a chair, and sat down. "I rode right past the rubble of the church. Took a Greyhound from Chicago to Selma. Then walked to Birmingham." She grimaced. "I was going to change the world."

He held out his hand across the table. "Toby Brown."

She didn't hesitate. "I'm Maggie Kendall." Toby's palm closed against hers, warm and dry, with no hint of calluses.

A waiter approached. "I'll have mineral water with a slice of lemon," Maggie said.

Toby pointed to his glass. He folded his newspaper, sat back, and studied her. "So you were going to save us po' colored folk, huh?" He grinned briefly as if mocking her.

"Yep. 'Fraid so." Maggie smiled back, mocking herself.

The waiter brought their drinks, sloshing Toby's beer across the table. He wiped up the puddle with a rag that looked older than he was and left, taking Toby's empty glass with him.

"So what happened?" Toby asked as he brushed his hand over his short-clipped curls.

"What do you mean? What happened on the march from

45

Selma to Birmingham, or did I really save the world?"

"Both, I guess." Toby chuckled, his teeth square and white beneath his short, black mustache.

"The march happened like they showed on TV. Singing and praying one minute, police dogs and fire hoses the next." Maggie sipped her mineral water. "We weren't encouraged to stay around Birmingham after the cops dragged the hoses into the street. I was practicing nonviolent resistance and feeling pretty righteous when a couple of rednecks in police uniforms pulled me from the crowd and threw me into a paddy wagon with some other marchers. They drove us to the bus station and separated out the ones they didn't recognize. The white women like me."

She took a breath. "They said, if we got on the bus headed north, any bus headed north, they'd take off our handcuffs. I tried to crawl back to the paddy wagon, but one guy had a pretty persuasive night stick. Finally he shoved me onto the bus and told the driver, 'Don't let her off before you cross the state line.' I had two cracked ribs. It was a long ride back to Chicago."

"Chicago, huh? I was there, too. Before Selma."

"And after Selma?"

Toby swallowed a slug of beer. "Let's say the police weren't as concerned about my personal safety as they were about yours. I did hard time before it was over."

Toby pulled out a pack of cigarettes, tapped it on the table, offered her one.

"No, thanks," she said, "I don't smoke."

He glanced at the cigarettes as if surprised. "I don't either. First ones I've bought in the last fifteen years or so." His long fingers caressed the unopened pack before he stuck it in the pocket of his pants.

"First cigarettes in approximately fourteen years, ten months, six days, and three hours?" Maggie asked.

He laughed. "Something like that."

"So why are you starting up again?"

"I'm not." Toby glanced over her shoulder at the bar behind her, flagged down the waiter, and ordered a plate of nachos.

The men at the two tables at the front of the bar exploded in laughter. They shoved back their chairs and staggered out the door.

"Think I'll stay here a little longer and let those boys drive themselves into a ditch without my help," Toby said. "Do you want a refill on your mineral water? Or something stronger?"

"Water's fine. Thanks."

He stared at her, his face a question.

"I'm in town for a few days. Staying at the motel across the way."

"I wondered how you ended up in this bar. You don't look like one of the usual crowd."

"Never have been." Against her will, Maggie's face stiffened. "But that's an old story." She pointed to the newspaper. "Were you thinking about Selma when I walked in?"

Toby stared at the picture of the bombed-out church. "I was thinking about those four little girls." His voice was gruff. "Not just them, but little black girls in general. When I was a boy, girls were special; you had to treat them with respect. My momma always kept after my sisters. 'Make something of yourself,' she'd say. 'Don't let anyone get his hands near you until you're married.' "

He pushed the newspaper away. "Now I drive through my neighborhood and what do I see? Girls no older than the ones who were killed in that church. Girls with makeup and skin-tight clothes, long painted nails. Little black girls with little black babies trailing after them.

"Where are their mommas? Who says 'better yourself' to them? Anyone? I want little girls to stay little girls for a while.

47

They'll get to be mommas soon enough." Toby stopped, put his face in his hands. After a long minute he looked up. "Sorry. It's been on my mind lately. My granddaughter—" He folded his hands on the table and stopped talking.

"Sure."

He studied her a little more closely as if memorizing her face. "So, Maggie, tell me. Why did you sit down at my table?"

"You were the only person in the entire place who wasn't smoking."

"I guess that'll do for now. I don't believe you." Toby fingered his mustache. "But it'll do for now." He turned in his seat. The bar was almost empty. "Want to dance?"

"Sure. Do we need music?"

He laughed, a full, rich, deep boom that warmed her and drove away the chill that had settled in her bones while she watched the policemen from the window of her cab.

Toby walked over to the bar, talked to the bartender. By the time he got back to their table, Duke Ellington drifted from a pair of speakers perched next to the TV.

They danced across the floor in silence.

"So why did you come here tonight, Maggie Kendall?" he murmured in her ear after the song changed. "Were you searching for me or would any black man do?"

She stopped dancing, squared her shoulders, and looked him in the eye. "I need a gun, Toby. One that can't be traced to me." She fell back a step. "When I walked in here and saw you, well, I guess I hoped you could help me out."

His arms dropped to his sides. "Help you get a gun? Oh, baby." He put his Southern drawl between them like a steel wall. "Because I'm a black man, you mean? You think I should be able to walk over to the phone and call someone, or better yet, open up the trunk of my car and pull out a gun for you?" He stared at her for a heartbeat. "You're crazy, lady."

"No," she whispered. "Not crazy. Scared. Scared to death."

"Well, you go get yourself another boy, Miz Kendall, 'cause this boy's got troubles enough." Toby grabbed his jacket. "I'm not getting myself mixed up with some crazy-scared, white lady, whether she marched to Birmingham or not."

He kicked his chair against the table and dropped two twenty-dollar bills next to his empty glass. He leaned close and said, "I'm going to remember your face, Maggie Kendall. Anything goes down around here and I'm calling the cops. You got that?"

Without waiting for an answer, he walked across the room and out the door.

Chilled again, Maggie groped blindly for her coat.

CHAPTER EIGHT:
MAGGIE

Zillah, Indiana. Tuesday, September 2, 1952

"Why, it's beautiful," Maggie exclaimed as Bennett steered his father's car along the sweeping arc of the hospital driveway. His mother sat beside him on the bench seat. Maggie sat in the rear. Ellie was sleeping at home, and Louisa's kitchen girl was sitting next to the stove and reading *Photoplay.*

Tonight was Maggie's first real chance to meet the physicians she would be working with. She hoped they would like her, would understand what she wanted to achieve. Already she missed the easy camaraderie of the childbirth clinic and the certainty that her work mattered.

Bennett slowed the Oldsmobile to a crawl and caught Maggie's eyes in the rearview mirror. A cocky grin lit his face. She smiled back.

"Not bad for a little farm town, is it?" He pointed to the parking lot on the south side of the hospital. "That's where we'll build the new surgical center. When it's finished, Zillah will have the finest operating theater north of Indianapolis."

"The Bennett M. Kendall, Sr., Surgical Pavilion," Louisa interjected.

"What do you mean, Mother Kendall?" Maggie slid forward. Her taffeta skirt rustled like dry leaves.

Louisa didn't answer.

Per usual. Maggie couldn't decide whether Louisa meant to be rude or whether she was trying to push Maggie out of the picture so she could have Bennett and Ellie to herself. It didn't matter. Maggie was here to stay.

Bennett glanced at his mother and said, "We hope the hospital trustees will name the new wing for Doc."

"It's more than hope," Louisa snapped. "Your father dedicated his life to this town. It's the least they can do to repay him."

"Of course."

Maggie put her hands on the back of the front seat and peered through the windshield. She liked the symbolism of an old-fashioned brick hospital flanked by a modern surgical wing: a medical community rooted in the past but building for the future. In Zillah she'd create the medical practice she had dreamed of. She'd bring the latest advances in ob-gyn to women who otherwise could never afford them.

Holding fast to that image, Maggie settled back in her seat. Her hand brushed Louisa's mink stole. Louisa twitched and drew the fur tight around her shoulders.

Good grief! I don't have cooties.

The car rolled over a small branch on the gravel, and Louisa barked, "Watch where you're going, Junior."

"All right, Mother." Bennett stopped in front of the entrance as the clock in the tower on the northwest corner of the hospital chimed the hour. Maggie checked her watch. Seven o'clock and correct to the minute. In Chicago, the clock in the clinic had always run slow. What had been maddening then, now seemed endearing. She pushed back a wave of nostalgia and straightened her gloves. Time to meet her new colleagues.

A colored man wearing a porter's uniform stepped forward and opened Louisa's door. He extended his arm. "Ma'am?"

Maggie felt a flicker of irritation as Louisa climbed awkwardly from the passenger seat and struggled with her ebony cane. Her arthritis must be acting up again. If she'd lose twenty pounds as

Maggie suggested, she'd feel a million times better.

When Louisa stood on the sidewalk, stiff and square, the porter opened Maggie's door.

"Thank you," she said. He smiled tightly, a small smile that compressed his full lips into a narrow line. A goiter under his left jaw bulged over the tight collar of his uniform, the skin grayed by pressure. His thyroid should come out, Maggie decided. If he didn't have surgery scheduled already, she'd offer to do it gratis so she could keep her hand in. It wasn't a complicated operation, and she could save him the surgeon's fee. Maybe the hospital would reduce the room cost for an employee or take him as a charity case.

The porter helped Louisa into the lobby while Bennett drove the car to the parking lot. As she followed, Maggie studied her mother-in-law. Mourner or martyr? A month after Doc's death, Louisa still wore full mourning: black hat and veil, black silk dress, black stockings, and black shoes with Cuban heels. Her stiff carriage implied that even her corset was black. A necklace of jet beads glinted in the folds of her mink stole. The glass eyes of the topmost animal winked at Maggie.

Inside the stiff clothing, Louisa held herself as if she was limp with exhaustion. The fine skin under her eyes was dry and wrinkled, her jowls sagged. Face powder had collected in the deep lines from her nostrils to the corners of her grim mouth. Small beads of perspiration dotted her upper lip. Louisa dabbed them with a scrap of cambric trimmed in black tatting and tucked the handkerchief back into the sleeve of her dress.

"Would you like to sit down while we wait for Bennett, Mother Kendall?" Maggie asked.

Louisa straightened her back. "Don't be ridiculous." She clutched the strap of her purse, and her gloves strained over her swollen knuckles. She stared at Maggie's exposed cleavage. "You must be cold."

With a woman her own age, Maggie would have joked about the clothes Bennett had chosen for her. But Aunt Vessie had raised her to defer to her elders, so she murmured, "Yes, I am chilly," and pulled her chiffon stole around her shoulders.

In truth, Maggie felt exposed in her silly little New Look dress. Tight around her bust, it clung to her waist and then exploded into a black, rhinestone-studded skirt, which reached to mid-calf. Her elbow-length gloves, high-heeled shoes, her tiny hat and cocktail bag had been dyed to match her dress.

Her charm bracelet, a wedding present from Bennett, twisted around the rhinestone bracelet that matched her necklace and earrings. She wore two charms, her Phi Beta Kappa key and a gold caduceus.

The day before they left Chicago, Bennett had cashed his last paycheck from the VA and whisked her off for a shopping trip at Marshall Field's. It had been a mad, extravagant whirl, as unbelievable as a rocket trip to the moon.

At Louisa's house this afternoon, fastening the corset that narrowed her waist and thrust out her breasts, Maggie had felt like a harem girl primping for the sultan. "I should wear something simple," she told Bennett. "We're in mourning. And I don't want people to think I'm a floozy."

"You're not a floozy, sweetheart." He had spun her around and kissed her. "Besides, I want everyone to admire my pretty little wife."

Now Maggie smiled at the memory. Bennett strode through the front doors and grinned back. Even though the evening was mild, he wore Doc's topcoat, black fedora, and gloves—the very image of a successful professional man.

Maggie stifled a snort. No one could imagine how truly broke they were. Despite the GI Bill, they had borrowed thousands of dollars so Bennett could finish his residency, and Maggie still had her student loans to repay. No matter. As soon as they were settled in Zillah and back to work, they could clear away their debts. And buy a home of their own. She hadn't lived in a house with a real backyard since Iowa, since her parents died and Aunt Vessie had carted her back to live in Chicago. She'd plant a pair of purple lilacs to remember them by.

Bennett escorted Maggie and Louisa to the elevator, where he pulled out a small brass seat for his mother. The porter took them to the fourth floor and opened the door. Maggie waited in the hallway while Bennett helped Louisa from the seat.

She heard laughter. The sound of clinking glasses drifted from an open door, borne on a cloud of cigar smoke. Louisa clung stiffly to Bennett's right arm and fumbled with her cane.

He extended his left hand to Maggie. "Tonight I'm stepping high, wide, and handsome with my two best girls." He squeezed Maggie close. "I'm a lucky guy."

Louisa stared straight ahead without answering. Maggie wanted to pinch her. Bennett was so happy tonight, like a little boy with a new truck. Why couldn't his mother be kind for once?

A brass tablet had been mounted on the wall next to the boardroom door, but before Maggie could read it, Bennett swept them into the crowded room. Maggie took one look at the other women and her heart sank. They wore wool crepe or gabardine suits with prim organdy blouses. No cleavage anywhere. With each step, her taffeta skirt swished against her silk stockings and whispered *floozy, floozy.*

They stopped beside a heavy man with the face of a cold cream model: rosy, sculpted lips; thick, white skin; icy-blue eyes behind gold-rimmed glasses. Maggie felt a flutter of distrust. The wide satin lapels of his black tuxedo gleamed dully as he held Louisa's hands for a moment before turning to Maggie.

"Maggie, this is Dr. Grandheim," Bennett said, "the chairman of the hospital trustees. Dr. Grandheim, may I present my wife, Margaret Kendall."

"Ah, Mrs. Kendall." Grandheim's voice was surprisingly high for such a large man.

"Dr. Kendall," Maggie replied with a level stare. Just because she had dressed like a floozy didn't mean she would be treated like one.

"Indeed." Grandheim took her gloved hand. "Bennett, why don't you help your mother with the buffet?" He nodded to a student nurse holding a silver platter of martinis. "Your wife and I will have a cocktail and get acquainted." He released Maggie's hand and turned his back on Bennett, who flashed her an imploring look.

Grandheim picked two glasses from the tray and gave one to Maggie. She took a small sip and wondered how to broach the subject of the porter's goiter. She didn't want to sound critical, especially if he were Dr. Grandheim's patient. But something had to be done. She decided to start with a neutral topic.

"I understand Community Memorial Hospital is scheduled to open a new surgical pavilion next year."

"Yes, indeed." Grandheim bent toward her with an old-fashioned bow, and she caught a whiff of Bay Rum. "It's my passion, you know, getting that wing built. It's key to a vision I've cherished for a long time."

"A vision?"

"Yes. There's no reason why Zillah can't become the center for modern medical practice in northern Indiana. The new surgical wing is only the first step, my dear. Only the first step. Once it's built, we can attract the finest specialists the country has to offer."

"Bennett's mother hopes the new building will be named for her husband."

Dr. Grandheim rocked back on his heels. "The hospital trustees are sympathetic to dear Louisa, but, of course, we must bow to the wishes of our donors."

"Of course."

Grandheim finished his drink and handed the glass back to one of the nursing students.

"So, Margaret Mueller Kendall." Grandheim's gaze swept up and down her body with open appraisal, and Maggie felt a sudden impulse to cover her bosom with both hands. "I've heard a lot about you. Yes, indeed." He folded his hands over his stomach and rocked back on his heels.

"From Bennett?"

"No, from my sister's boy." Grandheim's bald head bobbed up and down. His soft jowls quivered. "My nephew started medical school with you at the University of Illinois." He cleared his throat and peered at her over the top of his bifocals. "He was going to join my practice when he graduated. That boy would have made a fine doctor, let me tell you. A fine doctor."

"Would have made?" Maggie lifted her eyebrows in polite inquiry. "Has he been drafted?"

"No." Grandheim's tongue protruded between his full red lips as he lowered his chin and paused. "No, he was not promoted at the end of his second year."

"Oh." Sensing a trap, she studied Grandheim's face. "What's your nephew's name?"

"Allen Cook."

"I'm sorry, I don't remember him."

Grandheim smiled with tightly pursed lips. "He remembers you, though. Told us all about the brilliant Margaret Mueller who was always at the top of her class. 'Brilliant and beautiful,' he said."

A warm glow crept up Maggie's neck. "Thank you, Dr. Grandheim."

Grandheim let his cold stare rest on the tops of her breasts. "Allen said he never knew whether he lost out to your brains or to your pretty little face."

Maggie flinched as if he'd slapped her. A hundred men—and three women—had been in her class in medical school. Did Grandheim really blame his nephew's failure on her? Or was he trying to intimidate her?

It didn't matter. It was time to take the bull by the horns and let Grandheim know she planned to practice her brand of medicine in this town, with his blessing or without.

"I noticed the hospital porter's goiter."

"Indeed."

"Is he scheduled for a thyroidectomy?"

"Who? Old Tom?" Grandheim chuckled. "Oh, no. He doesn't want surgery."

"I don't understand. It's such a simple procedure."

"He can't afford it, my dear."

"Can't the hospital take him as a charity case?"

"All of our charity cases are referred by local ministers. I don't suppose any of them would know Old Tom from Old Nick." Grandheim smiled, pleased with his mild joke.

"Which church does he attend? I could speak to the pastor."

Grandheim stared at her, astonishment written across his face. "Which church? Well, bless my heart, how should I know? It's got to be one of the two colored churches down by the river, but I can't keep them straight. As for the pastor, those people don't have a regular minister, can't afford it. You'd have to talk to a lay brother, a ditch digger or some such, who wouldn't understand a surgical procedure if you drew him a full-color picture."

Maggie straightened her shoulders. She was beginning to despise this man. "I believe doctors should take care of people whether they can pay or not. As soon as I'm admitted to practice at the hospital, Dr. Grandheim, I plan to schedule Tom for surgery."

"As soon as you're admitted." Grandheim glanced down at her through his gold-rimmed glasses. "Hasn't your husband spoken to you yet, Mrs. Kendall?"

CHAPTER NINE:
MAGGIE

"Has Bennett spoken to me?" Maggie's eyes narrowed. "What do you mean?"

Instead of answering, Dr. Grandheim glanced past her. "I see Senator Jenner has arrived. Excuse me, Mrs. Kendall."

Clearly, the sultan had better things to do than debate a harem girl. He darted through the crowd, his heavy body surprisingly light on his tiny feet in their patent leather slippers. Maggie itched to stick out her leg and trip him.

She searched the room for Bennett. Why hadn't he warned her about Grandheim? She saw him standing on the other side of the buffet table and talking with an elderly lady, who gestured as she spoke. Louisa sat next to him, her hand clutching his sleeve. It wasn't going to be easy to pry him loose. Maggie pressed through the crowd anyway.

A few feet from the door, she bumped into one of the student nurses and knocked her tray of canapés to the floor.

Maggie swore under her breath as she bent to retrieve the small sandwiches.

"Dr. Kendall?" A hand touched her shoulder. "The girl will clean it up."

"Yes. Please, let me." The student nurse had already swept most of the appetizers onto the tray and covered them with a linen napkin.

Maggie stood and smoothed her taffeta skirt. A tall man stood in front of her, beaming as he held out a hand.

"We haven't been properly introduced, but welcome to Zillah. I'm Peter Grandheim, Dr. Grandheim's son."

The contrast between father and son could not have been more complete. Although he limped slightly, Peter stood two or three inches taller than any other man in the room. His brown hair, bleached gold by the sun, framed a strong, tanned face and marine blue eyes. He seemed more suited to a Cinerama screen than a small-town cocktail party.

"I'm pleased to meet you, Mr. Grandheim." Maggie glanced at Bennett, who was still engrossed in his conversation. With an internal shrug, she turned to Peter Grandheim.

"How do you like Zillah so far, Dr. Kendall?"

Maggie struggled for a polite response and felt herself blush. Peter grinned as if he could read her mind. "Don't answer. I can guess."

Maggie smiled back. *You're too damn attractive and you know it. But you're the first person in this town to call me doctor without tripping over your tongue.* "What do you do, Mr. Grandheim?"

"Me? I'm a legislative aide for Senator William E. Jenner." Peter Grandheim nodded over his shoulder at the noisy cluster of men by the door. "There he is now, talking with the hospital trustees."

"His aide?" Maggie stumbled over the words, unable to control a moue of distaste. "You work for the Indiana McCarthy?"

"Yes. There's a lot of folks hereabouts who believe Joe McCarthy and Bill Jenner are the last bulwarks against communism in this great nation of ours."

What did she hear in his voice—a trace of irony or a warning? "What do you believe, Mr. Grandheim?"

"Call me Peter." He grinned again. "And, ma'am, I believe I'm no more anxious to answer that question than you are to give me your impressions of Zillah."

"Touché." Maggie sipped her martini. "Can you tell me why Senator Jenner would care about the hospital in this little town?"

"You haven't heard him speak, have you, Dr. Kendall?" Peter took her empty glass and set it on a nearby table. "Bill Jenner believes farm towns are the real heart of America. Besides," Peter lowered his voice, "he's the biggest hypochondriac on Capitol Hill. If he ever gets sick around here, he wants to make sure the hospital is up to snuff."

Maggie laughed.

"May I introduce you?" Peter reached for her hand. "The senator always wants to meet the prettiest lady in the room."

"Meet Bill Jenner? No, of course not." Maggie pushed down a surge of repulsion. She had learned everything she needed to know about Jenner from her Aunt Vessie, a professor at Roosevelt College in Chicago, one of the most progressive schools on the face of the earth and one of the first to hire women. Three years ago, in 1949, Vessie had testified before Jenner's subcommittee on the control of subversive activities. Despite knowing that teachers in Boston and New York had been fired after Jenner's committee got through with them, she had testified against two bills that would have required members of the Communist Party to register with the Federal government.

When Jenner asked, "Are you now or have you ever been a member of the Communist Party?" she took the Fifth Amendment. To no one's surprise, Jenner had urged the college administration to fire her. To Maggie's surprise, the college had refused. Enrollment in Vessie's classes soared to an all-time high. No one but Maggie knew the toll the conflict had taken on her aunt. The thought of meeting Senator Jenner tonight made her physically ill.

"Sorry." Peter studied her face for a minute, and Maggie wondered again if he could read her mind. Well, let him! She wasn't going to change her opinions to suit Peter any more than she'd change her profession to please his father. They'd have to learn to live with who she was.

"Let me get you another cocktail, and I promise—" Peter sketched a Boy Scout salute "—I won't mention politics again."

"Thank you."

He drew her into a curtained alcove by a window. "Wait here."

"Doesn't your boss need you?" Maggie couldn't resist a verbal poke, but Peter took her words at face value.

"Not until it's time to drive home."

He disappeared into the crowd. Maggie drifted to the open window and stared at the town laid out below her like an illustration from a children's book. The sun had set. She heard the lonely whistle of the Monon train as it chugged through Zillah, its Cyclops eye glowing. Several blocks away, a dozen lights illuminated the statue of a Civil War soldier in the courthouse square. Elsewhere the town was twilight dark except for the neon sign that blinked "Packaged Liquor."

Despite the laughter in the room behind her, the clatter of plates and silverware, the cigarette smoke, and the gin warming her stomach, Maggie stood alone and isolated, like a princess trapped behind high castle walls. She wanted to be down there, down on the ground where real people lived and worked— sweaty men with dirty hands, mothers who scrubbed floors and slept without dreaming. If the hospital trustees had served ginger ale and Saltines instead of martinis and caviar, they could have saved enough money to pay for the porter's operation.

"Dr. Kendall?" Despite his limp, Peter had managed to balance a small plate of canapés as well as two cocktail glasses.

"Please, call me Maggie." She took the olive from her glass and set it next to the canapé dish. "Were you in the war, Peter?"

"No, I was 4F." He tapped his thigh. "Polio. I was lucky,

though. Doc—you know, Bennett's father—heard of Sister Kenny's hot packs and massages long before they were accepted in the states. He persuaded my father to try them. Afterward, Dad would have done anything for Doc."

"I guess a lot of folks around here worshipped Bennett's father." Maggie picked out a shrimp puff. "What was it like to grow up in Zillah?"

"Let me show you." Peter put his hands on her shoulders and gently turned her so she faced the window. His palms felt firm and strong against her bare skin. As she looked out, Peter described the scenic attractions of Zillah: Meyer's feed store, the Deep Valley Grange, the Odd Fellows Hall, and something he called the smallest slum in the free world, a ramshackle collection of wooden shacks on the riverbank. It was too dark to see clearly, but his descriptions were gently ironic and unexpectedly sweet.

Peter finished his cocktail. "Enough about me. Where did you practice medicine before you came to Zillah?"

"I was the attending physician at an obstetrical clinic for indigent women in Chicago."

"Tell me about it."

Peter turned out to be as good a listener as he was a raconteur. As she described the clinic on Maxwell Street, he laughed at the right moments and asked intelligent questions about her patients. It was the type of conversation she had hoped to have tonight, but with a colleague, not a politician.

"So, after all that, you landed in Zillah." Peter offered her the last toast point, heaped with black caviar. "Do you plan to open a clinic here?" He leaned close and whispered, "I warn you, the hospital frowns on competition."

His breath was laden with gin. Maggie pulled away. "Of course not. I'm going to partner with Bennett. What's your ambition, Peter?"

"I intend to become attorney general of the great state of Indiana."

"Really?" She couldn't tell if he was kidding.

"Working with Senator Jenner has given me a taste for politics." Peter straightened his tie. "I have some pretty strong ideas about what's wrong with this country. With Bill's support, I may get the chance to try them out." He stuck his hands in his pockets and gave her that smile again, the one that said she was beautiful and he was interested.

"Peter, you old skirt chaser! I knew you'd be here." Bennett stepped between them and put a possessive arm around Maggie's waist.

Peter winked at her, lazy and knowing. Maggie felt an unexpected flush of guilt, as if she were six years old again and had been caught stealing cookies.

CHAPTER TEN:
MAGGIE

"Nepotism?" Maggie slipped her aching feet from her shoes and rubbed her insteps, one after the other, as Bennett steered Doc's Oldsmobile out of the hospital parking lot. In the front seat, Louisa sat next to him, her back poker stiff. "That's what Dr. Grandheim said? What did he mean?"

Bennett pulled into the street. A car passed going in the opposite direction. Its headlights flickered across Bennett's face and lit up his bald spot. He grimaced. "The hospital trustees have a policy forbidding nepotism. It means that you won't be admitted to practice as long as I'm on staff."

"But Bennett." Maggie gripped the back of his seat. The car accelerated around the corner. She slid sideways in a rush of panic, as if the ground had shifted under her feet. "If I can't admit patients to the hospital, there's no way I can work as a doctor in Zillah. Why didn't you tell me before the reception?"

Bennett scowled in the rearview mirror. "Because I think it's a Mickey-Mouse policy. Because I hoped Dr. Grandheim might relent once he met you. Because—" He glanced back at the road and sighed. "Because I feel like an all-American chump, sweetheart."

"You have to talk to Grandheim again."

"There's no point in bellyaching." Bennett sounded tired and defeated. "He won't listen to me."

Louisa turned in her seat and glared at Maggie. "What do you expect, Margaret? The hospital trustees to change their

65

policy to suit your convenience?"

"I expected to practice medicine with my husband, Mother Kendall." Maggie's temples throbbed. "I'll bet that policy is so new the ink isn't dry yet."

"Please, Maggie," Bennett started.

Louisa interrupted. "You could have asked me, Junior." She sniffed. "I knew what the trustees would say." She touched her lips with her handkerchief. "Doc always maintained that he never did find a female doctor he could trust. Women just aren't suited."

The blood pounded behind Maggie's eyes. She took a deep breath and said coldly, calmly, "Do you mean to tell me, Mother Kendall, before we moved to Zillah I knew I would not be admitted to practice at Community Memorial Hospital?"

This time Louisa didn't even turn her head. "Of course. Bennett should have known it, too."

Maggie couldn't answer. Louisa was right. If Bennett hadn't known, he must have guessed. And the deal they made in Chicago? When she agreed to give up the clinic so he could have his father's practice? He had betrayed her. That deal was over.

For a nickel I'd grab my daughter and hop on the train back to Chicago so fast that . . . No! Maggie sat up straight and pulled her shoes on. She wasn't going to let this bunch of patronizing dinosaurs defeat her. She was going to be a doctor in Zillah, one way or the other. They'd have to get used to the idea. And if they didn't? Too damn bad.

She stared out her window at the shuttered houses flitting by, at the dark streets made even darker by the branches of the elm trees that touched overhead. Peter seemed to understand what her work meant to her. And he was Grandheim's son. If Bennett wouldn't go to bat for her, maybe Peter would.

CHAPTER ELEVEN:
BENNETT

Friday, September 5, 1952

Three days after the cocktail reception at the hospital, Bennett drove home feeling at peace with the world. He rolled down the window of the Olds to let in the smell of sun-dried hay. It was good to be back in Zillah again. His office had been busy all week. Apparently none of his father's patients planned to change doctors. And a lucky thing, too.

Josef Grandheim had been right—there really wasn't enough business in Zillah to support another doctor. Maybe when the new hospital wing opened, but not before. Grandheim should have tried to educate Maggie about the economics of medicine in a small town instead of forcing through that policy on nepotism.

He entered the house, loosened his tie, and mopped the back of his neck with his handkerchief. In the long run, though, it didn't matter. Maggie was sensible. She'd get over her hurt feelings. And they could try for a son or two while they waited for Doc's practice to grow. Maybe in four or five years, by the time Ellie started first grade, Maggie could go back to work. If she still wanted to.

Bennett kissed his mother and glanced through the mail. Whistling, he strolled outside to find Maggie. He'd take her out for a nice dinner tomorrow night. They could afford it now. Someplace air-conditioned. She'd wear that sexy little black dress. They'd have a couple of dry martinis and then—

He smiled. Maggie's shoes stood outside the chicken coop. He pushed open the heavy wooden door and stepped across the threshold. The acrid smell of chicken droppings stung his nose. A narrow shaft of sunlight streamed into the building, gilding the hay motes and pinfeathers that hung in the still air. He tasted dust at the back of his throat.

He unfastened his cuff links and rolled up his shirtsleeves. As his eyes adjusted to the dimness, he saw Maggie at the back of the shed in her rubber boots, gathering eggs. She straightened when he called to her, but her hand lingered in one of the nest boxes that lined the wall. She put a brown egg into the galvanized zinc bucket standing upright in the straw and smiled at him, her mouth crooked. She looked beat to a frazzle.

She must have seen the letter from the medical school at Indiana U. Shit. His hopes for a romantic evening faded away.

He crossed the chicken house in half-a-dozen strides and put his arms around her. "I'm sorry, sweetheart."

"It's not right." Maggie rested her head against his chest and wiped her nose with the ruffled shoulder strap of her apron. She fit against his body like she belonged there. "I called the dean as soon as I read his letter."

Bennett tightened his arms around her. "What did he say?"

"He said he knew I was at the top of my class in med school, that I had been at the top all four years." She beat her closed fist against his chest. It sounded like the tapping of a child's drum. "But he said grades aren't everything. He said I don't need a residency because I'm a wife and mother. He has only two positions in obstetrics, and he's going to give them to men who will be full-time doctors."

"Veterans?"

"I suppose so. And they have families to support." Maggie stooped and picked up the handle of the pail. "Did you ask Dr. Grandheim to reconsider?"

"Yes." Bennett took the bucket. The eggs clinked against each other. "Josef Grandheim is adamant."

"Damn! If his son were a physician, I'll bet the trustees would change the policy in a minute."

"Maybe so." There was no point in rehashing that issue. He nuzzled her hair. It smelled like summer flowers. He could lose himself in the smell of her.

Maggie pulled away. "Grandheim!" It sounded like a curse.

"What did you two talk about at the reception the other night? His hackles went up the minute I said your name."

"His nephew flunked out of medical school while I was there. Dr. Grandheim seemed to think it was my fault." Maggie rubbed her eyes and shrugged. "He and the dean certainly make a fine pair, the old reprobates. They hate women like me."

"Ignore them, sweetheart. Once the new surgical wing is complete, the hospital will need more doctors. I'm sure I can get the trustees to reconsider by then." Bennett wanted to cross his fingers behind his back, but he reached for her waist instead.

Maggie stepped to the side, neatly evading his hand. "I'm not going to wait. Forget the residency. The state medical board will let me qualify for a license without it. I'm driving to the public health clinic in West Lafayette on Monday. Peter said they are looking for a general practitioner, and they may be willing to consider a woman."

"Not Peter Grandheim?" *Peter needs to learn to keep his nose out of my business.*

"Yes. He called this morning. He seems to like doing favors." She shrugged. "Even for a Stevenson Democrat like me."

If a woman is sexy enough, Peter doesn't give a damn about politics. "Maggie, you can't work at the public health clinic."

"Why not?"

"For one thing, it's a forty-five-minute drive each way."

"I used to spend an hour on the El every day, Bennett."

"But what about Ellie? What if you bring home lice or TB or polio?"

"Stop it. If working at a public health clinic is the only way I can have a medical practice in Indiana, that's what I'm going to do. I agreed to move to Zillah with you, Bennett. I did not agree to give up being a physician." She turned on her heel.

Without answering, he studied her as she crossed the hen house and opened the lower half of the Dutch door that led to the chicken yard. With that walk of hers, it'd take more than rubber boots and an apron to turn his glamour puss into a farm girl. He'd like to snatch her and carry her up to bed right now, galoshes and all.

"Chick, chick. Here chick, chick," she called as she scattered cracked corn across the floor.

The rooster stalked in first, dignified and slow. He glared at Bennett. His comb and wattle swelled as he lifted his head and crowed, challenging the male intruder. The hens scurried around the rooster, raising dust and clucking anxiously as they hopped into the empty nest boxes, fluffed their speckled feathers, and settled in the straw.

Maggie closed the Dutch door. "Is that what the dean saw when I talked to him? A speckled hen running around, flapping my wings, squawking hysterically when I'd be better off sitting on my nest and hatching chicks?" She grinned ruefully. "Is that what you see?"

"No, of course not." Bennett grabbed her wrist with one hand and the feed sack with the other. "I see my brilliant and beautiful wife, and I want her to be very happy living in Zillah with me. Let's talk about the public health clinic after supper."

He squashed a kiss against her cheek and followed her outside. She stopped next to the door, pulled off her rubber boots, and rinsed them under the spigot. "Are your shoes clean?"

Bennett lifted one foot and then the other to inspect his soles. "They're fine."

She stooped to pull on her shoes and tie the laces. Her long brown curls hid her face and muffled her voice. "How did you find out?"

He sighed. "How did I learn about the residency?"

"Yes. Did Dr. Grandheim tell you the dean turned me down? Does word get around town that fast?" Maggie straightened and pushed the hair away from her face.

"No, sweetheart." There was no point in stonewalling. "Mother mentioned it."

"But I didn't tell her. I wanted to talk to you first." Maggie paused. "She opens my mail."

"What's the big deal? It's Mother's house, and she's used to handling the mail. It's what she always did for Doc."

"She did more than open my letter. She read it." Maggie bent and shut off the water spigot, twisting the handle until her knuckles whitened. "I'm not your father, Bennett. I'm your wife. And I don't want your mother going through my mail. You tell her to stop or I will."

"Can't it wait?" Pain shot through his stomach. "Until things settle down a little?" He leaned against the wall and panted quietly in short, shallow breaths. No need to scare her.

"That's absurd." Maggie looked up. "Bennett, what's wrong? You're as pale as a ghost." She took his wrist and counted the seconds on her watch. "Your pulse is jumping around like crazy."

"It's nothing, sweetheart." Bennett yanked his arm away and picked up the bucket of eggs. "I'm hungry, that's all."

"But—"

"Junior!" his mother shouted from the back porch. "Dinner's ready!" The screen door slammed shut.

Bennett gave Maggie an impatient push toward the house. Before he closed the door to the chicken coop, he studied the hens. They clucked contentedly in their nests. He watched the red-breasted rooster with his gleaming tail feathers pace back and forth as he guarded his harem. *I love her,* he thought, *but what I really need is a sweet, plump, placid little wife and homemade bread rising in the oven. Maybe once Maggie's pregnant again, she'll calm down.*

CHAPTER TWELVE:
MAGGIE

September 6, 1952

Post Office Box 44

Zillah, Indiana

Dear Aunt Vessie,

As you see, I have a new post office box. I don't want to go into the particulars, but please write me at this address until further notice.

I survived my introduction to Zillah and the medical society—barely. Bennett thrust me into the cocktail reception at the hospital dressed in my new finery and, with his usual optimism, expected me to wow the old sourpusses. (Oh, yes, it was the fitted black dress with practically no bodice at all. You should have seen the stares! I've included a picture from the society pages of the *Zillah Courier*. Mother Kendall is the woman on the left glaring down the front of my dress.)

Despite all my blatantly exposed charms, Dr. Grandheim, who runs the hospital with an iron fist, absolutely refuses to allow me to admit patients to his hospital. He's using a trumped-up policy on nepotism as his excuse.

To make matters worse, who else do you suppose was at the cocktail party? None other than Senator William E. Jenner, Indiana's own Joe McCarthy. It appears he's a bigwig in Zillah, someone who can help get the new hospital wing built.

Anyway, I need your help. At the party, I met Dr. Grand-heim's son, Peter, who is a legislative aide to Senator Jenner. Despite working for that right-wing bigot, Peter seems very pleasant, intelligent, and, most important of all, liberal-minded where lady doctors are concerned. I want him to persuade his father to reconsider the nepotism rule.

Before I ask Peter for assistance, however, I need to know what went on between you and Jenner. I don't want to trip over any sleeping dogs!

Your loving niece, Maggie

P.S. Don't forget my new address

CHAPTER THIRTEEN:
BENNETT

Wednesday, September 10, 1952

Bennett came home from the hospital at eight-thirty that night, tired and hungry. He had skipped lunch to drive twenty miles east of town to check on a farmhand who'd fallen off a hay wagon and fractured his tibia. The kid was doing okay, but he'd have to lay off the booze before he got into serious trouble.

As Bennett tiptoed into the house, he thought about all the nights he had lain awake in his bedroom upstairs, listening for his father's footsteps. He'd promised himself that his children's lives would be different, but here he was, repeating the same old pattern. He hadn't seen Ellie at all today and probably wouldn't see her tomorrow. Good thing Maggie was around. The girl needed her mother.

He should move into hospital administration, where he could work from nine to five and still make good do-re-mi, but the job wouldn't open up until the new medical center was built. Which could take years, even if the board of trustees was willing to appoint him.

He trudged into the kitchen and dropped his black bag next to the Frigidaire. His mother gave him a quick hug before she opened the oven door and lifted the cover from the plate of pork chops and mashed potatoes she had kept warm for him. It smelled so good he groaned.

He remembered standing on the deck of the troop ship on his way home from New Guinea and tossing his last box of

C-rations into the ocean. At that moment, if anyone had asked him what they'd fought for, he would have said a home-cooked meal served on a china plate. Tonight he still felt that way. He slumped into a seat at the table, and Louisa poured him a glass of milk.

"You've got to do something about that wife of yours, Junior. Or you aren't going to have any patients left." She put the bottle of milk in the refrigerator and slammed the door.

"What's wrong, Mother?" Bennett touched his stomach. The burning had started as soon as he sat down. He gulped half the milk, and the pain subsided.

Louisa bustled around the kitchen without looking at him. "I took your wife to the garden club today out of the sheer goodness of my heart. She's been moping around here since the public health clinic turned her down until I thought I'd go mad." Louisa made an impatient gesture as she sat across the table from him.

Bennett chowed down a forkful of mashed potatoes. There was no point in saying anything until Mother got it all off her chest.

"Mrs. Cominski was complaining that her food backs up on her most days. That wife of yours told her to put her fork down and go for a walk if she wanted to feel better. I mean really!"

Bennett bit back a smile. That sounded like Maggie, all right. Damn the torpedoes and full speed ahead. And it wasn't bad advice. Just the wrong time and the wrong place.

"Her husband's on the hospital board. You know that, don't you, Junior?"

Bennett nodded, well aware of the implied message. Mother was right. He couldn't afford to have Maggie antagonize Cominski, especially if she wanted the board to take her seriously. Somehow he'd have to smooth things over.

Louisa spooned more gravy on his meat. "I wish your father

was alive, Junior. He'd know what to do with her. You're too soft where Margaret is concerned."

"Maybe so." Bennett finished his milk and wiped his mouth. "I'll give it a shot, Mother. See if I can make her understand how things work around here."

She raised both eyebrows and shot him a skeptical look. "Exactly how do you propose to do that?"

Mindful of Maggie's fury about her opened mail, he didn't know either. "Let me talk to her." Time to change the subject. "Dinner was wonderful, Mother."

Louisa jumped up and refilled his glass. "That's another thing. That wife of yours didn't eat a single bite of the meal I fixed."

"She's never liked pork. You know that."

"It's good healthy food. She should eat it." Louisa sat down again, pulled a handkerchief from her sleeve and patted the perspiration on her upper lip. "I don't know what she wants. Margaret has everything any sensible person could need. A roof over her head, a little girl who's smart as a whip, and a Christian husband who's a war hero to boot."

"I wasn't a hero, Mother. I did my bit like everyone else."

"You're too modest." Louisa reached across the table and squeezed his fingers until he was forced to look at her. "All I want is for you to be happy, Junior. The whole time you were overseas, I couldn't go anywhere but some sweet young thing would come up to me and ask how you were doing. I must have given your address to a dozen of them."

"I know." Bennett pulled his hand away and cut another pork chop. "Thanks to you, I got more scented letters than any other guy in my unit."

"You could have married any girl in this county. Any one of them. If Margaret hadn't trapped you."

"Trapped me?" *Damn. Couldn't he eat in peace for once?* "What are you talking about?"

"I may not be a doctor, but I'm nobody's fool." Louisa pinched her lips together. "Eleanor wasn't born two months early. Margaret was already in the family way when you married her."

"But, Mother." Bennett stopped. He couldn't explain how he had gone all out to win Maggie. Her pregnancy, unexpected and unplanned, had been the best thing that ever happened to him. He'd felt like the luckiest guy in the world.

Louisa sat back in her chair and folded her hands in her lap. Bennett finished his meal and laid down his knife and fork.

"What kind of pie do you want? There's apple or cherry. Or I could heat the leftover cobbler."

"Nothing, thanks. I'm all in." Bennett stood and picked up his plate. Hunger satisfied, he wanted to get his hands on his wife. *I hope she waited up for me.*

"Stop that." Louisa grabbed the dish out of his hands. "I'll clean up. You go right upstairs and get your rest." She set his plate on the table and reached up to stroke his cheek. "I'm so glad you came back to Zillah, Junior. I wish your father could see you now."

"Me, too." Bennett slipped away from her and picked up his black bag. He hurried across the kitchen, but paused in the doorway to the living room. Upstairs Maggie waited for him, but with Doc gone, his mother had no one else to talk to. It wouldn't hurt to spend another minute shooting the breeze.

He leaned against the doorjamb. "I really miss him, Mother. Every time I go into his office, I expect Doc to be sitting there, reviewing some patient's chart and chewing that old cigar."

"Me too." Louisa pleated her apron between her fingers as her eyes teared up. Bennett studied the coarse gray threads in her brown hair, the faint mustache on her upper lip, the blue pouches under her eyes. She looked completely washed out. He felt sad and protective.

He turned his head away, toward the kitchen window, toward the dark fields outside. But all he saw was himself, a wavering reflection distorted by the old glass. "I want to be a good country doctor like Doc was. That's all."

Louisa wiped her eyes with the hem of her apron. "With your brains and your training, you could be even more, Junior. You could be the head of the new medical center in Zillah."

Yes. But he didn't want to queer the deal by talking about it. "We'll cross that bridge when we come to it, Mother. Sleep well."

Duty done, he hurried through the living room and climbed the stairs. His mother was right. He'd have to get Maggie settled down before the board would consider appointing him hospital administrator.

In the upper hall, the house was several degrees warmer, and Bennett wiped fresh sweat from his forehead. He saw a ribbon of light under the bedroom door. Maggie. She'd waited up for him. Anticipation built in his throat. He was ready to fraternize with the enemy all right.

Maggie jumped from her chair and spoke in a fierce whisper as he entered the bedroom. "I have to get out of here." She unbuttoned her housedress and kicked off her shoes. They bounced against the wall.

Shit! Not more trouble. Bennett shut the door. "What's the matter, sweetheart?" He pulled off his tie and tossed his jacket and bag onto a chair.

"I've been trying to play the role of the good doctor's wife, that's what. But I won't do it anymore." Maggie hung her dress in the closet. "This is a town of narrow-minded old ladies who gossip from morning to night, who go from bridge parties to the garden club and back again without having a single intelligent thought all day long."

How could she still be so slender? He watched her stride across the bedroom as she undressed. Pregnancy and childbirth had left barely a mark on the firm abdomen between her brassiere and her half-slip. Her white garter belt made a faint outline beneath her slip, the fasteners as knobby and provocative as bare nipples. He unfastened his cuff links and dropped them into a china bowl on the dresser.

"That may be what doctors' wives are supposed to do, but it's stupid, a waste of time. I can't stand it. I have to go back to work."

As Bennett listened, he pictured her smooth muscles moving with every step she took. He loved her muscles, her soft skin, her strong, square shoulders, but most of all he loved to caress the white striations on her abdomen, stretch marks from pregnancy so tiny that he had to find them with his fingertips before he could touch them with his tongue.

Maggie stopped next to the bed. Her voice softened. "This isn't what we planned, Bennett. It's not what you promised when we moved here."

"What do you want, Maggie?" He hated to be yanked away from his fantasy. "Instead of living in this grand old house, do you want to move back to Chicago, to a basement apartment?"

Maggie's face crumpled. *Too bad.* She had to understand.

"You could hang diapers above our bed again and boil water so it's fit to drink. Is that what you want?" He unbuttoned his shirt, pulled it off, and threw it at the clothes hamper.

"Yes," she said. "No." Maggie hugged herself. "I want our family to stay together."

"We are together. I'm here, sweetheart, and Ellie's sleeping right next door. All hands safe and accounted for." Bennett took her into his arms, stroking her spine, playing with the hooks and eyes of her brassiere, caressing the musculature of her shoulders. She pulled down the neck of his undershirt and rubbed her face in the hollow of his throat.

"You don't appreciate how lucky we are, Maggie. One month out of residency and already I'm supporting us and Mother, too. And you can stay home with our daughter."

Maggie pulled away from the circle of his arms. "This isn't about Ellie, Bennett. I love her. I'd kill to protect her if I had to. I wouldn't hesitate a minute."

"Hush." He touched his finger to her lips. "Don't go off the deep end, sweetheart."

"Okay. But between your mother and the kitchen girl, Ellie doesn't need me at home all day." Maggie ran her fingers through her hair. She pulled out the bobby pins and shook the curls free. "I don't belong here. Not in Zillah, not in this house."

Fire began to bubble in Bennett's stomach. "What do you mean?"

"I'm tired. Tired of feeling useless. Tired of being useless."

"I've got something for that." He released her. Maggie dropped to the bed and leaned against the iron bars of the headboard. He took the black bag from the chair, the medical bag with his father's initials stamped in gold. He opened it and searched inside.

"I found these in Doc's desk." Bennett held out a white envelope. "Take one in the morning with a glass of orange juice."

She took the envelope and opened it. "What are they?" She fingered the small white tablets.

"Miltown."

"Tranquilizers?"

"Yeah."

"No! I don't need happy pills." She crumpled the envelope and flung it at him. It tumbled in the air and fell softly on the bedspread. "There's nothing wrong with me. I just need to go back to work."

81

"Okay." Bennett sighed. All of a sudden, he wasn't sure she'd go for his plan. He turned to the window and pushed the sash up. Hot, humid air layered the house like a blanket, thick and soft, unmoving. Tornado weather. He leaned over the sill and breathed in. *Do I tell her or not?* The air smelled harvest ripe, full of promise. A bomber's moon shone over the fields, casting shadows under the pear trees. An owl hooted, and he saw a flicker of wings as it dived at the ground.

He drew in another deep breath. God, he loved Indiana. Loved the sounds and smells of it, the taste of it on his tongue. After that bloody war in New Guinea, he was glad to be home, more than glad. He belonged here, fitted in as smooth and snug as a peg in a hole. Not like Maggie. Vessie had taken her in after her folks died, but Maggie didn't have roots like he did, no deep attachment to a place. That was something he could give her.

He turned around and saw her frown at him. "I have an idea, sweetheart. It'd be duck soup for someone like you."

"Tell me."

Bennett pulled off his undershirt and wiped his armpits. "I ran into an old friend of mine today, Janet Davis. She's the fourth-grade teacher at the elementary school. She said they can't find a school nurse."

"I could fill in." Maggie's face brightened. She stood up. "What's involved?"

"They need someone to give the kids physicals." He dropped his undershirt into the clothes hamper. "You'd have to get cracking, though. They're way behind schedule."

"Tomorrow." Maggie snapped her fingers. "I'll skip the Junior League breakfast and be at the school by eight." She looked poised for flight.

She'd bought it! His heart raced. She sauntered over and twined her fingers through his belt loops. "Thanks, honey."

He watched a bead of sweat inch between her breasts and disappear under the lace edging of her brassiere. "It will give you a chance to bump elbows with people who don't play bridge. And the physicals are important. It's the only time some of these farm kids ever see a doctor." He chuckled. "Besides, it won't hurt to remind folks that Doc's boy is back in town."

Maggie's eyes danced, and his body responded. "This is honest, pro bono work, isn't it, Dr. Kendall?" she said. "Not advertising. You do know the AMA forbids advertising, don't you?"

"Yes, Dr. Kendall, I know the code of conduct." He spread his hands around her narrow hips, hips smooth and silky under the nylon slip, and pulled her against his groin. Her skin smelled faintly of roses, of lush wild roses, their deep red petals opening wide under the hot sun. Maggie made him feel strong and powerful. She was the only person who could do that.

His hands moved under her slip and found the top of her stockings. She leaned back, her eyes dark and heavy lidded. He groaned and drew her down to the bed. The nylon slip flowed through his hands like summer rain. He wanted to keep her, to put her in a glass box and keep her safe and beautiful, ready for him, in a beautiful glass box. And he'd have the only key.

Zillah Courier. *Thursday, September 11, 1952*

Sen. William E. Jenner, R-Ind., will address the Northern Indiana Medical Society, on Saturday, Sept. 13, at the Deep Valley Grange in Zillah, the senator's legislative aide, Peter Grandheim, announced today.

Jenner will speak on the Communist menace and the threat of socialized medicine, Grandheim said. The senator is campaigning for reelection, and the $25-a-plate dinner is a fund-raising event.

A straw poll recently conducted by the *Indianapolis Star* found that Jenner is in a tight race with his Democratic opponent, Indiana Gov. Henry F. Schricker.

"Stevenson liberals are flooding our state with tainted money in a desperate attempt to buy the election for Governor Schricker and cripple Senator Jenner's noble struggle against the forces of Communism," Grandheim said at a press conference yesterday.

The meeting will begin with a cocktail reception at 6 p.m., followed by dinner. Jenner will speak at 7:30 p.m. Tickets may be purchased at the door.

CHAPTER FOURTEEN: MAGGIE

Friday, September 12, 1952

By eleven-thirty, the smell of fried fish had permeated Pulaski Elementary School, causing Maggie to wonder if cooking grease was coating her face. It had taken all morning to examine the third-graders, who were not as intimidated by her white lab coat and stethoscope as the younger children had been the day before. While her back was turned, one girl had opened Maggie's black bag, unrolled several yards of sterile gauze, and draped it over her head like a wedding veil.

Maggie didn't mind. It felt good to be working again—even as a substitute school nurse. She wrote follow-up slips while she waited for the next class to arrive. One of the first-grade boys almost certainly had hookworms, but his family doctor could deal with that. So far, she had seen no signs of polio or TB, and no rickets, which had been common in the slums of Chicago.

Pulaski Elementary was a beautiful school, new and already overcrowded. Classrooms built for twenty children were packed with thirty, and the lunchroom operated in shifts. Books filled only a third of the shelves in the library, however, and the nurse's office, which still smelled of fresh paint, stood empty, aside from the brass plate on the door and the scale in the corner. Hopefully the school would be better equipped by the time Ellie started kindergarten.

The custodian, a one-armed colored man, had fetched Maggie a stool from the principal's office. She sat on it, sipping

Coca-Cola from a Dixie Cup, and riffled through the forms from the state health department.

Janet Davis, the fourth-grade teacher, had been a pleasant surprise. Tall, athletic, with a cloud of short curls and golden-brown eyes, she had taken Maggie on a tour of the school Thursday morning before classes started. The excursion ended in a fit of giggles outside the principal's office when Janet whispered, "Mr. Cominski is a pompous old fart. Avoid him like the plague."

For the first time since arriving in Zillah, Maggie had made a friend. She'd sensed Janet didn't feel truly comfortable in Zillah either, even though she had been born here. Another outsider. *We should stick together.*

As she finished her soda, Maggie heard shuffling and whispers in the hallway. Janet rapped on the door twice and called out, "Dr. Kendall? We're ready."

Maggie dropped the paper cup in the wastepaper basket and opened the door. The fourth graders stood in two restless lines, boys on the left, girls on the right. She smiled. "Hello, children. My name is Dr. Kendall."

Under Janet's sharp eye, they answered, "Hello, Dr. Kendall," in a ragged cadence.

"I'm going to ask you to come in here one at a time. First a girl and then a boy. I'll check your eyes and ears with my little light." Maggie turned her penlight on for a second. "Then I'll listen to your heart—" she waved her stethoscope "—and check that your spine isn't curved." A couple of girls straightened nervously. "Then I'll weigh you and measure you and send you back to your classroom."

She surveyed the line of clean and well-mannered children with pleasure. This school would be perfect for Ellie. "Any questions?"

No one moved. Maggie beckoned the first girl into the office and began. Fifteen minutes and five children later, a boy stepped through the door. She thought he looked younger than the other fourth graders, pale and thin beneath his flannel shirt and denim jeans. Like many of the children at Pulaski Elementary, his clothes appeared to have been handed down a time or two. His shirt was neatly darned, and the legs of his pants had been lengthened with several inches of new denim. He smelled like a bushel of apples left standing too long in the rain—musty, sweet, and a little damp. Possibly a bed wetter?

"What's your name, dear?"

"Zeke Whittaker." He stood at parade rest, his hands clasped behind his back. His brass belt buckle gleamed. "Folks call me Zeke."

Maggie smiled as she checked his name on her list. "I'll bet your daddy was in the war."

"Yes, ma'am!" He saluted her. "U.S. Army Corps of Engineers, ma'am."

"Well, Zeke, what do you like to do at school?" she asked as she checked his eyes and ears.

"Draw mostly, ma'am."

"That's nice." She looked into his throat: no sign of strep or diphtheria, no scars from mumps. "Good." She listened to his heart. It beat with a steady, reassuring thump. "Please lift your shirt so I can check your spine, Zeke."

He pulled his shirttails out of his pants and held the plaid flannel over his head. Maggie winced. His back was crisscrossed by red lines, fresh welts raised on his transparent white skin. The welts overlapped other lines, thin and white, old scars. She felt sick. In Chicago, she had seen children who had been whipped, but she hadn't expected to find them in Zillah.

She dug inside herself for calm. She knew exactly what to do. First, cleanse the wounds, then stop the beating.

She opened a bottle of witch hazel, moistened a cotton ball, and gently washed the boy's back. Zeke flinched, but said nothing. When she was done, Maggie pulled his shirt down and turned him around.

"What are those marks?"

"Don't rightly know, ma'am." His voice was muffled as he bent his head, intent on making sure his shirt was tucked tightly back in place.

Maggie put a finger under his chin and tilted his head. His eyes, as green as corn sprouts, were touched with flecks of gold.

"Zeke? Do you ever wet the bed at night?"

He looked over her shoulder. His eyes seemed to jump back and forth.

"You can tell me. I'm a doctor. I can help you."

She watched his jaw muscles work as if he were trying not to cry.

"Who whipped you, son?"

He pinched his mouth shut and shook his head.

She hadn't really expected him to answer. They both knew if he named the person who beat him, his punishment would be worse the next time. *First, do no harm.* Maggie couldn't afford to interfere unless she could absolutely guarantee the boy's safety. And she didn't know how to protect him. Not in Zillah.

But Janet might.

"Wait here, Zeke." She hoisted the lightweight boy onto her chair and poured him a cup of soda pop.

His eyes widened as she held out the cup. "For me?"

"Yes." Maggie stepped into the hall and shut the door behind her. "It's time for lunch, children," she said to the remaining fourth graders. "Go back to your classroom, and we'll finish the examinations this afternoon."

One boy raised his hand.

"Yes?"

"Where's Zeke, Dr. Kendall?"

"He's going to stay here for a minute. Go back to class."

Like a collie snapping at the heels of reluctant lambs, she turned them back. She followed the children down the hall and waited outside the classroom door for Janet to dismiss them for lunch. The custodian was mopping the floor in front of the boys' bathroom now. Despite missing his left arm, he seemed to work quickly and easily. The new linoleum gleamed.

Principal Cominski emerged from his office across the hall. He was one of those red-faced, rotund men whose stomach precedes them into every conversation, an enormous expanse of gut ornamented with a gold watch chain. Hypertensive from over-indulgence, Maggie thought with distaste.

"Ah, Mrs. Kendall." He panted as he marched toward her. "I need to have a word with you."

"Yes, Mr. Cominski?" She tried to keep the impatience out of her voice. She glanced towards the nurse's office, not sure how long Zeke could sit still.

Cominski puffed a little and bounced on the balls of his feet. "I hope you can come back Monday to do the coloreds. My report to the state board of health is already overdue."

"What are you talking about?"

"The coloreds. There's a column for them on the form."

"But I haven't seen any Negro children."

He bounced again. "I told the teachers to keep them in the classroom while you checked the other children. I imagine you have a separate set of instruments for them." Sweat gleamed on his broad cheeks. "I hope coming back Monday is agreeable."

"Separate instruments for the Negro children? You mean, like a different stethoscope?"

He nodded, exasperation clear in his pink face. "Can you come back?"

"That's ridiculous. I don't have separate instruments for Negroes. No responsible doctor would." Irritated, she shook her head. How could he fuss about that nonsense when one of his students was being beaten? "You do have a real problem in this school, however." She described the marks on Zeke's back.

"Zeke Whittaker?" Cominski shrugged. "His father has been known to use a switch."

"You mean his father whips him and you know about it?" Rage blurred her vision. "That's got to be stopped."

"Stopped?"

"Yes. Stopped right now. If you're sure the father's at fault, I'll call the sheriff." Maggie started across the hallway. "Is the telephone in your office?"

"Now wait a minute." Cominski grabbed Maggie's arm. His cheeks were mottled with purple splotches. "Corporal punishment is not against the law."

Maggie tried to shake her arm free. "If whipping a child is not against the law in this state, it should be."

His fingers tightened. "I know the family. His father is the football coach at the high school and his mother teaches Sunday School."

Her heart thumped. "But he beats his son!"

"Proverbs 13:24," Cominski said as if that settled the argument.

Stunned, Maggie searched her memory for a rebuttal. He must have seen her frown, because he continued in a condescending tone. " 'He that spareth his rod hateth his son: but he that loveth him chasteneth him.' And Proverbs 23:14: 'Thou shalt beat him with the rod and shalt deliver his soul from hell.' " His head bobbed up and down on his short, fleshy neck. "And Proverbs 19:18: 'Chasten thy son—' "

"Shut up, you fat-headed fool!"

Cominski jerked as if she had struck him, and Maggie heard a clatter behind her. The custodian had dropped his mop. The principal whipped off his glasses and wiped his eyes with a handkerchief. He glared at the custodian, who picked up the mop handle and turned his back.

Oh, God. Bad move. "I apologize," Maggie said quickly. "I'm very worried about the boy." She spread her hands. "I shouldn't have insulted you."

Cominski pulled himself together, slowly, with dignity. He settled the heavy, horn-rimmed glasses on his nose. "No, Mrs. Kendall, you shouldn't have." His eyes glinted behind the thick lenses. "Especially not while delivering a lecture against corporal discipline. I'm afraid your behavior makes a very poor case for your philosophy."

He appeared to be more concerned about preserving his self-respect than the welts on Zeke's back. She'd have to go around him to help the boy, but she didn't want to lose her position at the school. Who knew how many other children were being beaten?

"Please, sir." *I sound like Oliver Twist begging for more gruel, not a doctor,* she thought, appalled. "I would like to come back on Monday. I need to finish the examinations."

"We shall see." Cominski straightened his waistcoat and his tie, twisting his fat neck as if the starched collar of his shirt were strangling him. "But for now, I suggest you vacate the school premises before I am forced to summon the sheriff to escort you out." He brushed invisible dust from his lapels, slowly, deliberately, and pulled down his cuffs until they hung exactly half an inch below the sleeves of his jacket.

Maggie heard a noise on the other side of the hall. She glanced up as Janet opened the door of her classroom. The children filed out in two noisy lines, which quieted as soon as they saw the principal. A colored boy brought up the rear.

"Miss Davis," Cominski said, his voice full and deep. "Please send a child to escort Zeke Whittaker to the lunchroom. Mrs. Kendall is leaving now."

Without waiting for a response, he disappeared into his office. Maggie would have liked nothing better than to throw a rock through the frosted glass window of his closed door. Instead she waited grimly as Janet directed the children to the cafeteria.

As soon as they were alone in the hall, Janet turned to her. "You're leaving? What happened?"

"Can we meet after school today? I need your help. Zeke's father beats him, and I have to stop it. No matter what the principal says."

"Me? Go up against Mr. Cominski?" Janet stepped back, and Maggie's heart fell. *Doesn't anyone in this town want to do the right thing?*

"I'm sorry, Maggie. I can't afford to lose my job. Really, I can't." Janet took a deep breath. "I'll give you one piece of advice, though. Talk to your husband before the principal does. Cominski's one of the hospital trustees, and he's got a mean streak a mile wide."

Chapter Fifteen:
Maggie

September 12, 1952

Dear Aunt Vessie,

Thank you for sending me the copy of your testimony before Senator Eastland's committee. Jenner's threat to have you fired from Roosevelt College was outrageous. If there's any justice in this world, both Jenner and McCarthy will be voted out of office in November.

I make a point of wearing my Stevenson button ("All The Way With Adlai," the one with the union label) whenever I go out. It's too bad that "I Like Ike" is so euphonious! You can imagine the looks I get in downtown Zillah. And the sniffs from Mother Kendall!

Actually, there are moments when I feel sorry for Louisa. She's going through the change of life as well as trying to adjust to widowhood. As much as she wants Bennett to assume his father's role in the community, she's afraid I'll usurp her position as la grande dame de Zillah. She can't conceive that I don't care about the Garden Club or the Junior League. I only want to practice medicine! But Louisa is wonderful to Ellie, so I try (not very successfully) to be patient with her.

After the disastrous cocktail party at the hospital, I decided the best thing I could do was complete a residency in obstetrics. I applied at I.U. and was promptly turned down. The two positions were awarded to veterans. Next I tried for a very low-paying position at a public health clinic forty miles away only to lose out—you guessed it—to a male doctor. By then, I was in such a state that I jumped at the chance to give the students at the local elementary school their annual physicals.

This morning I examined a fourth grader whose back was crisscrossed with scars. When I told the principal, I learned that men who whip their children in Zillah are not to be reprimanded, at least not by the new lady doctor. But somehow, I will put a stop to the beating.

On the credit side of the ledger, I've made two friends: Janet Davis, who is both the fourth-grade teacher and the sheriff's daughter (everybody in town serves double duty, one actor for two personae, like a high-school production of *Twelfth Night*), and Peter Grandheim, whom I mentioned before. I discovered Peter didn't work for Senator Jenner in 1949. He was finishing up law school—at Harvard. Pretty good for a farm boy! I wonder how well he fit in with those east-coast, Stevenson liberals. He doesn't talk about his time at Harvard at all.

I honestly don't know if Peter believes all of the McCarthy hysteria or whether he sees Senator Jenner as a stepping-stone for his own ambitions. (Peter plans to run for attorney general of Indiana in two years.) Talking to him makes me feel daring, as if I'm juggling hot coals. He, at least, has no problem with a lady doctor, and he told me about the job at the public health clinic. He has agreed to speak to his father about the hospital's nepotism rule as soon as the election is over. Keep your fingers crossed. I am determined to make some changes in Zillah or die trying!

Meanwhile, Ellie is growing like Topsy. Fresh milk and eggs certainly agree with her. She has taken to eating corn on the cob until the butter runs down her chin. The pinafores and anklets you sent fit perfectly. Please remember me to Dr. Samuelson. I miss the clinic more than I can say.

Love, Maggie

"What in the world were you thinking?"

"Bennett, don't shout! You'll scare Ellie." Standing in the hallway of Louisa's house, Maggie felt like a truant schoolgirl summoned to the woodshed.

Janet Davis had been right. After leaving Pulaski Elementary, Maggie had stopped at the post office to check her mail box and drop off her letter to Aunt Vessie. By the time she got home, Bennett knew all about her fight with Mr. Cominski. She had caught a glimpse of Louisa as her mother-in-law whisked Ellie upstairs, and Maggie hadn't missed the spiteful, knowing look on her face, either.

Maggie fingered the letter from Dr. Samuelson in her skirt pocket. She couldn't have picked a worse time to tell Bennett her news. But after meeting Zeke, she had to get back to work as soon as possible. She smiled grimly. The good citizens of Zillah needed her whether they knew it or not.

"So you admit you called the school principal names?"

"For goodness sake, Bennett, you sound like Hamilton Berger from *Perry Mason*. I'm not on trial here." Maggie opened the door to Doc's office and marched inside. "Let's discuss what happened in a civilized manner. But I warn you—" she glanced back at him "—your precious Zillah is going to change."

Bennett threw his hands in the air, but he followed her into the study and sat behind Doc's desk, ensconced in Doc's chair. Heavily carved and high-backed, with a leather seat and brass filigrees, it looked like an ancient throne.

Maggie shut the door behind her and drew a ladder-back

95

chair in front of his desk.

"Okay." His fingers tapped the blotter. "Tell me what happened at the school."

She crossed her legs and surveyed the dim room as she put her thoughts in order. Doc's office was on the ground floor in the southeast corner of the house. Bookshelves covered one wall from top to bottom. She had spent several long afternoons browsing through them while Ellie napped. All of Doc's old medical books stood on the middle shelf near his deck. They were out of date, of course, written before the Second World War, before penicillin was widely used, before Atabrine for malaria, before blood banks and gamma globulin.

Bennett had placed a picture of her and Ellie on the desk, but otherwise, the study looked ready for Doc to walk in and start work. Pictures of Doc's mother and wife hung above the fireplace, and the heavy, closed drapes still held the smell of his cigars.

This room is more like a shrine than an office. Bennett should toss out those old books or give them to a museum.

Bennett cleared his throat and rapped on the desktop. "Maggie? I thought you were going to tell me what happened."

Briefly, she described what she had seen on Zeke Whittaker's back, what she had said, what she had done.

"Oh, my God. You actually called Mr. Cominski an idiot?" Bennett buried his head in his hands. "It's worse than Mother thought." He glanced up. "You're going to ruin my practice, Maggie. You can't get into a flap about every little thing."

"Get into a flap?" Blood pounded in her temples. "You missed the point, Bennett. That boy is being punished because he's suffering from enuresis. Whipping him isn't going to help. He needs to see a doctor."

"You're right, sweetheart, but—" Bennett groaned. "Parents have the right to discipline their kids. When I was a boy, if a teacher spanked me at school, I got another wallop from Doc when I got home."

"A spanking, yes. But Doc never left welts, did he? Or scars? Besides, bed-wetting is a medical problem, not bad behavior."

The telephone rang. Bennett picked up the extension on his desk. "Doctor Kendall." He paused. "Here she is." He handed the receiver to Maggie and sat back in his chair. His fingers tapped the blotter again.

"Maggie, it's Janet Davis. I talked to my dad. You know that he's the county sheriff?"

"Yes."

"He said the same thing Cominski did, corporal punishment is not against the law. But he agreed to chat with Coach Whittaker informally. At the lodge meeting this week."

"Be sure your father tells the coach to take Zeke to a doctor. Punishing him will only make his bed-wetting worse."

"Okay." Janet sighed. "I promise you, I'll keep an eye on that boy myself and call Dad if he's beaten again. And Mr. Cominski said you can come back and finish the physicals on Monday."

"Thanks, Janet," Maggie said with a surge of triumph. An informal chat wasn't a perfect solution. But Zeke's father was a lot more likely to listen to the sheriff than to Maggie.

"Would you and your daughter like to picnic with me tomorrow?" Janet continued. "There's a lovely pawpaw patch near the river."

Maggie grinned. "That would be wonderful."

After Janet hung up, Maggie held the receiver for a moment until she heard the faint click of the extension phone in Louisa's bedroom. She touched the envelope in her pocket again. Between what Bennett made and her new salary, they should be able to qualify for a VA loan and move out of here. And finally have some privacy.

"What was the phone call about, sweetheart?"

Maggie stood and smiled down at Bennett. "Janet talked to her father. Sheriff Davis will speak privately to Coach Whittaker, and Janet's going to watch out for Zeke."

"Great." Bennett pushed the wooden throne back and pulled her onto his lap. "I'm glad you got everything squared away." He put his arms around her waist and nuzzled her hair. She tried to relax. Maybe now would be a good time to talk. Before she could decide, Bennett asked, "What else are you and Janet cooking up?"

"We're taking Ellie on a picnic tomorrow."

"You can't do that." Bennett straightened, and she almost slipped off his knees. "Tomorrow is the medical society dinner. Senator Jenner's fund-raiser. I bought three tickets."

"I'm not going."

"You have to."

"No, Bennett." Maggie made her voice as firm as possible. "I will not support Senator Jenner and that's final." She heard Louisa call them and slid to her feet. "It's time to eat."

Half an hour later, they had finished their meal. In the chair opposite Maggie, Ellie concentrated on scooping the last kernels of buttered corn onto her spoon. Her cheeks and forehead were pink, just this side of sunburn. Bennett sat at the head of the table and Louisa at the foot. As Louisa pushed back her chair, Bernadette, the kitchen girl, swooped in and carried Ellie off for her bath.

"I have an announcement to make." Maggie touched the letter in the pocket of her skirt.

"In a minute, Margaret. Sanka, anyone?" Louisa asked, halfway to the kitchen.

"Thank you, Mother." Behind her back, Bennett grimaced for Maggie's benefit. That was another thing they would have in their own home. Real coffee. She stretched her arm to him. He reached out, touched her fingertips, and pantomimed a kiss.

Louisa carried the chrome-plated coffee pot into the dining room and filled their china cups. She placed the pot on the Queen Anne sideboard next to the sugar bowl and creamer and sat at the table again, unfolding her damask napkin and spreading it on her lap as carefully as if she was celebrating communion.

"Well, Maggie, what's your announcement?" Bennett grinned, handsomely expectant. Maggie's heart lodged in her throat. *Good God, he thinks I'm pregnant.* But it was too late to retreat.

She unfolded the letter. Her palms were sweaty. The thin paper crinkled as she spread it on the tabletop. She looked at Bennett and tried to smile. "Dr. Samuelson wants me to start a clinic in Zillah like the one I managed in Chicago."

"A free clinic?" Louisa rose abruptly and shut the door to the living room as if she was afraid Bernadette would hear their voices. She sat down again, heavy and awkward because of her gouty knee, and glared at Bennett.

"Yes. It's the perfect opportunity." Maggie realized her voice sounded too loud, too bright, too cheerful. "The foundation wants to test whether a clinic can help poor families in a rural community like it does in Chicago. If Bennett will persuade the hospital trustees to support me—" she winked at him "—Dr. Samuelson promises I can open the doors in a few weeks."

"Socialized medicine," Louisa snapped, her lips drawn tight as she lifted her coffee cup.

"What?" Maggie glanced at Bennett for help, but he was tracing the design on the tablecloth with his forefinger.

"That's what Doc always called it," Louisa said when Bennett didn't respond. "Socialized medicine. It's Roosevelt and his gang of crooks trying to take control of our lives. The next thing you know, the Bolsheviks will be telling you how to practice medicine and Zillah will be no different from Russia."

"Mother Kendall."

Louisa refused to acknowledge her. Maggie wanted to pound the coffee pot against the sideboard until Louisa looked up. "Mother Kendall, President Roosevelt has been dead for over five years."

"So what? His toady is still in the White House." Louisa turned toward Bennett. "Junior, you can't let your wife open a clinic in Zillah. What will happen to Eleanor if her mother goes through with this harebrained scheme?"

"In Chicago, Ellie sometimes came to the clinic with me, Mother Kendall. She loved it."

Louisa shot Maggie a look of pure venom. "No grandchild of mine is going to visit a public health clinic." She cleared her throat and barked, "It's communism, plain and simple."

"A clinic doesn't have anything to do with communism, Mother Kendall. It's health care for mothers and children too poor to go to the doctor."

"If people can't afford a doctor, they shouldn't be having children." Louisa folded her hands on the table. "Right, Junior?"

Bennett studied the tablecloth without answering.

I should have known. He'll never stand up to her.

Maggie forged ahead. "Mother Kendall, do you know how many American babies died here at home during the war? Almost a million. That's more than all the American soldiers who were killed on the battlefield. It's not right."

"Well, maybe those babies were meant to die. Did you ever think about that?" Louisa pushed back from the table and glared at her son. "Junior, your father always said the weak ones should be allowed to die off. The epileptics, the diabetics, and the feeble-minded. It's what God intended. Natural selection. Survival of the fittest."

"What about Ellie?" Maggie interrupted, so outraged she could hardly speak. "When she had whooping cough, should I have let her choke to death?"

"Don't be ridiculous. Eleanor's a healthy child from good stock, even if she does have that ridiculous name. It's people like you and Junior who should be reproducing, not the ne'er-do-wells and niggers who will flock to your clinic."

Maggie slapped the table. "Don't say nigger!"

"Why not? It's my house, isn't it? I'll use whatever words I want in my own home."

"Then it's time for us to move out."

Louisa froze. A flush crept up her neck. Her ears turned fiery red and her cheeks quivered.

"That's enough." Bennett looked up.

Finally.

"Maggie, we'll discuss Dr. Samuelson's proposal after dinner. Mother, thank you for a delicious meal."

Louisa swept from the room, her coffee cup held high on its china saucer, her balky knee suddenly under control, her carriage magnificent.

Maggie pushed back her chair. Her whole body was shaking with anger. Bennett took her arm and steered her outside to the screened-in front porch. His other hand rubbed against his stomach. Sweat plastered his shirt to his body. He smelled hot.

The porch was cool and dark. Maggie took a deep breath and tried to relax. Bennett shut the door to the house, loosened his tie, and took off his cufflinks and slipped them into his pants pocket. He rolled up his sleeves and sat next to Maggie on the wooden swing. June bugs pinged as they flew into the screen surrounding the porch. Night-blooming nicotiana released its sweet seductive scent. She could be happy here—

"That's better." Bennett ran a finger inside his collar and sighed.

"Your mother hates me."

"Only because you keep fighting with her." Bennett took

Maggie's hand. "Be patient. Mother hasn't recovered from losing Doc yet, sweetheart. She worshipped him."

"She worships you, too." Maggie settled against the back of the swing and pushed the hair from her face. Her bangs were damp with sweat. She stretched her legs and pulled her gathered cotton skirt up to her knees. She should have changed into pedal pushers after school.

"I try, but I can't replace my father." Bennett leaned back and stretched his arms along the top board of the swing.

They pressed against each other in the darkness and sat without talking. Maggie heard the rattle of plates as Bernadette cleared the dishes from the table and ran water into the sink. Bennett must have heard it too because he said, "There wasn't any running water here when Mother and Doc got married, you know. There was a hand pump in the kitchen and an old wooden scrub board."

He shifted in his seat. Another wave of heat rolled off his body. "Did your mother use a scrub board, too?"

"Stop evading the issue, Bennett." Maggie straightened her shoulders. "I can't believe those things your mother said. I suppose when my parents died from the flu and left me an orphan at five, that was natural selection, too."

"I guess she'd say the Lord works in mysterious ways. Even you have to admit something good came out of your parents' deaths."

"What?"

"It made you the dedicated doctor you are today. Think of all those poor women you helped in Chicago. You saved more lives than you'll ever know, Maggie."

"That's why I need your support. I want to start the clinic in Zillah no matter what your mother thinks."

"I know what you want. But don't forget, I want things, too. I want what I fought for." Bennett folded his hands over his head, locking his stubby fingers over the bald spot on his crown. He leaned back in the swing, his face stony in the half light. "I want to have more children. I want to go to church and to have a garden. I want to be a good doctor to these good people. I don't want to fight with my mother and her oldest friends." He frowned at her. "And I don't want you to fight with them, either. I had enough fighting in New Guinea to last me a lifetime."

"But, Bennett—"

"Sweetheart, can't we live in peace and forget the clinic? You put in your time in Chicago. Now, can't you just settle down and be my wife?"

Maggie stood up and moved to the screen door that led to the front walk. "I can't live in peace when I know little boys are being beaten. When I can't practice medicine." She took a deep breath. "I can't."

Bennett stepped next to her and put his arm around her waist. "Maggie, even if I supported you, you can't start that clinic. Not in this town. They'll fight you every step of the way."

"Who? The doctors?"

"Of course. They don't want to lose patients to you."

"So it comes down to money?"

"It always does. They won't admit it, but that's the heart of the problem."

"Dr. Samuelson said the clinic will pay the hospital."

"What?"

"The foundation offered to contract with the doctors at Community Memorial to provide medical services for the clinic's patients when they need to go to the hospital. Dr. Samuelson suggested I budget three thousand dollars a year for the first three years."

Bennett didn't answer right away. Maggie watched the moon rise behind the sycamore trees at the horizon. A block away, a truck rumbled over the railroad tracks. Finally, Bennett pulled her down on the swing next to him. He leaned forward, propped his elbows on his knees, and rubbed his hands together. She heard the whisper of his palms.

When he spoke it was as if he were talking to a stranger. "The money is a nice sop to throw to the doctors, Maggie, but it's not enough. They're worried about keeping their patients, of course, but it's more than that. There are principles involved. They don't want anyone telling them how to practice medicine, especially not a bunch of do-gooders from Chicago. Mother's right. Everyone will call you a socialist—or worse. It will kill any chance I have to head up the new hospital. You've got to bail out now. I can't let you go through with it."

"You can't let me?" The words hung between them in the damp night.

Bennett didn't answer, didn't look at her.

"Let me?" Maggie repeated. She heard the shrill note in her voice. "Bennett, starting this clinic is an important job. I can do it better than anyone else."

"No." It was lighter now, but she couldn't see his face. He said again, "No. There'll be hell to pay if you go through with this crackpot idea."

"You have to support me, Bennett." Maggie stood. She clenched both fists so she wouldn't cry or scream or throw something at him. "If you don't," she said, her voice cool and collected, "I'll take Ellie and go back to Chicago. It's your choice." She strode into the house, and the screen door banged behind her.

CHAPTER SIXTEEN: MAGGIE

Saturday, September 13, 1952

At nine-thirty, Maggie sat in the living room reading the latest issue of *JAMA* and idly scratching her mosquito bites from the picnic by the river. After lunch, Janet had taught Ellie how to suck the sweet, yellow flesh of pawpaws from their prickly brown skins. Later, while Ellie splashed in the shallows of the river and chased minnows, the women talked. Janet didn't have any ideas about how to make Zillah accept Maggie's clinic, but still, it had been a glorious day.

Bennett and Louisa were still at Senator Jenner's fund-raising dinner when the telephone rang. Maggie bumped against the leather hassock as she jumped up to answer. "Dr. Kendall here."

"It's Luther Pierce, ma'am. Miss Davis over at the school, she said to call you." The man gulped. "It's my sister. She's bleeding." His voice broke. "I think she's going to die."

"Bleeding where?" Maggie grabbed a pencil and an envelope and started making notes.

"She had a miscarriage." Something in his voice sounded false.

"Where is she?"

He gave her the address. "It's right by the river, ma'am. The north shore."

"Have you called an ambulance?"

"No, ma'am. The colored hospital is in Indianapolis." Maggie thought she heard a motorcycle roar at the other end of the line. "I don't think she'll last long enough to get there."

"Where are you?"

"At the gas station, ma'am. The corner of Twenty-Eighth and Maple."

"Wait there for me."

Maggie ran upstairs for her black bag, mentally ticking through her checklist for house calls. In the kitchen, she grabbed a flashlight and a handful of newspapers. She wrote a note to Bennett and propped it against the small vase of orange zinnias on the kitchen table. She filled a baby bottle with cool water. She brought her Studebaker to the front of the house and threw her supplies on the floor behind the driver's seat. She ran upstairs for Ellie, wrapped her in a blanket, and laid her on the rear seat of the car. Ellie whimpered and went back to sleep, her raggedy old Teddy bear tucked under her arm.

Ten minutes later, Maggie stopped in front of the Conoco Gas station. A one-armed man ran awkwardly in front of the car. In the headlights, she recognized his sweaty face. She leaned across the front seat and unlocked the passenger door. "You're the custodian at the elementary school."

"Yes, ma'am. I'm Luther Pierce." He shook her hand. "Thank you for coming." He glanced in back. "Your girl?"

"Yes."

Luther folded himself into the narrow seat and closed the door. "Turn left here."

They drove for three blocks and stopped in front of a wooden shack. White paint hung in long strips from the bare boards. Shadows moved back and forth behind the sheets hung in the windows.

Maggie smelled the river: dead fish and sewage. As she stepped from the car, mud squished over the tops of her shoes. She shivered as if she had stepped off the end of the world.

From inside the house, a woman cried out. Luther plucked

Maggie's bag from her hand. "Hurry, Doc."

"Grab the newspapers from the car," Maggie said. She picked up Ellie and followed him through the door.

The small front room held a table, four chairs, and a dry sink. A stack of firewood stood in the far corner next to a cast-iron stove. A rocking chair with an afghan folded on its rush seat was pushed against the wall. The floor boards were bare and newly swept.

How in the world do they manage to keep it so clean here by the river?

Luther opened the door next to the stove. In the back room, a young colored girl lay on an iron bedstead under a pile of thin cotton quilts. A kerosene lamp threw shadows on the wall. A tin button reading "Remember Dorie Miller" hung from a black ribbon nailed next to the mirror. Dorie Miller. During the attack on Pearl Harbor he had helped move injured sailors through oil and water to the quarterdeck of his torpedoed ship, saving countless lives. Afterwards, he was awarded the Navy Cross for bravery, the first-ever Negro to receive that high honor.

A couple of tattered movie magazines covered a small table next to the bed. Luther cleared the surface of the table with a sweep of his arm and set down Maggie's bag. The room smelled fetid like the river and coldly metallic like fresh blood. Maggie glanced at the girl's pale face and her heart sank.

"This here's Dr. Kendall," Luther said. He gestured to two women who stood by the bed. "My mama, Reba, and my grandma."

Maggie straightened her shoulders. Time to get to work. "Mrs. Pierce?"

Reba Pierce clung to the girl's hand. "Yes?"

"I need to examine your daughter." Maggie shifted Ellie to her shoulder. "Could someone hold my child?"

107

The other woman, Luther's grandmother, had been wiping the sweat from the girl's face. She turned to Maggie. She was so stooped and worn that she seemed almost invisible except for the whites of her eyes. They shone in the steady yellow glow of the lamp. "I'll take care of her."

"Thank you." Maggie looked at Luther. "I need more space. Would you and your grandmother wait in the front room? Boil some water, please. I'll want to sterilize my instruments."

"Sure, Doc." They left slowly, reluctantly, with backward glances, as if stumbling away from a grave.

The girl's breathing sounded shallow, rough. Maggie lifted her eyelids, and her eyes reacted sluggishly to the light. Maggie touched Mrs. Pierce's shoulder. "What's your daughter's name?"

"Sadie."

"How old is she?"

"Fifteen."

"Does she have any allergies? Any medical problems?"

Sadie's mother shook her head.

"When did her periods begin?"

"About a year ago."

"When was her last one?"

The woman looked away. "At the start of summer."

"When did she have the miscarriage?"

"Three days ago."

Maggie pulled down the covers and lifted Sadie's thin shift. The sheets were stained with blood, but the girl's legs, groin, and sparse pubic hair had been washed clean. *She's only a child,* Maggie thought as she palpated Sadie's thin, flat stomach. The girl's skin was as soft as Ellie's.

Maggie dampened a cotton ball with rubbing alcohol and wiped her thermometer. She shook it down and put it in Sadie's armpit. As Maggie pressed the girl's arm against the thermometer, she checked her pulse. It felt weak and rapid, and her forehead was clammy. Shock. She turned to Sadie's mother. "We need to keep her warm."

Reba pulled the covers over the girl's chest and up to her chin. Sadie moaned. Her head jerked left and right. Her shoulders twitched.

Maggie pulled out the thermometer and held it close to the kerosene lamp. One hundred-three-point-three. An infection, a bad one. She wiped the thermometer with rubbing alcohol and put it back in its case. She stepped to the foot of the bed. She pushed the blankets up to the girl's waist and said, "Hand me my flashlight, please. It's in my bag."

Maggie lifted Sadie's legs and shoved a pillow under her bony hips. She covered the sheet underneath her with news-papers.

There was a knock at the door. "The water's boiling," Luther called.

"Keep her like this," Maggie said. She hurried into the front room, slipped on her rubber gloves, and held the speculum in the water for two minutes. She came back into the bedroom and set it on a clean newspaper.

Then she took the thin brown ankles and gently forced them back toward Sadie's hips so her knees lifted and her thighs spread open. She waited a minute for the speculum to cool and inserted it into the girl's narrow vagina. She wiped away a trickle of blood and squatted down to look. Was the cervix lacerated?

She moved the speculum and palpated Sadie's lower abdo-men with her fingertips. The girl cried out and pulled away. A tear ran down her mother's cheek, but she kept a steady grip on Sadie's ankles. Maggie packed the wound with sterile dressings.

She straightened and wiped her forehead. "Let her go." Sadie's legs flopped to one side. Maggie drew the quilt down and covered the girl's feet. She dug her fingernails into her palms and tried to push aside her rage. Whoever had done this to the girl should be shot. The abortionist and the man who had knocked her up. What kind of a person would have sex with a child? She took a deep breath and turned to Reba.

"Mrs. Pierce, someone put something up inside her. There's a good chance her uterus has been perforated." She stared into Reba's eyes. "Do you understand what I'm saying?"

"Yes, ma'am."

"I'm going to take her to the hospital. If it's as bad as I think, Sadie will have to have an emergency hysterectomy. Do you know what that is?"

"You're going to take out her female parts."

"Only if I have to, Mrs. Pierce. If I take her uterus out, she won't be able to have children. But if it's perforated and we don't operate, she's going to die."

Reba gripped Maggie's arm. "Are you sure?"

"No. I won't know for sure until I open her up." Maggie took the woman's hands and squeezed them. "I'll do what's best for your daughter, I promise." *And I'll get the man who raped her.* Mrs. Pierce nodded. Tears streamed down her face. Sadie moaned. Her mother brushed the tears away and bent over her, crooning softly as she stroked her daughter's hair. Maggie turned around. "Luther?"

"Yes, ma'am." He stood in the doorway.

"We're going to take Sadie to Community Memorial."

"But—"

"I'll handle it, Luther. Will your grandma watch Ellie for me?"

"Yes, ma'am."

Luther's grandmother handed Maggie a couple of white rags that had been wrung out in the boiling water. She quickly cleaned Sadie and her instruments and washed the girl's blood from her hands. She used the last piece of cloth to wipe her own face.

"Luther, we have to talk." Maggie backed out of the bedroom and shut the door.

Luther leaned against the wall as if he were ready to collapse. The kettle of water on the cookstove was still boiling. Maggie dampened the fire. The room felt hot and steamy, as if all the fresh air had been sucked away.

"This is a bad business. Who did the abortion?"

Luther shook his head.

"I have to report it."

"I know."

Five minutes later, Maggie stopped at the service station. She telephoned the hospital operator. "This is Dr. Kendall. Get a hold of whoever's on call. I have an emergency hysterectomy coming in. We'll be there in ten minutes."

Chapter Seventeen: Maggie

"She's your patient?" Dr. Grandheim stood in front of the admissions desk and blocked the hallway to the emergency room. "She's the case the operator called me about?"

"Yes, sir." Maggie looked over her shoulder. Luther and the porter staggered through the door to the hospital, carrying Sadie between them. Reba Pierce followed close behind. "I think she has a perforated uterus."

"You can't admit her, Maggie," Grandheim snapped. "You know that."

Sadie groaned and fell sideways. With only one arm, Luther couldn't hold her, and she slid to the floor. Her mother knelt beside her.

"We don't admit colored patients," Grandheim said. "Take her to Indianapolis."

"She won't survive the trip, dammit! If you don't operate now, you might as well throw her out behind the hospital and shoot her. Look, if it's the money, don't worry. I'll pay. Every dime. She's not a charity case, Doctor."

Sadie groaned again. Her mother looked up at Grandheim. Grandheim sighed.

"All right." He growled at the porter, "Get a gurney. Move it."

Maggie allowed herself a moment of elation as she dialed the sheriff's office from the telephone at the receptionist's desk. A minute later, she followed Sadie into the emergency room.

Grandheim handed a pair of rubber gloves to Maggie. "Let's see what we have here." He motioned for the nurse to cap Sadie's hair. "So, little Sadie Pierce, whatever happened to you, child?" He glanced at Maggie. "Do you know her?"

"No, sir."

"Her mama, Reba, is our housekeeper. Sadie's been underfoot every summer since she was a little pickaninny." As Grandheim talked, he took the girl's pulse.

So that's why he admitted her. But why did Luther call me instead of Grandheim?

The nurse undressed Sadie and draped her. She pulled a tray with a basin of soapy water, a straight razor, and a towel next to the bed, and shaved Sadie's pubic hair in long, rapid strokes.

Grandheim said, "Make a note. Her pulse is one-twenty and weak."

Maggie wrote it and the time on Sadie's chart.

Grandheim tested Sadie's reflexes, checked her temperature, and listened to her chest, talking softly as he worked. "Her grandma is the head cook and bottle washer at the hospital. Makes the best pig knuckles and sauerkraut I ever tasted. She's worked here longer than I have." He held the thermometer to the light. "One hundred-three-point-three. Is that what you got, Doctor?"

"Yes, sir." Maggie made another note on the chart.

Grandheim lifted Sadie's feet into the stirrups and motioned for a nurse to hold them in place. He removed Maggie's packing and inserted the speculum. Sadie mewed like a sick cat. Her skin had grayed in the past half hour. Maggie checked her blood pressure. It was falling.

We got here just in time.

Grandheim's examination was swift and thorough. He took out the speculum and palpated the girl's abdomen. Finally he dropped his rubber gloves into the sink.

"We need to operate. Let's get Reba's consent." He looked back at the girl. "Poor little Sadie."

They pushed through the first set of double doors that led to the waiting room. Maggie's muddy shoes had left footprints on the floor. Next to the linen closet, Grandheim pulled Maggie aside. "Now, tell me straight." His icy blue eyes pierced her. "Did you do that abortion?"

"No, sir."

"You might have thought you were helping the girl."

Maggie straightened her shoulders and stared back at him, making her eyes as cold as his. "Dr. Grandheim, I swore the same oath you did. My job is to save lives, not to take them. Sir."

"Okay." He sighed. "I have to notify the police."

"I already did, sir. I called Sheriff Davis and told him about the abortion. And I told him she had been assaulted."

Grandheim looked startled. "Do you know that for a fact? Is that what her mother said?"

"No, sir. But as far as I'm concerned, pregnancy in a fifteen-year-old girl is prima facie evidence of rape."

Grandheim put his hands in his pockets of his lab coat and shook his head. "You don't know these people, Maggie. Colored girls, girls like little Sadie here, they mature faster than women like you. She could have a common-law husband somewhere, maybe even Luther—"

"He's her brother."

"That's what I'm trying to say. The good Lord made these people different than He made you and me. You don't know what they're like, down there by the river, living like animals, a bunch of dirty kids running around all over the place, no sanitation. It's worse than Russia."

"You're wrong about Luther, sir." Angered by the monstrous accusation, Maggie could barely push the words out. "He

114

wouldn't do that."

The nurse opened the door behind them. "Dr. Grandheim. The patient's ready for surgery."

"Okay." He turned to Maggie. "Will you assist me, Dr. Kendall?"

She frowned at him, sensing a trap. "I don't have privileges here, sir." *As you very well know.*

He waved his hand, brushing her objection aside. "For God's sake! I realize that. But you're competent aren't you? I don't want to get anybody else involved."

"Yes, sir, I'm competent."

"Okay. Let's get that consent."

They entered the waiting room as Maggie's husband and mother-in-law burst through the front door. Dr. Grandheim nodded to them as he sat down next to Sadie's mother. He pulled a paper from his jacket pocket and began to talk to her. Luther stood next to his mother, listening intently.

"Where have you been?" Bennett hustled Maggie into a corner by the exit. "We've driven all over town looking for you."

Maggie brushed his arm away. "I left you a note."

"Where's Eleanor?" Louisa grabbed Maggie's wrist. A flush crept up the wrinkled skin of her neck. "Where's my grand-daughter?"

Maggie shook free and stepped back. She held up her hands. "Wait a minute! I brought a patient for emergency surgery. We're going to operate now." Maggie swept her hand through her hair. "Ellie's back at the house."

Louisa stepped closer and hissed. "No, she's not." Spittle flew across Maggie's face.

"I meant Ellie's with my patient's grandmother. At Luther's house."

"Luther? Who's he?" Louisa's fingers dug into Maggie's arm. "Tell me where Eleanor is."

"I don't know the address. I could drive to it, but I can't leave now."

"You left your daughter with a complete stranger?"

Maggie paused. In her headlong rush to get Sadie to the hospital, had she put Ellie in danger? She remembered that house, those faces. No, she had done the right thing. She took another step backward. "Ask Luther where he lives. He's sitting over there."

"You are the worst—"

"Wait, Mother." Bennett put his arm around Louisa's shoulder. "If Maggie's going to operate, she has to get cracking. We can't bother her now." He pulled Louisa toward him. "Come on. We'll find Ellie and take her home. It'll be all right."

"Well, I never." Louisa pulled a handkerchief from her sleeve and wiped the perspiration from her face. Her thin, gnarled fingers trembled.

Maggie reached for compassion. Louisa adored Ellie. "I'm sorry, Mother Kendall. I didn't mean to worry you."

Louisa glared at her and stalked away. Bennett shrugged helplessly at Maggie and followed his mother out of the hospital. Surprised that Bennett had stood up to his mother even that much, Maggie turned to look for Dr. Grandheim.

Across the room, he stood and took his pen from Reba Pierce. She must have signed the consent for surgery. He handed the paper to the receptionist and beckoned to Maggie. Mrs. Pierce bowed her head. Luther sat beside his mother and put his arm around her shoulders. He closed his eyes. His lips moved as if he was praying.

Maggie thought of the difficult surgery ahead. Pray for me, too, Luther. Dr. Grandheim and I have to figure out how to work together if we're going to save your sister. And I'm not sure we can.

Chapter Eighteen:
Bennett

It was close to midnight when Bennett and Louisa arrived at Luther's house. The full moon cast shadows across the fog that blanketed the river, and the steady yellow light of a kerosene lantern shone through the sheets over the windows.

Bennett parked the car on the rutted road. Louisa tightened her lips and gripped the purse in her lap. Bennett sighed as he got out of the car. His mother would never forgive Maggie for tonight. And sooner or later, Maggie would give Louisa a taste of her own medicine. Then there'd be hell to pay. He'd have to choose sides whether he wanted to or not. His stomach burned. He couldn't bear to lose either one of them.

He knocked on the door of the little shack, and an old black woman opened it. She held Ellie against her hip. As the girl slept, her pink and white hands clutched the woman's flaccid breast.

"Come in," the woman whispered, and Bennett obeyed, feeling as if he had wandered into a fairy tale—the old woman, the sleeping child, the miasma of decay rising from the river.

Inside, the front room looked surprisingly neat and clean. He sat in a straight-backed chair, and the woman handed Ellie to him. She laid a small bundle wrapped in newspapers on the floor next to the chair. "Her diaper," she whispered. "I washed it out and put a clean cloth on her."

Bennett nodded. That homey detail made the fairy tale seem more real than ever, transforming the white-haired woman into a kindly witch.

"How's my grandbaby doing?"

"Your grandbaby?" For a moment, Bennett blanked. Then he wiped his eyes and said, "Sadie's going to be fine," without knowing if it was true. "You can visit her tomorrow."

The woman hobbled past him. Her slippers whispered against the wooden floor. She sat in the rocking chair with a sigh. "I knew Doc would save her."

"Doc?" Bennett echoed. Even in this fairy-tale world, Doc—his father, Doc—was dead.

"She seems like a mighty fine woman, Doc does. I'm glad you brought her to town."

Maggie, he thought. That's who she's calling Doc.

He stood and held Ellie against his shoulder. "I have to go now."

"Yes, sir." She handed him the newspaper bundle. "Good night, sir."

The house darkened as he pulled away. He turned onto Maple Street, and Louisa whispered in a soft voice like a hiss, "Margaret's deceiving you, Junior."

Bennett's stomach twisted. He glanced at his mother. She sat beside him in the passenger seat, holding Ellie tight in her arms. As he drove, the streetlights created bars of black and white that flickered across Louisa's face. Her eyes glittered. "She's deceiving you."

"No, she isn't."

"Well, what about this?" Louisa shifted Ellie and pulled an envelope from her purse. "When Margaret said she had a letter from that Jew doctor in Chicago, I figured she must have fixed herself up with a mailbox somewhere. Larry over at the post office told me she did. He gave me this letter for her." Louisa waved it at him. "It's from Peter Grandheim."

Bennett kept his eyes on the road. "Maggie doesn't want you

to open her mail, Mother. That's why she got the P.O. box."

"Well, she could have said so." Louisa sniffed. "She didn't need to get herself a mailbox. There's no call to be sneaking around behind her husband's back."

"Maggie didn't sneak around. She asked me to talk to you." Bennett steered the car around a corner. "But I didn't."

"All I can say is, no Christian woman I ever knew had any need to be getting her own mailbox unless she had something to hide." Louisa handed the letter from Peter Grandheim to Bennett. "I didn't open this. Give it to your wife and see what she's got to say for herself."

Bennett's stomach roared and hissed as if he had swallowed battery acid. *No. I'm not going to interrogate my wife. Either I trust her or I don't.*

Ellie twitched in her sleep. He glanced at her and saw the crude diaper. He thought of the old black woman in the shack. She had called Maggie "Doc." Bennett tightened his hands on the steering wheel. *Because that's who Maggie is and always will be.*

CHAPTER NINETEEN: MAGGIE

"Is that you, Maggie?"

Maggie stopped halfway across the dark front porch. Bennett stood in the lighted door of Louisa's house as if blocking her way. "Yes, it's me." She set down her black bag. "Did you pick up Ellie from Luther's grandmother?"

Bennett nodded. "She's upstairs asleep."

"Good." Maggie studied him as if she were watching a play, sitting in the front row, almost but not quite close enough to touch the man on stage.

"Why didn't you leave a message for me before you took off?" His jaw tightened. "Don't you know I'd be worried sick?"

"We've been through this, Bennett. I did leave a note. On the kitchen table."

"Well, I didn't see it."

"I'm sorry." Maggie picked up her bag. It felt like it was packed with lead. "The hysterectomy was successful. If you care."

"Of course, I care. But honestly? I wouldn't risk your safety to rescue anyone." He took the bag from her. She stumbled into the living room and dropped onto the couch, too tired to climb the stairs, too tired to argue with him. She heard Ellie whimper.

"Wait here." Bennett ran upstairs. Maggie saw a soft beam of light as he opened the door to the nursery. She heard Ellie's music box start. She heard a shuffle and then whispers. Louisa was checking on the baby, too. The grandfather clock struck the quarter hour, and Maggie shut her eyes.

She awoke with a start. Bennett had turned on the floor lamp. He sat facing her.

"Who was your patient?"

Maggie rubbed her eyes and stretched. "Sadie Pierce. Her brother, Luther, is custodian at the school. Janet Davis told him to call me."

"I can't believe you took Ellie and drove to a stranger's house in the middle of the night."

"It was an emergency. She needed help." Why was Bennett demanding an explanation? He made house calls all the time.

"But, Maggie. You don't know these people. What if he was after narcotics or—"

"Bennett, that's a chance every doctor has to take." Maggie closed her eyes and leaned back against the couch. She was too tired for this ridiculous argument. She heard him sigh. He took her hand. He stroked her fingers and straightened her wedding ring.

"I'm sorry, sweetheart. I should have gone to the mat for you and I didn't."

Startled, she opened her eyes. Bennett was running his index finger along the edges of her short nails. "What do you mean?"

"I think you're the best doctor this town has ever seen. It's crazy that you can't work here." She watched his muscles twitch as he clenched his teeth. "Things have got to change."

"Really, Bennett?" Maggie felt lightheaded, drunk. "Do you mean it?"

"Wait, I'll be right back." She shut her eyes again and listened to him step into Doc's study. She heard several faint clicks, and then he came back to the living room. She opened her eyes and sat up as something rattled on the coffee table in front of her: a gun and a handful of bullets.

"Good God, Bennett. What's that?"

"A revolver. A Lady Smith. Doc bought it for you when he heard about your job." Bennett grinned. "He was worried about you running around in the slums in Chicago. I told him you knew how to shoot. You do, don't you?"

"Of course. Aunt Vessie taught me. On the Indiana dunes." Maggie gave him a tired smile. "In case the Nazis invaded the Midwest." She picked up the revolver, unlocked the cylinder, and checked the chambers. They were empty. She closed the gun, pointed the barrel at the floor, and squeezed the trigger. "It's nice." She stroked the smooth rosewood grip. "It fits like a glove."

"Good. Doc thought you'd like it. It was supposed to be your Christmas present. I'll set up some hay bales in the barn so you can practice with it."

"But, Bennett. Do you really think we should have a revolver around the house?"

"It's not for the house, it's for you." He frowned and added, "Please, sweetheart. Keep the gun with you. Lock it in the glove box of your car if you want, but keep it with you. Once your clinic has opened, you'll need protection if you're going to start making house calls again."

"House calls?" Maggie's whole body bubbled like champagne. "Are you going to talk to Grandheim about the clinic?"

"Yes, ma'am, Dr. Kendall. I'll call him first thing in the morning." Bennett sounded triumphant. "I'll make him put you on the agenda for the trustees' meeting Monday morning." He grinned at her. Despite his red-rimmed eyes and his unshaven cheeks, it was that same old cocky grin.

Her heart turned over. He understood. Despite all his worries. All his complaining. Despite his mother. She reached out to him. "I love you so much."

"You'll knock 'em dead, sweetheart," Bennett said.

CHAPTER TWENTY:
MAGGIE

Monday, September 15, 1952

Bennett and Maggie left the house for the hospital trustees' meeting at eight o'clock sharp. Louisa had complained of heart palpitations, so Bennett served her breakfast in bed while Maggie helped Ellie get dressed and brush her teeth.

"I want Grandma," Ellie fussed as Maggie led her into the kitchen.

"I'm sorry, sweetie, but Grandma's not feeling well, so you're going to help Bernadette instead." Maggie lifted Ellie into her chair and pulled it up to the table. "I hope that's okay, Bernadette. Do you mind?"

"No, ma'am." Bernadette was a big-boned countrywoman who had cooked and cleaned for Louisa and Doc over the past decade. Her husband had been killed during the invasion of Normandy, and her only child, a son, had died of pneumonia a few weeks later. After the war, her sister had married George Whittaker, the high school football coach. Bernadette boarded with her sister's family and hiked the two miles to Louisa's every day. "Walking keeps me young," she'd said with a laugh the first time Maggie offered her a ride home.

Maggie didn't know if Bernadette was aware that her brother-in-law whipped his son, Zeke, or that Maggie had put a stop to it. She sensed Bernadette would have been distressed if she had to choose between her loyalty to Coach Whittaker and her job, so Maggie had decided to keep quiet, deferring, at least this once, to Zillah's outdated and inconsistent moral code.

Bernadette treated Ellie like a princess but enforced a clear standard of right and wrong without laying a finger on her. Maggie hoped she'd be willing to help out with Ellie after they moved into their own home, maybe even live with them if they could afford a big enough house.

Bernadette poured Ellie a glass of orange juice. "I'll make you a stack of hot cakes and then we'll bake a pie. How does that sound?"

"Me help. Bye-bye, Mommy."

With Ellie safely settled, Maggie rushed upstairs for her hat and gloves, brimming with energy. Today was the day. Once the trustees approved the contract with the Samuelson Foundation, she could start negotiating for a building. With any luck, she'd open the clinic in a week or so and get back to work at last.

At the hospital, Mrs. Richardson, Dr. Grandheim's rabbitty secretary, all buckteeth and freckles, asked Maggie to wait in the corridor. Bennett brushed her cheek with a kiss and followed Mrs. Richardson into the boardroom.

Maggie straightened her hat and checked the seams of her stockings. She wore a gray rayon suit dress and carried a black leather folder with Dr. Samuelson's letter, the proposed three-year budget for the Zillah clinic, the most recent annual report for the Chicago clinic, and a testimonial from Mrs. Marshall Fields, chairwoman of the Chicago clinic during Maggie's tenure.

Relaxed and confident, Maggie counted off the five hospital trustees. She and Dr. Grandheim had worked well together during Sadie's operation; surely he couldn't doubt her competency. And Bennett had said that Mr. Ebersol, the chairman of the trustees, always followed Grandheim's lead, so that was two men in her corner.

Bennett would be elected to fill his father's position on the board this morning, so she had one more strong advocate, and, despite Janet's warning, she couldn't imagine a pompous fool like Mr. Cominski would carry much weight with the other men.

Best of all, except for yesterday, she had sat in the front pew of church every Sunday since they moved to Zillah, in full sight of the Reverend Archibald Mosley, the fifth trustee.

Yesterday, Bennett had begged off going to church, telling his mother he needed to bring his father's files up to date. As soon as Louisa and Ellie drove off, he and Maggie had spent the morning making love—long, lazy, luxurious lovemaking that healed the fissures between them and filled her with a sense of well-being and optimism.

Sunday afternoon, Maggie had driven to the hospital to visit Sadie. She had discovered how pretty the girl was, long limbed and slender, with smooth chocolate skin over elegant cheekbones and wide brown eyes. She'd been annoyed to find Sadie relegated to a makeshift room in the basement, but her mother, who had spent the night in a chair by her bed, said Dr. Grandheim had checked on her every four hours after surgery.

While Maggie was there, Janet's father, Sheriff Davis, showed up to interview Sadie, but she had refused to name the abortionist. Exasperated, the sheriff threatened to charge her with seeking an abortion, a felony under Indiana state law. Sadie had clamped her mouth shut, and Maggie pulled him into the hallway.

"She's only fifteen, Sheriff, almost a child. The person you should be looking for is the man who impregnated her. If you prosecute Sadie for seeking an abortion, I'll refuse to present the medical evidence, and your case will collapse." Maggie bit her lip and hoped the sheriff wouldn't call her bluff. Dr. Grandheim could testify, and he probably would.

"It's the district attorney who decides to bring charges, Dr. Kendall, not me. I'll tell him what you said." The sheriff gave her a tired smile. "I've got a couple of daughters myself, and this kind of thing makes me sick. But I can't do much if Sadie won't talk. Forget it. We won't prosecute her."

For such small things, let us be grateful, O Lord. But Sheriff Davis hadn't seemed anxious to go after the man—or boy—who had raped Sadie. Maybe, like Dr. Grandheim, he felt it was none of his business what "those people by the river" did. She'd have to ask Janet.

She opened her purse to make a note to talk to Janet, and a well-polished brass plaque mounted on the wall outside the hospital board room caught her eye. It read:

Dedicated this 4th day of July, 1924
to D. C. Stephenson
Grand Dragon of the Ku Klux Klan
and to the Members of the Ku Klux Klan of Indiana
and the Queens of the Golden Mask
Who Raised the Funds Necessary
to Build this Great Hospital
to Serve the People of Zillah

Maggie rubbed her arms. Doc had founded Community Memorial. Had he been a member of the Klan? What about Louisa? Had she been a Queen of the Golden Mask—whatever the hell that was? Maggie shivered as if a north wind had blown through the hospital corridor.

Mrs. Richardson opened the door and beckoned. "We're ready for you now." She clasped her hands at her waist and gave Maggie a nervous smile. "Good luck, hon."

"Thank you." Maggie took a deep breath and strode into the boardroom. The men around the table stood as she entered. She examined their faces with new interest. Had they been

Klan members, too?

"Dr. Kendall, welcome." A gray-haired man at the head of the table moved forward to shake her hand. "We met at the reception, but for the record, I'm Hamilton Ebersol, chairman of the hospital's board of trustees and president of First National Bank of Zillah."

Ebersol's speech was hesitant and broken, his gait unsteady. Maggie diagnosed Parkinson's. *What a shame.* He seemed otherwise healthy.

He took Maggie's elbow and steered her to the open seat on his left. "Please, sit down."

The boardroom presented a more formal appearance than it had the night of the cocktail party. The mahogany table gleamed as if newly waxed. The heavy yellow curtains, pulled back from the open windows, swayed in the draft of a large electric fan that stood in one corner. Opposite the windows, an American flag fluttered from a brass pole. She heard a lawnmower and caught a whiff of freshly cut grass.

Mr. Ebersol sat down heavily. "Now, my dear, I hope you've met the other trustees."

"Yes, I have." Maggie glanced at the men as they resumed their seats. Except for Bennett, they could have been brothers or cousins, heavy-set men with freshly shaven jowls, ruddy complexions and thinning hair. Their suits were pressed, their shirts starched, and they wore gold jewelry—watch chains, diamond tie clips, a pinky ring or two. Ten years from now, she realized with a twinge, Bennett would fit right in.

They nodded to her politely, even Mr. Cominski. Bennett winked at her and grinned.

"Thank you, Mr. Ebersol." Maggie set her purse on the floor, pulled off her short gray gloves and folded them. She opened the leather folder and looked up. "I'm ready." She hoped he couldn't hear the pounding of her heart.

Mr. Ebersol tapped a walnut gavel. "Mrs. Richardson, please have the minutes show the meeting reconvened at nine-fifteen. Will you read the next item on the agenda?" His fingertips trembled against the mimeographed paper in front of him.

"Of course, Mr. Ebersol." Mrs. Richardson patted her strawberry-blond curls. "Be it resolved that Community Memorial Hospital will enter into a contract with the Samuelson Foundation to provide medical services for a health clinic for needy families in Zillah, Indiana."

"Thank you, Mrs. Richardson." Mr. Ebersol's thumb and forefinger jerked together. He turned to Bennett. "Dr. Kendall, would you like to address the trustees?"

Dr. Grandheim cleared his throat. "May I interject, Mr. Ebersol?"

At Hamilton's nod, Grandheim said, "Gentlemen, we are in the enviable position of having two Doctors Kendall with us this morning. For the sake of clarity and to make minute-taking a little easier for Mrs. Richardson, I suggest we address Dr. Margaret Kendall as Mrs. Kendall."

There was a murmur of accord. "A sensible suggestion," Mr. Ebersol said. "Do you agree, my dear?"

Maggie felt a prickle of irritation, but she ignored it. She had come, hat in hand, to get their support. She couldn't afford to provoke them over a trifle. "I prefer to be addressed as Dr. Kendall, sir, but I understand the trustees' position."

"Thank you, Mrs. Kendall." Mr. Ebersol turned to Bennett. "Now, Dr. Kendall, please proceed."

"Thank you, sir." Bennett smiled anxiously at the older men. "My wife, Dr. Margaret Kendall, graduated magna cum laude from Knox College and received her medical degree cum laude from the University of Illinois. Until our marriage and relocation to Zillah this past August, my wife practiced at the Maxwell Street Clinic in Chicago."

Outside the window, the lawnmower coughed and died.

"Recently my wife learned the Samuelson Foundation is exploring whether its program of pre- and postnatal care would be as effective in preventing premature births and reducing infant mortality in a rural community as it has proven to be in Chicago. To address this question, the foundation proposes to fund a free clinic in Zillah to be headed by my wife."

He paused and took a sip of water. "You have a mimeographed copy of Dr. Samuelson's letter in front of you. The foundation proposes a three-year budget, which would be adequate to hire staff and outfit the clinic."

Bennett looked around the room. "In order to ensure the health and well-being of its patients, the foundation requires the director of the clinic to sign an agreement with a fully accredited hospital to provide emergency hospital care, should that become necessary. The foundation has authorized an annual retainer of three thousand dollars to the hospital for these services, whether or not they are required. Any actual hospital costs incurred will be borne by the foundation."

He faced Mr. Ebersol. "To open the discussion, therefore, I move that the board of trustees of Community Memorial Hospital adopt the resolution as proposed." Bennett grinned at Maggie. "Thank you, gentlemen."

"Thank you, Dr. Kendall." Mr. Ebersol held the gavel poised over the agenda and looked around the boardroom.. "However, as you are not yet a trustee of this hospital, you may not introduce a motion."

What? Maggie stole a glance at the agenda and saw the new trustee wouldn't be elected until after they acted on the clinic. Her confidence, already shaken by Grandheim's unexpected demand that she be addressed as "Mrs. Kendall," wavered even more.

The Reverend Archibald Mosley cleared his throat and said,

"So moved."

"Second."

To Maggie's surprise, Principal Cominski had seconded the motion. For a moment she wondered if he would support the clinic after all, but one look at his stony face and she decided his action was merely *pro forma*.

"Thank you, Mr. Cominski," Mr. Ebersol said. "Is there any further discussion?"

For a minute the room lay still under an air of heavy expectancy. Then Dr. Grandheim pushed back his chair and stood, unbuttoning his suit jacket and exposing the old-fashioned watch chain strung across his vest. He inflated his lungs and nodded coolly at Maggie. Her heart sank.

"Gentlemen and Mrs. Kendall, it is indeed an honor to have such a distinguished organization as the Samuelson Foundation cast its eye upon our little community. For that reason, it is doubly regrettable that a representative of the foundation could not attend our deliberations today."

Maggie bit her lip. *You old goat. The board refused to invite Dr. Samuelson and you know it.*

Dr. Grandheim lowered his gold-rimmed spectacles and studied her over the rim. "First, let me say how deeply appreciative I am that this charming young woman, after living in our little town for less than a month, has discovered a need for medical services, which has escaped the notice of the local doctors during all the years we have lived and practiced in this community."

The lawnmower started up again, choked, and stopped.

Grandheim raised his voice. "I, myself, have labored five decades in Zillah, five decades during which I have turned no one away from my door, five decades during which I have visited, first by horse and buggy, and now by automobile, almost every house and farm in our little county."

Even the Negro houses by the river?

He poured a glass of water from the pitcher in front of him and took a long swallow. The other trustees sat so silently that Maggie heard the faint clicks of her wristwatch as it ticked away the seconds. It was like waiting for a grenade to explode.

"As I have said, I am grateful to Dr. Bennett Kendall, Jr., the son of my greatest friend, and to his lovely wife, Mrs. Margaret Kendall, for calling our attention to what she perceives is a deeply felt need for medical care for the indigent, and, due to Mrs. Kendall's connections with the great outside world, care that could be available at no apparent cost to the hard-working citizens of Zillah."

Dr. Grandheim pulled a monogrammed handkerchief from his vest pocket and patted his forehead, although Maggie saw no signs of perspiration.

"But I tell you, my esteemed colleagues, there is indeed a price to be paid." He looked around the room slowly, expectantly, his well-shaped eyebrows arched.

He must pluck them, Maggie thought. And then, *Pay attention! Don't let him hypnotize you.*

"A price that we may not see until it is too late, a price that we cannot and must not pay in these perilous times, and that price, my friends—" he leaned forward, propping his hands on the table, balancing his great weight, and peering into each face in turn "—is the price of freedom."

Good grief. It's just a clinic for women and babies.

Grandheim settled back into his chair, arms crossed over his massive chest, his cold, white face expectant.

Mr. Ebersol tapped the gavel. "Dr. Grandheim, I think the trustees are anxious to understand why this clinic might threaten our freedom." His left hand quivered furiously.

"All right." Grandheim pushed himself to his feet and, with a flourish, pulled a thin blue book from the inner pocket of his jacket and held it at arm's length. "This little book, prepared by the AMA, eloquently and lucidly describes the dangers of social-ized medicine." He turned to face Maggie. "This clinic of yours, Mrs. Kendall, bears all the hallmarks of that insidious practice."

"I object." Bennett stood. He cleared his throat several times. "With all due respect, Dr. Grandheim, my wife is not a social-ist." His voice rose on the last word as if asking a question.

Mr. Ebersol rapped the gavel again. "Now, now, Bennett. No one has said a word about your lovely wife. She will have a chance to respond in due course." He pointed the gavel at Dr. Grandheim. "Please proceed."

Defeated, Bennett sank into his chair. Grandheim continued without missing a beat. "Mrs. Kendall, you say you will serve the needy of this community. Before I vote on the motion, I must first ask you, what will prevent destitute women and children all across the state from racing to our little town to obtain free medical care?"

Maggie opened her mouth, but Grandheim silenced her by raising a forefinger. "Second, how will you determine which indigent families deserve free care and which ones, poor only because of their own indolence, should not be allowed access to your clinic?"

He raised another finger. "Third, how do you propose to ensure that families who can afford the excellent medical care they are used to receiving from the doctors in this room will not suddenly abandon their long-term relationships to avail themselves of your free services?

"Fourth," he continued, "I am not acquainted with the Sam-uelson Foundation. None of my friends or associates is familiar with this organization. Its very name, however, must lead any thinking person to inquire whether this clinic, no matter how described, is intended to establish a foothold for the Jewish religion in our community."

He looked around the room. It felt as if the trustees, even Bennett, had stopped breathing. "Gentlemen, would you want your wife attended by a physician from a Semitic clinic? Would you not ask yourself what ceremonies might be performed before your newborn son is delivered safely into the bosom of his family?"

The men began talking at once.

Dr. Grandheim held up his hand. They fell silent. "In addition, gentlemen, I call your attention to the events of this past weekend. Despite the long-standing policy of this board, Mrs. Kendall deliberately forced Community Memorial Hospital to admit a colored patient."

Maggie could not remain quiet. "The girl would have died—"

Mr. Ebersol banged his gavel. "Mrs. Kendall, I repeat. You may respond at the appropriate time."

"But—"

"Already I have received a number of calls from my patients, families I have treated for many years, asking whether the policy of this hospital has been changed," Grandheim said, drowning her out. "Gentlemen, such flagrant disregard for well-established practice cannot and must not be tolerated."

Grandheim stretched both arms wide, looking for all the world like Billy Graham making his final appeal from the pulpit. "Finally, while I laud the tender, female heart that wants to bring a free clinic to Zillah, my own Christian heart—" he touched his right hand to his chest "—sternly educated by decades of medical service to this community, cannot support the proposal before us today."

There was a long moment of silence. Grandheim sat down and folded his hands on top of the table. Mrs. Richardson turned a page on her steno pad and looked up. Maggie pushed back her chair. "Mr. Ebersol, may I respond?"

He nodded and Maggie stood. "Members of the board of

trustees and Mrs. Richardson."

Startled, Grandheim's secretary glanced up, her brown eyes wide, a rabbit surprised in the kitchen garden.

Despite her pounding heart, Maggie forced herself to speak calmly, each word distinct. "I believe every American child has the right to a healthy life. I believe this right extends not only to our own children, but to all children, whether rich or poor, Negro or white, Protestant or Jewish or Catholic. This is not socialism, gentlemen. It is simply good medical practice.

"As Dr. Grandheim said, if you sign the contract with the clinic, it is indeed possible you will be forced to treat colored patients at Community Memorial Hospital.

"But gentlemen, on Saturday, a young colored girl in Zillah required emergency medical care. She was operated on. Here, in this very building. Dr. Grandheim saved her life. And, gentlemen, despite that violation of your long-established policy, Community Memorial Hospital is still standing.

"Despite the infamous basis upon which this hospital was established, despite the testimony of the plaque outside this very room, you, the trustees of this hospital, have the opportunity to lead Zillah into a new era, where every individual in our community has an equal chance to lead a healthy and productive life." She paused. "That, gentlemen, is the goal to which I have dedicated my life. I trust you, too, will share that goal."

Maggie sat down and folded her hands on the tabletop, deliberately mimicking Grandheim. The blood raced through her body, her fingers trembled, but she held her face perfectly still.

The Reverend Archibald Mosley cleared his throat. "I call for the motion."

"Very well." Mr. Ebersol tapped the gavel on the table. "If

there is no further discussion, all in favor will signify by saying 'Aye.' "

Bennett called out, "Aye."

"May I remind you, Dr. Kendall, that you cannot vote." Ebersol turned to the other trustees. The room thundered with silence.

"Opposed?"

With one voice, the men said, "Nay."

"I see we are unanimous, gentlemen. Mrs. Richardson, please let the minutes show that the motion failed on a vote of zero to four." Hamilton rose and turned to Maggie. "You may be excused, my dear. Thank you for joining us."

Maggie clutched her purse and gloves and stood. Her legs felt wooden, her eyes clouded, but she was determined not to cry. How could they all be lined up against her? Even the minister. It wasn't right. She straightened and pulled her dignity around her shoulders. "Thank you, gentlemen."

Mr. Ebersol opened the door. Stiff-legged, Maggie walked from the room. He closed the door behind her, and she leaned against the wall.

Now what?

"Are you okay, Maggie?" She felt a strong hand on her arm.

"Peter Grandheim! What are you doing here?"

"I'm agenda item number seven. The campaign's heating up, and Senator Jenner expects me to pry twenty-five thousand dollars out of the hospital board. If I can't persuade Dad and his cronies to cough up the money, I can kiss my political career good-bye." He frowned. "You look pale. Let me buy you a cup of coffee." Limping slightly, he steered her toward the elevator.

"Aren't you supposed to wait here?"

"Old Tom will find me when they need me." Peter glanced at the porter. "Won't you, Tom?"

"Yes, sir."

A minute later Maggie sat across from Peter in a corner of the cafeteria. She poured out the story of the board meeting. To her surprise, he smiled.

"You didn't once try to sweet-talk them, did you?"

"Sweet-talk them? No, of course not. I thought they should do the right thing."

"Most men don't appreciate being told what the right thing is."

"But without a contract with the hospital, the clinic can't open."

Peter folded his arms. "Does it have to be Community Memorial?"

"What do you mean?"

He leaned forward and grabbed her hands. "I just rolled in from a campaign stop in Gary, where I met with the hospital administrator." He grimaced and the dimple in his cheek deepened. "Raising money like always. I think he'd sign a contract with you. There's a lot of coloreds working in the steel mills. The hospital has set aside an entire floor for them."

"What about the public hospital in Indianapolis? It's closer."

"That's a snake pit. I wouldn't send anyone there."

Maggie could imagine Dr. Grandheim's angry reaction if she agreed to Peter's plan. And Bennett's. She pushed the images away. Somehow she'd smooth things over with Bennett. As for Josef Grandheim? *He had his chance.*

"Okay. When can I talk to the hospital administrator in Gary?"

"Wednesday. I'm driving up there to get the check. Come with me, and I'll make sure you get in front of the board." He squeezed her hands again. "I think they'll love your clinic, Maggie. Really I do."

"You're a life saver." She glanced up and, to her astonishment, saw Sadie Pierce staring at them from the other side of the steam tables. The girl's face twisted. Was she in pain? Before Maggie could react, Sadie vanished back into the kitchen, and Maggie remembered her grandmother was the head cook.

"What's the matter?"

"Nothing." She'd check on Sadie later. Maggie leaned back and studied Peter's face. "Why are you helping me? Your father will be furious."

His blue eyes twinkled. He reached out and tapped her nose with his index finger. "I expect you to be grateful, my child. Very grateful."

"Peter!" Bennett hurried out of the elevator. "We're waiting for you in the boardroom." He bent down and hugged Maggie. "I'm sorry, sweetheart. It's going to take longer than I thought to win the trustees over. Please, give me time."

Maggie glanced at Peter. "I may have found a solution."

"Good. We can talk about it after dinner." Bennett squeezed her shoulder. "Will I like it?"

"No." Maggie slumped in her seat. She felt a hundred years old. "Probably not."

CHAPTER TWENTY-ONE:
BENNETT

Monday, September 15, 1952

"Mother?" Bennett set his black bag on the floor and tapped on the heavy wooden door. He still felt awkward about stepping into his parents' bedroom. It had been off limits when he was growing up, a secret, adult place with foreign smells and odd noises, a place where little boys were not welcome and the door was always locked. "Are you feeling better?"

"I'm fine," Louisa called out. "Come and join us."

He opened the door, and Ellie ran to him, her yellow pinafore flying behind her. "Daddy, Daddy, Daddy." He swept her into his arms.

The bedroom looked exactly as it had when Doc was alive, twin beds on either side of a mahogany nightstand, the telephone extension within easy reach. The curtains of the bay window were open, and sunshine lit the silver-handled hairbrush and comb on his mother's dressing table.

"Look, Daddy. Tea party." Ellie squirmed down and jumped onto Doc's bed. Expecting to hear a reprimand, Bennett glanced at his mother. She was smiling.

He couldn't remember Louisa playing with him like this. She had read to him at bedtime, mostly Bible stories, and walked with him to the playground. But she had never allowed him to run in the house or shout or bring his Lincoln logs into her bedroom. He couldn't help but feel jealous that Ellie took all these privileges for granted.

"What a nice tea party, sweetie," he said. Ellie's dolls and her old Teddy bear sat in a circle on Doc's bed, propped up with pillows.

Tiny blue and white teacups lay scattered across the coverlet. Bennett picked up the china teapot. He turned it over. "Blue Willow?" He looked at his mother. "I've never seen this before."

"I bought the set at Marshall Field's when I was pregnant with you." Louisa sat on the edge of her bed and pulled Ellie into her lap. "Eleanor helped me unpack it a couple of weeks ago. We've been having tea every afternoon since."

"Daddy, eat cake." Ellie held out a cookie the size of a quarter. Its pink icing held small, grubby fingerprints.

He nibbled one edge. "Mmm. Delicious."

Downstairs the screen door slammed. "Mommy home," Ellie shrieked. She bounced out of Louisa's lap and raced down the hall to the stairway.

Louisa shut the door behind her. "Now, tell me what happened at the trustees' meeting, Junior." She pushed a chintz-covered footstool toward Bennett and started picking up the doll china, fitting each piece into place in a cardboard box.

Bennett sighed. Maggie had refused to discuss her plans for the clinic with him after the meeting. She needed to think about it, she'd said. He had worried all day. *Full steam ahead and damn the torpedoes. That was his gal, all right.*

"Well, Maggie made a fine presentation this morning," he started, "but—"

"I don't care about that!" Louisa slid the box of doll china under Doc's bed, fluffed the pillows and pulled the coverlet tight. She sat the stuffed bear against the headboard. "What about the new surgical wing? Did you vote on the name?"

"No, Mother. Grandheim refuses to talk about names until he has the money in hand, and we're still half a million dollars short. He's got a meeting with the head of Methodist Hospital in Indianapolis next week. They may be willing to loan us the funds. If not, he's going to talk with the state public health department and see if there's federal money available." Bennett leaned back and laced his fingers over his bald spot. "But only as a last resort. We all want to keep it a private hospital."

"But Josef Grandheim agrees it should be named for Doc, doesn't he?" Louisa slipped off her shoes and stretched her legs out on her bed. Under her heavy cotton stockings, her ankles were swollen. Her pumps had carved deep indentations across her arches.

Bennett drew the footstool to the end of the bed and bent down to massage her feet. "I think we have to give up on the name, Mother. If Methodist invests, they'll probably want to call it Methodist Hospital at Zillah, something like that. If we get federal money, who knows? Maybe the William E. Jenner wing."

"You can't allow that, Junior. Senator Jenner may be a great man, but he hasn't had anything to do with our hospital."

"I agree. But I think Grandheim would sell his soul to get the money. He had the architect sketch out what the whole medical complex could look like in another ten years. The campus would be huge, fifty acres or more. We'd have to lease the land behind the hospital to have enough room for expansion."

"That's the old Whittaker farm," Louisa said. "It belongs to his son, George, the coach over at the high school. You remember him, don't you? He and his wife have a whole passel of kids, and I know she wants to build a brand-new house west of town. Out on the bypass next to her parents."

"Well, if Grandheim gets his way, Whittaker will collect enough money to build his wife a new house every year if that's what she wants."

He patted her feet, moved over to sit on Doc's bed, and grinned. "Maybe Grandheim will decide to name the new surgical pavilion the Whittaker Wing. Sounds patriotic, doesn't it, like a squadron of bombers?"

"Don't try to be funny, Junior. You're supposed to make sure the trustees do the right thing."

"I don't think I can, Mother. I'm one vote, nothing more. We have to see what happens."

"I'm not going to wait. I'll see Josef Grandheim tomorrow and talk some sense into him." She clamped her lips together and folded her arms across her chest. *End of discussion.* He heard a clatter of dishes from the kitchen. Ellie must be helping Bernadette set the table for dinner.

"What happened with Margaret's clinic? Did the trustees turn her down flat?"

"Yeah, she was pretty disappointed. She's determined to get that clinic started, come hell or high water."

"I wish she were as determined to be a good wife to you."

"Come on, Mother. Maggie cares as much about being a doctor as I do, maybe more." He raised one eyebrow, drew in a breath, and glanced at Louisa. He probably looked like a little boy asking for another slice of cake with no expectation of getting it. "I have an idea."

"Yes?"

"Doc used to have his office here at home." Bennett stared at his hands as he rubbed his palms together. "What if we remodeled his study and made it into a medical office for Maggie?" He looked up. "She could hang out her shingle, and when she has patients who need to be hospitalized, I could admit them to Community Memorial. That'd give her something to do."

"Over my dead body!" Louisa's face flushed. She grabbed the headboard and pulled herself upright. "I absolutely forbid it, Junior. I don't want her kind of people running in and out of my house all day, stealing stuff, likely as not, bothering Eleanor, always underfoot. I'd be the laughing stock of the county and you would be, too."

Louisa's chest heaved. Her hand shook. The headboard clattered against the wall.

"What's wrong, Mother?"

Without answering, Louisa let go of the headboard, took off her glasses, and massaged the bridge of her nose. "What's more, if Margaret keeps on pestering people, stirring up trouble, she's going to turn the hospital trustees against you, Junior, and then they'll never name the new wing for Doc."

As she finished, Louisa gasped. The blood drained from her face. She leaned back, her hand over her heart, and fumbled for the handkerchief in her sleeve.

"Mother!" Bennett jumped to his feet. "Lie down." He grabbed his black bag from the hallway and pulled out his stethoscope. He put a pillow under her head and moved the bell of the stethoscope over her chest. She lay still, her face white and sweaty, her hands shaking.

There was a knock on the door, and Maggie sang out, "Dinner's ready."

Louisa gripped Bennett's wrist. Her knotted fingers felt like baling wire. "Don't you dare say a word to Margaret," she hissed. "Not one word! I don't trust her. She cares more about some dirty pickaninny working in the fields than she does about honoring your father's memory."

CHAPTER TWENTY-TWO:
MAGGIE

September 18, 1952

Dear Aunt Vessie,

Thanks for giving Dr. Samuelson my new P.O. box number. The foundation has decided to fund a clinic in a farm community, and he has chosen Zillah and me. I am so grateful.

Of course, things never go smoothly here. The foundation needs a hospital to provide backup medical services if there's ever an emergency at the clinic. I tried to persuade the trustees of Community Memorial to sign the contract, but they (along with Mother Kendall) think any plan to help poor people is a communist plot. Bennett was elected to fill his father's seat on the board, but only after they had given me the bum's rush.

Ever the happy optimist, Bennett insists it will be only a matter of time before the trustees capitulate, but I can't wait. If I don't get a contract signed by October 1, the foundation will choose another location for the clinic.

Fortunately, Peter Grandheim arranged for me to meet with a hospital in Gary. One of the big brass there is the grandfather of little Moses Kendall Johnson, so skillfully delivered by yours truly a month ago. Mr. Johnson, who owns the largest colored mortuary and insurance agency in East Chicago, sang my praises and (hallelujah!) the contract is signed.

Peter keeps popping up like a fairy godfather, solving all my problems in the twinkle of an eye. Yesterday, he drew up an agreement so I can lease the old elementary school for the clinic. He's busy trying to wheedle twenty-five thousand dollars for Senator Jenner's re-election campaign from the hospital. The trustees can't bear to part with that much money, especially since they're building a new surgical wing. Peter's been good to me, so I sympathize with his problems, but I sure wish he were raising money to defeat Jenner instead.

Meanwhile, I've hired Luther Pierce, a colored custodian from the new elementary school, to help me transform the old building into a medical clinic. Peter objected, but he wouldn't say why. In any event, much to everyone's astonishment, we plan to open our doors in a month. Can you come down for the ceremony? The train is slow but reliable, and I could meet you at the station.

Louisa is truly furious about the clinic, and Bennett wants to talk to the hospital trustees again, but at long last, I am making progress. Like General Patton, my motto is "Forward, always forward." (I expect shelling to start at any minute!)

Love, Maggie

CHAPTER TWENTY-THREE

Zillah Courier. *Friday, September 19, 1952*

Hospital Addition Funded!

Mr. Hamilton Ebersol, Chairman of the Board of Trustees of Community Memorial Hospital, announced today that an anonymous benefactor has contributed $500,000 to the building fund for the new surgical pavilion. With the donation in hand, Mr. Ebersol is confident that the new wing can open within a year.

The surgical pavilion will include four operating rooms, fully equipped with the latest medical technology, a radiological center, a state-of-the-art medical laboratory, and 20 additional patient beds.

Mr. Ebersol also announced that the hospital trustees have chosen to name the new building the Bennett M. Kendall, Sr., and Louisa J. Kendall Surgical Pavilion in honor of their many years of service to Zillah. The community is invited to attend the ground-breaking ceremony at 1:00 p.m., Sunday, September 28, at the hospital.

A local building firm, Grandheim & Whittaker Construction, has been awarded the contract for the addition.

CHAPTER TWENTY-FOUR:
LUTHER

Two Weeks Later. Thursday, October 2, 1952

Luther stopped in the doorway of Dr. Kendall's office in the prenatal clinic, push broom in hand. He was ready to get back to work. No lazing around for this man, no sir. He had already put in a full day at Pulaski Elementary, and he wanted to finish up here and get home for dinner. But first, he paused to look at the slender, brown-haired woman behind the wooden desk. She seemed so young, only a few years older than Luther himself. *I'll bet she misses being at home with her baby.*

Dr. Kendall sat in a circle of light created by a goose-necked lamp, reading a small book. The top of the desk was covered with papers. They looked like government forms—thin paper, tiny print. As the sun set, a gust of wind swirled a small tornado of brown and yellow leaves against the windows behind her.

He and Dr. Kendall had worked for two weeks turning the old elementary school into a medical clinic. She had taken the kindergarten room for her office because it had a sink in the corner. Luther had built bookshelves next to the cloak closet, and the Samuelson Foundation had sent them glass-fronted equipment cabinets, an examination table, and boxes of medical supplies.

For now, urine and blood samples would go to the hospital in Gary, but Dr. Kendall planned to set up a lab in the first-grade classroom as soon as she found a part-time technician. She could test for pregnancy right here in the clinic, though. He had built two cages by the back door to house rabbit does and set up a tin-topped table for slaughtering them. Dr. Kendall said her microscope was powerful enough to examine the rabbit's ovaries without sending the samples to a lab.

The small schoolhouse was in good condition for being almost fifty years old. There were five rooms on the first floor: the principal's office, the library, kindergarten, first grade, and second grade. The other four grades were upstairs. The fire escape from the second floor, an enclosed metal slide, snaked down the side of the brick building and emptied onto the asphalt-covered playground, which still had monkey bars and a rusty swing set that groaned in the wind.

Luther rapped twice on the open door. "Shall I turn your lights on, Dr. Kendall?"

She swept back the curls that had escaped her bobby pins. Her face looked tired and lined. He saw a dirt mark on her cheek as dark as a faded bruise. "Thank you, Luther." She smiled and motioned toward the clock mounted on the wall. "I didn't know it was so late."

"Must be a pretty good book." Luther flipped the switch by the door. Overhead, the fluorescent lights blinked twice. The harsh glow lit Dr. Kendall's office as if it were a display window in a department store and she a mannequin. "Let me adjust the shades for you."

Luther set the handle of his broom against the door and moved across the room quickly and quietly, his work boots, worn but spit-polished, barely touching the floor. With his right arm, he lifted the eight-foot pole that stood in the corner next to the steam pipes. Bracing it against his shoulder, he inserted the metal hook into the grommet at the bottom edge of the nearest shade, which was tightly rolled against the ceiling.

With a swift, sure motion, Luther pulled the shades down, one after another, and the room grew even quieter, even more intimate. For a brief moment, he felt nervous, alone in this small room with a white woman. But Dr. Kendall seemed at ease. He replaced the pole in the corner, where it jangled against the pipes.

"Thanks, Luther. I can't manage the shades by myself."

He grinned. "It takes a special knack, ma'am."

Luther marched past her desk, back to the push broom, back to the sinks and toilets to be cleaned, back to the mop bucket and the lye soap. As he passed, he glanced at the book Dr. Kendall had been reading in the small circle of golden light.

"Gwendolyn Brooks?"

"Yes, it's *Annie Allen,* the poems that won the Pulitzer. Would you like to see it?" She slipped a scrap of paper inside to mark her place and handed the book to him. Luther took it awkwardly. She pulled a chair close to her desk. "Why don't you sit down?"

"No, ma'am. I should get back to work." Luther laid the thin volume on her blotter; the harsh lights overhead bleached its cover. He stepped away. "I never did thank you properly, Dr. Kendall, for taking care of Sadie."

"When is she coming home from the hospital?"

"Tomorrow."

"Well, remind her that she needs to schedule a follow-up visit with me."

"Yes, ma'am." Luther studied the floor. "Thank you for paying Sadie's hospital bill, Dr. Kendall. And for letting me work it off here at the clinic."

"I got the best of the bargain, Luther. I couldn't have managed without you." She touched the book. "I'll leave *Annie Allen* here. Feel free to borrow it."

"Thank you, ma'am. I haven't had time to read poetry as much as I'd like. It's not one of those things Congress intended to pay for on the GI Bill."

"Are you going to college, Luther?"

"Yes, ma'am. I'll start at Howard next year. I aim to be a newspaper reporter."

"A reporter?" Her face lit up, almost but not quite erasing the strained look around her eyes. "That's wonderful."

"Yes, ma'am. I've been reading what the papers have to say about the colored soldiers in Korea and all, and I decided someone needs to tell the true story. Somebody, like me, who was really there."

"Is that where you lost your arm, Luther?"

"Yes, ma'am." He touched the sleeve pinned over his stump, pinned where his elbow should be. "This here's my souvenir of the Iron Triangle."

"How did it happen?"

He looked at the clock. It was past seven and his dinner would be getting cold. "Are you sure you want to know?"

"Yes."

He heard her firm, calm voice and behind it, the wind blowing twigs against the windows. It made him feel as if they floated together, insulated, in a time and space where the normal rules of the world were suspended, floated in a place where he could tell his story and she could hear it.

Dr. Kendall rested her arms on her blotter and pointed to the chair next to her desk. "Sit down," she said again.

"No, ma'am. This is a story I have to tell standing up or I can't tell it at all." He looked past her at the row of medical books and read the gilt letters on the fat spines: Pathology, Anatomy, Surgery, Histology. He loved to see a row of books like that, neat but well thumbed, with worn spots on the covers and cracks in the spines. He knew what his room would look like when he started college: quiet and orderly, the room of a scholar, with a single good lamp and a row of well-thumbed books.

"Luther?"

"Yes, ma'am." He stood behind the empty chair at parade rest, his right arm behind his back and the sleeve for his left arm hanging straight down. He began to talk, his voice in as flat a monotone as he could manage, a neutral reporter.

"I enlisted, you know, right out of high school. After I finished basic training, my unit got sent to Japan. We'd been there about six months when the North Koreans pushed past the thirty-eighth parallel. The first I heard of it was when the brass said we were shipping out to Korea. A little police action, they said, we'd be gone for five days, a week at most. The captain ordered us to leave all our personal stuff in Tokyo."

Luther heard his voice rise and crack. He flattened it again. He was the reporter, nothing more.

"It took our boat almost five days to cross the Sea of Japan. The wind blew the waves so high we couldn't see the other troopships steaming beside us. They tried to keep order, but when you've got four hundred men puking below board and another four hundred hanging over the rails, discipline goes to hell.

"Our Japanese stevedores rode in the stern. At first I felt sorry for them, huddled in back, exposed like they were to the wind and the rain, but when we landed and crawled over the side and down the scramble nets, I looked up and realized the Japs felt sorry for us. They were going home again. We weren't."

Luther gripped the back of the chair as he remembered climbing down those nets, slipping in the spray of the surf, swaying against the side of the ship, his pack going one way, his feet the other. He swallowed.

"We rode across country that night in a pouring rain. After the boat, it felt good to be in a truck again. We were edgy, none of us had been in combat before, but we started to feel like real soldiers.

"One of the guys asked our platoon leader, 'How long will it take to sort out these gooks?' I could tell the sergeant didn't know any more than we did, he'd never been in combat either, but we wanted to believe he had the inside dope.

" 'A couple of days,' the sergeant said and grinned. 'Then back to Tokyo and the mama-sans.'

"We cracked jokes about the bar girls, jokes I can't tell you, ma'am, but you know. We were just kids when we went to Japan, and it was our first time away from home.

"It was pitch-dark when we arrived where we were going and pouring rain. We spread across the foot of a hill and dug ourselves in for the night. The ground was rock hard. All I could manage was to scrape out a depression in the dirt, not a real fox hole, and finally I went to sleep, curled around my gear, sleeping in the mud, like I was a little boy again."

Luther looked at Dr. Kendall. She had begun to rub her hands up and down her arms as if she were cold. *I'll bet she's sorry she ever asked.* But he didn't want to stop now, couldn't stop now. He let go of the chair and stood straighter.

"The North Koreans arrived with the light, a line of tanks coming down the road straight at us. We tried to hold our position, Lord we tried, but our old guns were useless against those tanks. They kept coming and shooting and coming and shooting, and the men on either side of me fell, spurting blood and screaming.

"Ben, who believed in God and wouldn't touch a Japanese girl, and Jack who didn't and did, they were both hit. I ducked down, laid on my stomach, and crawled through the muddy blood in the dirt, from one to the other, trying to do something, to stop the bleeding, to keep them breathing, to find a medic. The rain was still coming down."

Dr. Kendall stood and touched his shoulder. Through the fabric of his shirt, her hand felt warm and alive. "Stop a minute." She crossed her office to the tiny sink by the cloak closet. She lit a Bunsen burner, filled the kettle with water and set it to boil while she heated the teapot with hot water from the tap. As soon as the kettle whistled, she made tea and stirred in two heaping spoons full of sugar. "Drink this." She handed Luther a cup and saucer.

"Thank you, Dr. Kendall." The china clattered as he carefully set it on her desk.

"Please, call me Maggie."

No ma'am.

Dr. Kendall nudged him into the chair beside her desk. He took a swallow of tea and a deep breath.

"I got away somehow, a couple of us did. At first we carried Jack. Ben died where he fell, but pretty soon we could tell Jack was dead, too. We stopped running. Some wanted to take his body with us, some didn't. I couldn't say anything. I was the only colored boy left. I would have carried him myself if they had said to, he wasn't so big, nothing but a boney, freckled, red-headed kid straight out of the mountains of North Carolina. The other men finally decided we had to leave him. One of them said a prayer and we laid him in a ditch so he wouldn't be run over by the tanks. We walked on."

Luther turned to look at Dr. Kendall. "Did I tell you how Korea smelled? Smelled like the old outhouse that stood behind my grandma's shack down south that no one had ever cleaned out since my granddaddy died before I was born. Korea smelled like that.

"We kept marching south, keeping off the roads and hiding from the tanks, sloshing through the rice paddies, trying to stay on the dikes but slipping and sliding in the mud and falling down and coming back up again with that same smell of B.M. all over us.

"The night we landed, someone said the Koreans put their own B.M. on the fields for fertilizer and that's what we smelled.

We laughed at him, but it was true."

Luther finished his tea. He set the cup and saucer on Dr. Kendall's desk. The china was covered with tiny pink rosebuds. The rim of the cup was gilded like the titles on the spines of her books.

"More tea?" Dr. Kendall asked, lifting the pot from the blotter on her desk.

"No, ma'am. I'm fine." Luther paused, held up a finger. He had heard a sound. Maybe a dog had stumbled in the gravel outside Dr. Kendall's window. He listened without breathing. He heard the wind whip through the maple trees, tossing leaves and branches against the tall windows in front of him. The bottom of a shade suddenly billowed as if a gust had slipped through the loose wooden frames, and Luther remembered he had planned to put up the storm windows. Yesterday he had carried them one by one from the basement, washed them, and set them in the hallway to dry.

He shook himself and thought back to Korea again. "It took us three days of crawling through the rice paddies before we found the rest of our company." Luther cleared his throat. "We didn't have anything to eat but what we could find, bamboo, grass. We passed a little village on the second day. A bunch of shacks, bent over and dirty, filled with old people as bent over and dirty as their huts.

"There were five of us left by that time, and the rest of them decided I should see if I could find anything to eat. Nobody spoke Korean. The only words we knew in Japanese were dirty words, the words that you used to talk to bar girls and such. I don't know why they picked me except that I was the only colored boy and I was bigger than any of them."

Luther shifted in his seat. "When I got near I saw there was no one in the village but a couple of old people, men or women, it was hard to tell, and some babies. Finally one of the old

153

people dragged out a bamboo basket with turnip roots in it, and I took five. I said thanks and left."

The hands of the clock on the wall above the cloak closet clicked into place. Eight o'clock. He thought he heard the echo of a boot in the hallway.

"The guys weren't happy with turnip roots, but they were too scared to go back and try their luck. We all thought the men of the village must be hidden somewhere with guns—"

Glass crashed and broke in the hallway.

Luther leaped up and ran through the open door. He pulled a knife from his boot as he ran. Dr. Kendall cried out behind him. A thousand shards lay scattered across the tile floor. The front door slammed.

Dr. Kendall stopped beside him and put her hand on his arm. "What happened?"

"It's the storm windows, ma'am." He heard the roar of a car engine. "They must have fallen down."

"That's not true."

"No, ma'am."

"Someone broke them, didn't they? Deliberately."

"Yes, ma'am." Luther heard himself panting. He took a deep breath. *Steady down. Take care of Doc.*

"Did you see who it was?"

"No, ma'am."

"What's that in your hand?"

Luther looked down. "A knife, ma'am. I brought it back from the war." He put it back in his boot.

A piece of paper fluttered in the corner of the hall. He stepped through the glass. It crunched under his heavy work boots. He held the paper so Dr. Kendall could read it. The letters were big and black: NIGGER LOVER GET OUT.

Dr. Kendall pressed her lips together. "The clinic will open Monday morning, right on schedule." She paused. "I have no intention of being scared away. You get a dustpan. I'll call the sheriff."

"Yes, ma'am." Something hard and heavy had landed in the pit of Luther's stomach. Not fear exactly, but a sense of knowing, like riding in the back of that truck across Korea in the dark and smelling B.M. everywhere.

CHAPTER TWENTY-FIVE:
BENNETT

Sunday, October 5, 1952

"Where did you get the money, Mother?" Bennett slammed the kitchen door behind him and tossed his black bag into the corner.

Louisa glanced up as she lifted the lid from a Dutch oven on top of the stove. "Did you get your dictation finished, Junior?" she said evenly, as if she hadn't heard him.

Bennett smelled chicken and noodles, hot and heavy with chicken fat. The odor clung to his face and coated his throat. His stomach burned. "Don't change the subject, Mother. I want to talk about the new hospital wing. Five hundred thousand dollars." Bennett banged the counter with his bare hand. It sounded like a shot in the quiet room. "Where'd the money come from?"

"Don't ask me." Louisa turned to the stove again.

Bennett stared at her broad back crisscrossed by her white apron straps, her stiff neck flushed with heat, at the sheer immovability of her. He wanted to grab her and shake her, would have done so if she had been anyone but his mother. "I found out at the hospital today. Grandheim finally spilled the beans. He congratulated me. Actually congratulated me. I couldn't believe it."

He threw his jacket at the table. It slid to the floor. "Where did you get the money?"

Louisa replaced the lid of the Dutch oven. She turned

deliberately, pulled her handkerchief from her sleeve, and patted the perspiration from her upper lip and neck. She folded her hands together and said, "I took out a loan."

"A loan? For five hundred thousand dollars?" He felt a flood of anger. The entire world had gone cockeyed. "Are you crazy? Who would loan you that kind of money?"

"Mr. Ebersol at the bank."

"What did you put up for security? You haven't got anything but the house and Doc's practice."

She stared at him, tight-lipped.

"Oh, my God. You didn't." Bennett dropped onto a chair as another wave of fire raced through his gut. "How much? What do we have to pay?"

Louisa turned her head away. "About two thousand dollars a month."

"You've lost your mind! I've seen the books. Doc's practice took in only thirty thousand last year. What are we going to live on?"

"It'll be tight for a while."

"Tight! My God." Bennett leaned back and shut his eyes. *We're stuck in this house forever,* he thought. *Maggie will go into a tailspin when she finds out.*

Louisa bent over the back of his chair and wrapped her arms around his shoulders. He felt the urge to jerk away but sat still. She kissed his bald spot and laid her cheek against his hair. "I know it seems like a lot, Junior. But it's an investment in your future. Once the new wing is built, Doc's practice will grow. I'm sure of it."

It's not Doc's practice, he wanted to shout. *It's mine.* But, of course, it wasn't.

"The practice will have to double." Bennett squeezed his eyes shut. "It'll take me the rest of my life to pay off that loan." He pushed his chair back, forcing her to move. "You had no right

157

to sign anything, Mother, without talking to me."

"I had every right in the world." She folded her arms across her chest. "Your father left his business to me. You're my employee." She wiped her eyes. "I promised Doc I'd put his name on that new surgical wing. And I will."

"Is that why you wanted me to move to Zillah, Mother? To be your slave?"

"Don't use that word!"

Bennett snorted. "Indentured servant, then. How's that?"

"I thought you wanted to come back home."

"I did. But—" His voice trailed off.

But not like this.

He had seen himself as a conquering hero, the brave warrior and his beautiful wife sweeping into Zillah and reviving his father's practice, the medical scientist in a white lab coat, saving lives while a brass band blared triumphantly in the background. Now he felt like a small animal, lured into a trap with stale cheese.

"Junior, I—"

"Forget it! What's done is done." Bennett folded his hands over his bald spot and examined the ceiling. "It's a good thing the clinic opens tomorrow, Mother. We'll need every dime of Maggie's salary to buy groceries."

The words echoed in the small, still kitchen.

"Did you hear what I said, Mother? You can thank your lucky stars Maggie has a job. You're going to be nice to her. Do you hear me? If you don't, I'll march right out of Zillah and you'll lose everything."

"You wouldn't."

"I mean it, Mother. This time I really do."

Louisa smiled, indulgent, and Bennett realized she didn't believe a single word he said.

CHAPTER TWENTY-SIX:
MAGGIE

October 8, 1952

P.O. Box 44

Zillah, Indiana

Dear Aunt Vessie,

I did it! The Zillah Clinic for Women and Children opened two days ago, and I'm as happy as I can be.

I'm sorry you couldn't come down for the grand opening—it was a very select affair. From the number of signatures in our guest book, I think about forty people stopped by for tea and cookies. Dr. Samuelson gave a short, rousing speech, and all of the school board members (including her honor, the mayor's wife) toured the building. They were astonished at how clean and tidy it is. Luther Pierce and I scrubbed for days.

Two lay-brothers from the Negro church politely (and very, very quietly) inquired whether the clinic could help with "bad blood." I promised to talk to the state public health director as soon as I get the lab set up. Can you imagine the look on Louisa's face when she finds out? Not only treating poor women, but colored men with VD. Heavens to Betsy. What is the world coming to?

Louisa felt too poorly to leave her bed for the grand opening, but otherwise, she's a changed person. This morning, she actually asked me about the clinic: how it's run, how I will select patients (anyone who comes through the

159

front door), and even how much the foundation pays me (a very paltry five hundred a month—but I'd do this job for free and Dr. Samuelson knows it). I'm pleased with her interest, and I've decided to believe we'll be friends. Maybe I'm being naïve, but miracles do happen. (Of course, it'll be much easier to be friendly when we aren't living in the same house anymore.)

Unfortunately, Peter Grandheim, who made the clinic possible, still hasn't convinced the hospital trustees to donate $25,000 to Senator Jenner's campaign. He thought they would loosen the purse strings once the funds for the new surgical wing were in hand (the newspaper cited "an anonymous benefactor"), but they still haven't coughed up a cent. With the election less than a month away, he's running out of time. The board meeting next Monday is Peter's last chance. Even though I despise Jenner, I can't help but feel sorry for Peter—especially since I'm so happy.

My very first patient showed up yesterday, referred by her sister, Bernadette, our kitchen girl. Olive is seven months along with her fifth child. (Olive, it turns out, is the mother of Zeke Whittaker, whom I met doing the physicals for the fourth graders. She doesn't seem to have any idea that I complained to the sheriff about her husband, the high-school football coach, who whipped Zeke. My goodness, this town is small.)

Olive hasn't seen a doctor, of course, and seems resigned to dropping the baby in the cornfield and going back to work. But her blood pressure is erratic and she has "this funny feeling." I gather neither Olive nor Mr. Whittaker is very excited about another mouth to feed. She douched religiously, but "it jus' don't seem to work none." As soon as she delivers, I'm going to quietly prescribe a diaphragm. Olive can decide to let her husband know—or not.

We had a little vandalism at the clinic before we opened and a nasty note. Sheriff Davis says it's the work of teen-age hoodlums. I hope that's all.

Meanwhile, Ellie toddles by my side as we walk to the clinic every morning. I take her home at noon for her nap, and, surprise of surprises, Louisa hasn't objected once. I set up Ellie's little table and chair in the corner of my office and stocked it with blocks and books. She chatters happily while I plow through my paperwork. When she's here, I feel as if I'm sitting next to a babbling brook sparkling with sunshine. I won't let anyone destroy that.

All my love, Maggie

CHAPTER TWENTY-SEVEN:
MAGGIE

Thursday, October 9, 1952

"No trace of infection, Sadie. Your incision is almost healed."

Maggie pulled the drape over the girl's abdomen. *I wish I had closed her up,* she thought as she helped Luther's sister sit on the table in the examination room at the clinic. Grandheim had left a scar like a brand across Sadie's narrow pelvis. "You can go back to school Monday."

"I'm done with school." Sadie folded her arms across her chest and puffed out her cheeks.

"What about the truant officer?" Maggie grinned at her as she peeled off her rubber gloves and dropped them into a basin of disinfectant.

"He doesn't come around our part of town."

Maggie sighed. Her attempt at a joke had failed. Every attempt she made to establish rapport with the girl had failed. She agreed with Sheriff Davis. They needed to find out who had impregnated her. If it was a boy her own age, well, that was one thing. But if he was an adult, there was a good chance he wouldn't stop with Sadie.

This was the hardest part of running a clinic. Not the blood and urine, not the long hours or the house calls in the middle of the night, but the feeling of responsibility, as if her duty to heal encompassed more than relieving physical pain. She looked at Luther's little sister, defiant and vulnerable, and felt her heart ache. *First, do no harm.*

Maggie pulled a stool close to the table and perched next to Sadie. Despite all the cleaning she and Luther had done, the examination room still smelled like first grade, as if crayons were stuck between the floor boards and chalk dust hung in the air.

The clock over the door clicked. She glanced at it. Three o'clock. Fifteen minutes ago, she had heard someone, presumably her next patient, Olive Whittaker, walk into the principal's office, now remodeled as a reception area. Maggie hadn't hired a secretary for the clinic yet, so she had taped a sign on the front door: PLEASE WAIT UNTIL CALLED.

"Why don't you want to go back to school, Sadie?" she began gently. "Are you afraid the other kids will tease you?"

"Them?" The single word encompassed a world of disdain. "I don't need any more school. I'm going to get married."

"Married? You can't get married."

"I can if I want."

"But you're only fifteen."

"Oh, that." Sadie tightened her arms across her chest. "My birthday's next month."

"Who will you marry, Sadie? The man who—" Maggie paused before she dragged out the last two words "—assaulted you?"

"Assaulted me? That's a dirty lie. You've gotta stop running around, telling everyone I was raped, Doc. It wasn't his fault I got pregnant. Besides, he loves me."

"He loves you?" Maggie stood and looked down at the girl. "Why did he drag you to that butcher, Sadie? Because he loves you?" She put her hand on Sadie's shoulder. "Besides, love doesn't change anything. You're under sixteen. According to Indiana law, you were raped. End of story. Even if he's a kid like you."

Sadie pulled away. "He's not a boy. He's a man. He's been to college and everything. And as soon as I turn sixteen, we're going to get hitched." She drew in a deep breath. Her lower lip trembled. "You can't stop me, Doc."

What kind of man marries a child like this? A dozen ugly pictures tumbled through Maggie's mind. "Who is he?"

Sadie pinched her lips together and stuck out her jaw. For a second, she looked like Louisa, darker, thinner, younger, but just as implacable.

Maggie closed her eyes. *Sorry, Sheriff. I struck out.* Back to medicine where she could do some good. "Are you still—" the next words caught in her throat "—dating him?"

Sadie answered, "Yes, ma'am," and stared at the far wall.

"I want you to avoid intercourse for another couple of weeks, Sadie. Until you're completely healed."

"Sure, Doc." She sat up, straight and powerful. "I can make him wait around on me a little while longer."

"Good." Maggie sighed. *She's so beautiful. And still so innocent, no matter what she's done.*

Sadie slid down from the examination table, clutching the drape to her chest, and reached for her dress.

Maggie held up her hand. "Wait a minute." She turned to the glass-fronted cabinet where she kept her instruments and pulled out a narrow drawer. She opened a small box and took out a handful of condoms. "Do you know what these are, Sadie?"

A deep blush blossomed under the girl's smooth chocolate cheeks. "He calls them safeties, ma'am."

"I'm going to give you all of these." Maggie put the condoms in a paper bag as she talked. "Make sure he wears one every time." She stopped and looked up, holding the last condom between her fingers. "Do you know how to test for leaks?"

Sadie made a noise, half laughter, half contempt. "I don't need those, Doc. You took out my female parts. Remember?"

"Yes, but there's still a chance of disease."

"Not with him." Sadie lifted her dress from the hook on the wall. "Am I still going to have my monthlies, Doc?"

"No. We had to remove your uterus, so you won't have your periods. We left everything we could."

"If I can't have babies, why didn't you take it all?"

"Because you're still young. Because you need those hormones to finish developing properly."

"He likes me the way I am." Sadie let the drape fall to the floor. Her white brassiere and panties clung to the lithe young body. She turned her head and stared at Maggie, her skinny torso twisted provocatively.

Maggie wanted to shake her. "You're a beautiful girl, Sadie, and you're going to grow into a beautiful woman. That's why—"

"Don't call me a girl, Dr. Kendall. After all I've been through, I'm a woman, and nobody can say different." She slipped the dress over her head. "And you tell Luther to lay off me about school. I know what I'm doing. I've got myself a man, and he won't mind about having no children. I know he won't. We're going to get married and find ourselves a nice house in Indianapolis." She tied the sash at her waist. "And I'm not coming back to this hick town ever again."

Maggie leaned against the cabinet as Sadie slipped her bare, calloused feet into her shoes. "Is that what he promised you, Sadie? Marriage?"

"Yep." She lifted her head defiantly. "He promised to take care of me."

"Then he told you a lie. No man worth his salt wants a sixteen-year-old girl with no education. You're going to end up like your mother, scrubbing floors in somebody else's house."

"No, I'm not!" Sadie's face crumpled. She covered her eyes with her hands. "Nobody else will have a girl who can't make babies. Damaged goods. That's what they'll call me."

Maggie wanted to pull Sadie to her shoulder, to hug her,

hold her, and let her cry. Instead she said, softly and evenly, "Sadie Pierce, you listen to me. Go back to school. Learn enough to take care of yourself. You have all the time in the world to find a man who wants a grown woman, not somebody who hankers after little girls."

Sadie took a step backward. "Lay off, Doc!" Tears brimmed in her eyes. "You want him for yourself."

"What are you talking about?"

Maggie heard a loud knock at the door to the examination room. The knob rattled.

"Dr. Kendall? Dr. Kendall, are you there? I have to be home in fifteen minutes."

Sadie yanked the door open and ran into the hallway like a small brown tornado. She elbowed past Olive Whittaker. Hugely pregnant, clumsy, Olive stumbled against the wall. She cried and fell backward. Her feet slipped on the shining linoleum, and her head hit the wainscoting.

"Oh, dear God." Maggie knelt beside Olive and felt for her pulse. The front door of the clinic banged shut.

CHAPTER TWENTY-EIGHT:
MAGGIE

Friday, October 10, 1952

A shadow passed across Maggie's desk. She looked up from Olive Whittaker's chart. Olive had suffered only a few bruises when she fell, but Maggie had ordered complete bed rest anyway. Coach Whittaker hadn't liked it, but Maggie didn't need the concurrence of a man who beat his son.

"Peter! You startled me."

He stood in the doorway to her office. The setting sun streamed into the hallway behind him, outlining him in a halo of gold. Maggie rose and held out her hand. "How about a tour of the clinic? I feel indebted for everything you did."

"Good." Peter clasped her hand a moment too long. Maggie pulled away. He set his black fedora on the shelf above the sink and bowed to her. "I'm at your disposal."

The tour took all of fifteen minutes and would have been even shorter if Maggie had not so scrupulously avoided brushing against him as he peered into the remodeled schoolrooms. They returned to Maggie's office just as Luther carried the mop bucket into the hallway.

"Good evening, Dr. Kendall."

"Hi, Luther. You've met Peter Grandheim, haven't you?"

"No, ma'am." Luther eyed Peter speculatively. "I've heard all about you, though."

Peter nodded once, his lips tight.

Maggie watched, surprised, but ready to spring between

them. Sadie's wild outburst and now Luther's grim animosity made Maggie wonder if Peter was the girl's lover. But it couldn't be Peter. He was too, well, too attractive and too intelligent, to take advantage of a child. And Sadie had never seen Maggie and Peter together, except for that one time in the hospital cafeteria. Maggie's heart sank as she remembered the look on Sadie's face. Not pain but jealousy?

No, that's crazy.

With a final cold glance at Peter, Luther uncovered his mop pail. Maggie checked her watch and followed Peter into her office. Four-thirty. It'd take her an hour to drive to Gary and deliver the lab specimens to the hospital. She needed to drop them off by six so she could have the results in the morning. Whatever Peter wanted to say, he'd have to talk fast.

As soon as she sat down, Peter pulled a handful of papers from his pocket and fanned them across her blotter. "The school board is going to revoke your lease on the building, Maggie. They have a developer who wants to build a service station on this corner."

"What?" Her stomach plummeted. "They can't evict my clinic. I signed a five-year lease. You drew it up."

Peter leaned back in the chair. "You'll get a kill fee, Maggie. It's all in the agreement."

She tried to read his face. "What's this about?"

He acted as if he hadn't heard her. He flipped through the papers and put his finger on one of the numbered paragraphs. "I'll make sure the school board pays your salary for six months and ships this stuff back to Chicago." He glanced around her office as if assessing it. "You could be out in less than a week."

"Didn't you hear me?" Maggie shoved her chair back and stood up. "I'm not going anywhere!"

Luther appeared in the doorway. "Did you call, Dr. Kendall?" His gaze rested on Peter's back.

"No, Luther. Thank you."

He disappeared. Maggie heard his mop clatter against the metal bucket. She slowly sank into her chair. "Okay, what's really going on?"

Peter closed the door to her office. He loosened his tie and leaned against the wall, facing her. "I'm sorry, Maggie."

"You're sorry about what?"

He took a silver cigarette case from his pants pocket and held it out to her. She shook her head. He lit a cigarette and took a couple of quick puffs. "The hospital trustees meet on Monday. It's my last chance to pry a campaign contribution out of them. If they don't hand the money over, my dear friend Senator Jenner will dump me." He made a wry face. "And I can kiss my political career good-bye."

"But you're an attorney. You can get a job anywhere."

"I have no intention of rotting away as a small-town shyster." He stubbed out his cigarette and threw it into the wastepaper basket. "Glad-handing the school board and kowtowing to every gyppo developer who waltzes into my office."

He pulled his chair next to hers, sat and took her hands. "I'm sorry, kid. I really liked you. You've done a great job here, but—"

"Don't call me kid." Maggie yanked her hands away. "What does my clinic have to do with the campaign contribution from the hospital?"

"Dad wants you gone. Not you personally, but the clinic. He thinks it'll kill his plan to make Zillah into a regional medical center."

He leaned forward in his chair, propped his elbows on his thighs, and steepled his hands. His fingernails turned white as he studied her face. He was trying to keep himself in check, she realized. Trying to dampen the ten thousand volts of energy he carried inside. "Dad said the hospital would give me the money if I got you out of here."

169

Maggie closed Olive's chart. "Is that why you helped me set up the clinic in the first place? To create a bargaining position with the hospital trustees?"

"I knew you were smart." Peter winked.

"You son of a bitch." She dragged the words out between clenched teeth. "Well, sorry. It's not going to work. I'm not going to shut down the clinic."

"Don't push me, Maggie."

"Push you?" She poured scorn into her voice. "You haven't seen anything yet. What do you think I am, some little girl you can push around? The foundation's lawyers reviewed the lease before I signed it. As long as this building is still standing, I have the right to occupy it for the next five years. Neither you, nor the board, can force me out."

She leaned back in her chair and crossed her legs, trying with every inch to look relaxed and confident. "I'll fight you every step of the way. And I'll win."

"You're making a bad decision, Maggie. You'll regret it."

"I don't think so." She stood and opened the door. "Get out, or I'll have Luther throw you out."

"That one-armed boy? You're really scraping the bottom of the barrel if you're relying on people like him. Or does slumming excite you, Maggie?"

"Get out."

Peter paused in the doorway. "I didn't want it to end like this, Maggie," he said, his voice maple-syrup thick. "I hoped we could be friends, more than friends. Why don't you think it over and call me in the morning?"

She pointed down the hall to the front door. "Leave."

Peter snapped his fingers. "I almost forgot. Dad said he'd let you work at the hospital after the clinic shuts. That's what you want, isn't it? To be a real doctor in a real hospital?"

"No, Peter. What I want is for you to get out of here. Now."

"You're a hellcat, Maggie. I like hellcats." He retrieved his fedora from the shelf and spun it on one finger before setting it at a jaunty angle over his left eye. "See you around, kid."

CHAPTER TWENTY-NINE

Zillah Courier. *Sunday, October 12, 1952*

On the Campaign Trail: "Stevenson in the Lead," Says Adlai's Man Springfield, Ill. (AP)—An associate of Gov. Adlai E. Stevenson says the Democrats have Gen. Dwight D. Eisenhower on the run and will win November's election with a surge of support from independent voters.

Clinic Director Accused of Socialism

Addressing the Indiana State Medical Society in Indianapolis yesterday, U.S. Sen. William Jenner, R-Ind., pointed a finger at the Zillah Clinic for Women and Children when asked to provide an example of communist infiltration into American life under President Truman.

Sen. Jenner promised that if re-elected, he will chair a Senate investigation into socialized medicine.

"We must stop all attempts to socialize the finest medical system in the world," he told an audience of more than 150 physicians and their wives. "Free choice is the God-given right of every American. I will not stand idly by while socialists and communists creep into the waiting rooms of America to interfere with the sacred privacy of the doctor–patient relationship."

In response to a question from the audience, Sen. Jenner cited the newly established health-care clinic for women and children in Zillah as an example of socialized medicine in Indiana. According to the senator, Dr. Margaret Mueller Kendall, clinic director, was well known to his Senate committee on Subversion in Education as a member of Young Socialists for Change at Roosevelt College.

Dr. Margaret Kendall's aunt, Professor Vessie Mueller, testified before the committee, testimony that Sen. Jenner labeled "unresponsive and unsatisfactory."

Neither Dr. Margaret Kendall nor Professor Mueller could be reached for comment.

CHAPTER THIRTY:
BENNETT

Sunday, October 12, 1952, Noon

"Why am I always the last to find out?" Bennett pulled the bedroom door shut behind him. "I hate that damned newspaper."

He glared at Maggie who sat at her dressing table taking off makeup. The hat she had worn to church that morning lay next to the open jar of cold cream. She had already rinsed out her stockings, girdle, and white gloves, and hung them on a towel over the back of her chair.

"Find out what?" Maggie studied her husband's flushed face as she wiped the cold cream from her forehead. Whatever had happened wasn't doing his ulcer any good. Assuming it was an ulcer. She'd have to make him get it looked at. And stop Louisa from frying everything.

Bennett held out the front page of the Sunday paper. "Read this."

As Maggie scanned *The Campaign Trail*, she felt as if a pit was slowly opening at her feet. She dropped the paper on the table and wiped her ink-soiled fingers on a tissue. "What are we going to do?"

"Do?" He spat out the word. "I've already called the editor. I told him Jenner's charges are absolutely false, that he has to print a full and complete retraction. On the front page. First thing tomorrow morning."

Bennett folded his arms and looked at her, grimly satisfied.

"The publisher is the biggest crap artist I've ever met, but I've got his number. He can't afford to push me around. Not unless he wants to talk about the penicillin treatment Doc gave him last year."

Maggie's heart sank. "A retraction?"

"Of course. I'll write a couple of paragraphs after dinner, and you can type them up. I told the editor I'd deliver it to his office by five o'clock this afternoon."

He folded the paper under his arm. "We can't afford a scandal, Maggie. It could ruin my practice. Mother's going to have a fit when she reads that article."

Maggie stood without answering and leaned against the dressing table.

"Maggie?" Bennett looked at her. "What's going on?"

She shook her head.

"It's that bolshie aunt of yours, isn't it?" Bennett slapped the wall with his open hand. "I knew it. Well, it doesn't matter what Vessie got up to when you were a kid." He tossed the newspaper at the closet door. The paper unfolded. The pages fanned over the braided rug like wind-blown leaves. "Where's my pen?"

Maggie straightened her shoulders. "Sit down, Bennett."

He straddled the chair to her dressing table, and she sat on the edge of the bed. One of her damp stockings caught on his watchband. He freed it before she said, "It's all true."

He half rose. "What the hell?"

Maggie motioned him down again. "I joined the Young Socialists during my sophomore year of college. It was the middle of the war. Stalin was our friend, remember? I quit after a couple of weeks because chem lab took up all my time, but I never formally resigned. I suppose my name is still on the membership list."

"What about Vessie?"

"She did testify before Jenner's committee." Maggie felt

175

herself grin and covered it with a cough. "I've read the transcript. Jenner didn't get much satisfaction from her. She made it clear that she despised the man and everything he stood for."

"You think this is funny, don't you?"

"Not funny. Baffling. Vessie testified over five years ago, Bennett. Why would someone connect Vessie Mueller with Dr. Margaret Kendall now?"

"What difference does it make? The point is we have to tell your side of the story and let the editor know he can't push—"

"It had to be Peter."

"Peter Grandheim? What does he have to do with this?"

"For one thing, Peter is Jenner's aide. He wasn't around when Vessie testified, but he could have read the committee's report easily enough."

"The only reason Peter can walk today is that Doc told his father about an experimental treatment for polio."

Maggie knew lots of people who worshipped Doc but weren't willing to give his daughter-in-law the time of day. "Peter wants the hospital trustees to approve that twenty-five thousand dollar campaign contribution for Jenner. Tomorrow's board meeting is his last chance. Somehow, Peter got the notion that if he destroys my clinic, the trustees will pony up the money." Maggie paused. "Is that true?"

"For God's sake, don't ask me. I feel like the low man on the totem pole around here. Nobody tells me anything."

"If I let the school board revoke the lease on the clinic, Peter guaranteed I'd be admitted to practice at the hospital."

"He can't promise that. The hospital trustees have to vote on any changes to the by-laws."

"Peter seemed pretty sure he could make it happen."

"If Peter's hatching some plot, all the more reason to get your side of the story to the paper pronto." Bennett checked his watch. "Dinner should be ready any minute. Hunt up some paper so we can get started."

"I want to talk to Peter first."

"Forget Peter. He's out barnstorming for Jenner. You'll never find him." Bennett stepped to his dresser and began to rummage in the top drawer.

"Nothing we tell the newspaper will make any difference, Bennett." Maggie squeezed her eyes shut for a second. "Not anymore."

As if he hadn't heard her, Bennett held out a small notepad. "Here we go." He sat down on the bed next to Maggie and uncapped his fountain pen. "I'm ready. How should we begin?"

"Bennett, I told you. I have to talk to Peter before we do anything."

Louisa rang the bell for dinner. "Go downstairs. Tell your mother I'll be there in a minute."

She turned her back on her husband so he couldn't see her pull a folded paper from her purse. She opened it. As soon as Bennett left the room, she dialed Peter's number.

Chapter Thirty-One:
Maggie

Maggie shivered as she stood in front of the open window in the dark boardroom at the hospital. She ran her hands up and down her arms, but she didn't feel cold. Her body hummed with tension, with excitement. She felt like Gary Cooper swaggering down Main Street. She glanced at the clock. Nine fifteen, not high noon.

"I won't be in Zillah until late," Peter had warned her over the phone. "Can you get away about nine?"

"Sure."

Maggie hadn't told Peter about the retraction Bennett had delivered to the office of the *Courier*. She hadn't told him about the impact of the story in the newspaper, either. The telephone had rung all afternoon as, one after the other, the husbands and fathers of her patients called to cancel the women's appointments, some telling polite lies, some sounding embarrassed, others outraged and breathing fire. The worst callers, though, were the anonymous ones who hissed at her and called her every rotten name in their small vocabularies: *commie, nigger-lover, traitor.*

Determined to force each caller to account for himself, Maggie insisted on answering the telephone. By supper time, when the calls finally stopped, she was trembling with exhaustion. She lay on her bed, a wet cloth on her forehead, the hot, humid darkness pressing against her chest like a heavy hand. She should tell Bennett she was going to meet Peter.

But she pictured Louisa, who had sat at the dinner table and muttered darkly, "Where there's smoke, there's fire. A U.S. senator wouldn't lie." Louisa hadn't cared about Maggie's explanation. Instead, she had picked up Ellie and cradled her as if protecting the child from the mother's taint. And Bennett hadn't said a word.

It had been a relief to hear the opening melody of *The Ed Sullivan Show*, a relief to disappear down the back stairs, to slip into her Studebaker and drive away to meet Peter.

He had asked her to meet him at the hospital, the one place where they could both come and go without comment. She felt disguised as she slipped into the marble lobby wearing slacks, a blouse, and a cardigan. It wasn't how a doctor should look, even on a Sunday night. Old Tom, at his usual post in the corner, hadn't bothered to greet her. Had he read the paper, too?

The boardroom was dark. Without turning on the lights, she eased past the table to stand in the alcove of the window that overlooked the small town—the window where, six weeks ago, she and Peter had flirted and laughed about the scenic attractions of Zillah.

She had connections to all of those landmarks—the Deep Valley Grange where Sheriff Davis had talked with Coach Whittaker about the welts on Zeke's back, the slum where Luther and Sadie lived, and Pulaski Elementary where Janet worked, surrounded by its new parking lot, which shone in the moonlight like an inland sea.

I'm putting down roots here, she realized with surprise. *Despite Louisa and the vicious rumors, I want to stay in Zillah. There's so much work that needs to be done. And I want Ellie to grow up here, loved and secure.*

Beyond the edge of town, she saw the cornfield, part of Whittaker's farm, where Dr. Grandheim proposed building a world-class medical center. Almost below her stood the square brick building that held her clinic. She saw a light in the lower window. Luther was cleaning her office. He didn't know her patients had deserted her.

"You sure didn't dress like a woman who's come to beg a favor."

Maggie gasped as the overhead lights flickered on. Peter's hat was shoved to the back of his head, his hands stuck carelessly in his pants pockets. "You look real warm, Maggie. Much too warm."

She felt mesmerized as Peter limped closer. He peeled the cardigan from her shoulders and tossed it onto a nearby chair with his hat and jacket. He loosened his tie and stretched. "That's better."

Maggie rubbed her bare arms and studied his face. Peter looked tired. For the first time she noticed the wrinkles around his blue eyes, the deep creases across his brow. Still, he had an air of controlled excitement, smugness. *Like the cat that got the cream. No, more like a cougar, satiated after a kill but still wild and dangerous.*

"Peter," she said. "I won't let you shut down the clinic. I'll get the money for Jenner's campaign, if that's what you want. You won't have to go back to the hospital board and work a deal." She tried to smile. "Please, Peter. Give me another twenty-four hours."

"Twenty-five thousand dollars." His smile broadened. "You've got that kind of cash under the mattress?" He moved closer. His breath smelled like rum, sweet and dissolute.

"Of course not." She wove her fingers together to keep from reaching out to him, to keep from begging. "I'll ask Bennett to borrow it. I'm sure we can."

He laughed. "Have you talked to Louisa?"

"No. Why?"

"You're a fool, Maggie. A lovely young fool." He pulled a cigarette case from his pants pocket, opened it, and held it out to her. She shook her head. "Anyway, it's not about the money anymore." He lit a cigarette and stared at her through the smoke.

"What?"

"I said, it's not about the money. I've got that sewed up. What else have you got to offer me?" He laid his cigarette on the edge of the table, put his hand on her shoulder, and caressed her neck with his thumb. "What else will you do to keep your clinic open?"

Maggie trembled. It wasn't the clinic. It had never been just the clinic between them. She turned her head away. The silence deepened.

"Maggie." Surely her name had never been said so softly, so knowingly. She looked up.

Peter laced his fingers in her hair, tightened his grip and pressed his mouth against hers. He held her, kissed her. He forced his tongue into her mouth.

She felt herself melt in his hands, sink against his arms. *No!* But it was Ellie she pictured, not Bennett. She tried to pull away.

The stubble around Peter's mouth scratched her lips, raked her chin. Her face burned.

He held her tightly. "I need you," he groaned. He pressed her hips against his groin. She felt him harden. Her knees gave way.

Peter curled around her and forced her into a tight embrace. His arms felt like a wall. She tried to push him away. He pressed her against the table. It jumped back. Peter stumbled, almost fell, almost brought her down with him.

Maggie looked over his shoulder. Outside the boardroom window, orange fingers shot into the sky.

She screamed and ran to the window. Two blocks away, the roof of her clinic burst into flames.

Chapter Thirty-Two:
Maggie

Maggie ran down the hospital stairwell. The soles of her loafers slid on the concrete steps. She heard Peter slip and fall behind her, but she didn't turn around.

She was listening for another sound, the sound of Luther's claptrap Ford. She hadn't heard him drive away from the clinic.

She burst through the steel door at the bottom of the stairs and raced across the hospital lobby. Old Tom jumped up from his stool in the corner. She shouted, "Call the fire department! The clinic's burning!"

She ran outside and down the street. The sky was filled with falling cinders. Smoke bit into her eyes and burned her throat. She looked for Luther's car, but a curtain of gray smoke shrouded the road.

The fire crackled across the rooftop. It sounded like breaking bones. She ran up the marble steps and grabbed the brass handle on the front door. The hot metal seared the palm of her hand. She pulled the door open and stood on the threshold, stunned. The floor wavered. Hot air roared down at her.

Flames engulfed the stairwell at the other end of the hall. The wooden wainscoting in the main hallway smoldered. To her left, the ceiling over the reception area groaned. A flaming desk fell through the ceiling and crashed to the floor. A shower of sparks flew past her face. She smelled burning hair.

She put her arm across her nose and cried, "Luther! Luther, where are you?"

She heard a fire truck scream to a stop outside. She stumbled toward her office. Yanked the door open. Dove inside. Shattered window panes lay across the floor. Bits of glass reflected the blaze dancing overhead. The sudden draft of air from the hallway pulled the fire down through a hole in the ceiling. The flames leaped to her bookcase.

"Luther!" she cried again. She grabbed the picture of Ellie from her desk. The metal frame burned her fingers. She turned to run and slipped on the broken glass. Overhead, a joist collapsed. It slammed across her shoulders. She fell to the floor. Her cheek was on fire. She slapped it, again and again.

The room roared red. It spun around her and disappeared into darkness.

CHAPTER THIRTY-THREE: PETER

Peter stared out the boardroom window. He still smelled smoke, but only a few tongues of flame flared up and died against the brick walls of the clinic. He heard the firemen call to each other and an engine start. The crowd on the sidewalk between the hospital and the clinic began to break apart. As people drifted home, they chattered in loud, excited voices.

A few small boys darted back and forth across the street, as if daring each other to touch the smoking ruin. A tall man in a fireman's jacket chased after them, cursing at the top of his lungs. The boys slipped into the shadows and disappeared.

Peter pulled the drapes shut. He had arrived at the clinic in time to see Luther carry Maggie through the front door, her body slung over his shoulder like a sack of flour. The stump of Luther's left arm had pushed obscenely against her hips. *That damn nigger! Touching her. Like he had a right to.*

Peter followed the ambulance back to the hospital, but Maggie had been whisked into the emergency room before he could talk to her. "Only family members are allowed to visit," the little nurse's aide had whispered to him and then blushed when he offered her a cigarette.

He had taken the elevator to the boardroom to retrieve his jacket and tie. Now he struggled to put them on, drained and bone-weary. His fingers slipped on the knot in his tie, his bad leg still ached from the fall in the stairwell.

He leaned against the wall for a minute and rotated his ankle until it popped. Then he slowly pushed his heel toward the floor and stretched his calf muscle. The pain didn't go away. He fumbled in the pocket of his jacket and pulled out a tin of Bayer aspirin, collected saliva in his mouth, and swallowed four tablets. The bitter taste lingered in his throat. He washed it away with a quick swallow from his pocket flask. He checked the clock. Almost midnight. Time to go home, time to get some sleep so he could be bright-eyed and bushy-tailed for the hospital board meeting in the morning.

Everything was falling into place. With Jenner's support, he'd be unbeatable in '56. The youngest attorney general in the history of the great state of Indiana. Satisfaction flooded his body, as potent as a slug of rum. He'd show them.

He remembered the first time he had thought, *I'll show them.* It was the second day at Harvard, in the commons, watching his new roommate imitate Peter's Midwestern twang and awkward gait for a group of Radcliff co-eds, not caring that Peter sat two tables away.

Peter had been the only student admitted to the law school that year from the vast grasslands west of Pittsburgh and east of Denver. He had been the only one who believed he would graduate from Harvard Law School, the only one not surprised when he made the Dean's list, the only one to turn down an offer from a Wall Street law firm. Better to reign in hell than serve in heaven, he decided and caught the first train home.

As soon as he heard his father's voice on the telephone this morning, an hour after the Sunday paper hit the newsstands, Peter knew he had won. The board members had called each other to approve the campaign contribution for Senator Jenner, to support his valiant stand against the encroachment of socialized medicine. Everyone knew the actual board meeting was just a formality—everyone except Bennett, of course. Nobody bothered to call him. His vote didn't matter.

How had Bennett ever ended up with a firebrand like Maggie? It must have been the uniform. And the medals. All the trappings of a hero but none of the drive.

He doesn't deserve her. I do. Two hours ago he had held her, had peeled her cardigan from her shoulders. The sweater still lay on the table. If it hadn't been for Luther and that damned fire, she'd be here, bare-armed, warm, and perfumed.

Peter relaxed against the wall and closed his eyes. He would have finished undressing Maggie. He would have unbuttoned her prim white blouse and unfastened the zipper of her flannel trousers. He would have unbuckled her belt. Her slacks would have fallen to the floor. He would have motioned her into a chair, trying hard not to notice her flimsy panties as he let his excitement build. He would have knelt on the carpet in front of her, stumbling a little on his aching leg, and pulled the penny loafers from her small, white feet.

She would have worn nylons, he decided, sheer nylon stockings held up by a tiny garter belt that matched her brassiere and panties so that when he took Maggie's hands and pulled her upright, she would have been a perfect symphony of firm, bare skin and white lace. Her rosy nipples would have pushed against the open pattern of her brassiere, and brown curls would have peeked out between her panties and her garter belt. He would have reached down and brushed his thumb across her pubis.

He would have stayed fully dressed as he touched her. Fully dressed, fully in control. She would have stood in front of him, trembling a little. Maybe tears would have glistened in her glazed eyes as he ran his hands up and down her bare arms, cupping her full breasts, tweaking her shy nipples between his fingertips.

He would have held her narrow waist, and then he would have pushed one hand between her legs as he moved the other down her spine to clasp her hips and hold them firmly in place.

Her thighs would have parted enough to let his fingers stroke her damp softness, and she would have sighed as he touched her, her breath stirring his hair. She would have begged to please him, begged to—

"Peter?"

At first the whisper, low and caressing, wove seamlessly into his dream. He felt himself harden.

"Peter." A hand touched his shoulder. He smelled lily of the valley and hair grease. He opened his eyes. Sadie stood in front of him, her lips parted, her eyes glazed, her skinny young body leaning toward him.

For a moment he felt only rage, and then he wanted to throw her to the floor, to push up her skirt so it covered her brown face, to take her on the spot.

Sadie moved a step away as if she had read his mind. "Peter, aren't you glad to see me?"

He took a deep breath, straightened his tie, put his hands in his pockets. "Go away."

"I want to be with you, sugar. That's why I snuck into the hospital, followed you here from the fire." She swayed closer. "I'm well again. Don't you want me?"

He saw tears in her eyes. Ignored them. His kingdom would collapse if they were found together. He stepped closer and repeated, "Go away, Sadie."

"No." She began to cry. Her smooth skin glistened under the fluorescent lights. Tears mixed with snot, her wide eyes turned red. Her nostrils flared.

He reached out and grabbed her upper arm. It felt like a twig in his hand, so light, so easily broken. All at once, he felt disgusted with himself, disgusted with her. He shoved her toward the door. "For Christ's sake, Sadie—"

"What's going on?"

Peter looked up. Luther stood in the doorway, filled it. Ashes streaked his face, his khaki work shirt was singed across his chest. He stepped into the room. "Sadie. What are you doing here, girl?"

With a gasp, Sadie shot from the room.

Luther lowered his head. The muscles of his neck strained the collar of his shirt. Peter took a step backward and stumbled on his bum leg.

"Leave my sister alone." Luther spat into the metal waste-paper basket. He trapped Peter's eyes for a long minute, then followed Sadie from the boardroom.

Peter's leg gave way. He collapsed onto the nearest chair. *What the hell am I going to do?* It was all Maggie's fault. If she hadn't gotten him so excited, he could have dealt with Sadie. And with Luther—that self-righteous bastard. Always interfering.

The clock clicked.

Midnight.

Chapter Thirty-Four:
Bennett

October 13, 1952
WESTERN UNION TELEGRAPH
DR. DAVID SAMUELSON
THE SAMUELSON FOUNDATION
147 MAXWELL STREET
CHICAGO, ILLINOIS

ZILLAH CLINIC DESTROYED IN FIRE STOP
WILL FIND NEW SITE THIS WEEK STOP SEND
INSURANCE FORMS STOP MARGARET KENDALL

Bennett wadded up the telegram and threw it in the wastebasket. "I won't send this. You can't rebuild the clinic. That's crazy."

Maggie struggled to sit upright in her hospital bed. "But Bennett—"

"Wait a minute." He shut the door to her private room and glanced at his wristwatch—one o'clock. Community Memorial Hospital slept quietly around them. He drew his chair close to her bed and took her hand. Maggie looked beautiful. Even with a bandage taped to her cheek and her eyebrows singed, even in that faded hospital gown, she looked beautiful.

"I love you, Maggie," he began. She started to speak but he held up his hand. "Wait a minute. Let me finish."

She leaned against the pillows and watched him, her brow furrowed as if trying to read his mind.

"When the emergency room receptionist called, I thought I had lost you." He squeezed her fingers until she winced. "I can't live without you, Maggie. Ellie and I need you. You have to give up the clinic, sweetheart. It's not worth dying for. Nothing is worth—"

A knock on the door interrupted him.

"Come in." Irritated, Bennett rubbed his bald spot.

Sheriff Davis opened the door. "Good evening." He nodded at Bennett but addressed Maggie. "I need to talk to you, Mrs. Kendall." He took off his hat and flipped it onto the bedside table next to the pitcher of ice water. He drew the other chair close to Maggie's bed and sat down, his body comfortably bulky. He was a tall man with the large hands of a farmer, who was never seen out of his khaki-green uniform and who cultivated a grave, blank demeanor, betrayed only by the crinkle of laugh lines around his eyes.

"Can't this wait?" Bennett said. "My wife's exhausted."

"I'm sorry, Dr. Kendall, but someone started that fire at the clinic. The sooner I question your wife, the sooner I'll find the arsonist."

"It's okay, Bennett." Maggie touched his hand.

"Good." Moving slowly and deliberately, Sheriff Davis pulled a pencil and a pad of paper from his pocket. He found a clean page in his notebook and licked the end of his pencil. "First, can you tell me when you decided to go to the clinic tonight, Mrs. Kendall, and why?"

As he watched the color drain from Maggie's face, Bennett's stomach burned. He hadn't had time to ask her those questions, but they'd nagged him as he drove to the hospital. What was Maggie up to now? Why hadn't she consulted him first? Had she stopped somewhere else before she drove to the clinic?

Maggie twisted her wedding band around her finger as she struggled to answer, and Bennett saw a chance to finally rein her in. He knew his wife. She was impetuous, determined to do what she thought was right, no matter what the cost. That's why he loved Maggie, and why he despaired of living with her.

But the sheriff didn't know Maggie like he did. He might try to turn her odd foray tonight into something sinister, something that would reflect badly on Bennett and his practice.

Bennett cleared his throat loudly and shifted his chair so he faced the sheriff. "My wife always goes to the clinic on Sunday night to catch up on paperwork." He spoke with the firm, sure voice of male authority. "It's part of our family routine. She must have left just before the fire broke out."

As he caught Maggie's quick look, puzzled and grateful, Bennett knew he had won. The whole damn clinic business was over.

CHAPTER THIRTY-FIVE: MAGGIE

October 13, 1952

P. O. Box 44

Zillah, Indiana

Dear Aunt Vessie,

Last night, someone set fire to my clinic and it burned to the ground. Fortunately, the volunteer firemen were able to keep the flames from spreading to the buildings next door, but I lost everything.

When I saw the fire break through on the roof, I thought my assistant, Luther Pierce, was trapped inside. I panicked and tried to rescue him. I didn't know he'd left for a prayer meeting. Thank God, he saw the flames and returned. He pulled me from the fire. He saved my life.

Don't worry, I don't have any serious injuries. My back and shoulders are covered with a mass of bruises from the ceiling crashing down on me. I look like I went ten rounds with Sugar Ray Robinson, but thankfully I don't have any broken bones. I'll have a burn mark on my cheek, though, about the size of my palm. I don't have any eyebrows left, my hair is singed, and my face is pitted with red marks from the flying cinders. Poor little Ellie! She screamed when she saw me. But I am grateful to be alive. The good Lord must still have work for me to do.

Sheriff Davis is investigating, but he doesn't expect to find the arsonist unless someone confesses. The morning of the fire, the publisher of the Zillah newspaper (may he rot in hell) printed a campaign speech by Sen. Jenner. I've enclosed the clipping. Jenner accused me of foisting socialized medicine on the good citizens of Zillah. (He also dug up all the old garbage about you—I'm so sorry.) It's nonsense, of course, but Bennett is worried the arsonist may strike again. He wants me to shut down the clinic and stay home.

I will not be intimidated. Until the newspaper article appeared, I had as many patients as I could handle. The women here need my help. I plan to reopen the clinic again as soon as I can.

Dr. Samuelson says the foundation will back me if I can find another building. And, he promised me the money to hire an RN and a receptionist. Luther says the two Negro churches are praying for my success—how can I fail?

The only thing that worries me is Ellie. Am I putting her in danger? I don't want to be overly melodramatic, but I don't think my enemies (whoever they are) will stop trying to shut the clinic down—especially now that I'm officially a pinko. I wish Ellie could stay with you until the furor blows over, but Bennett says no.

Meanwhile, I have pages and pages of insurance forms to fill out. In a way, it's soothing to deal with sheets of clean white paper filled with small type and tiny, numbered boxes. I need to complete them. As soon as the company pays the claim, I can start scouting a new location for the clinic. Keep your fingers crossed.

Love, Maggie

CHAPTER THIRTY-SIX:
MAGGIE

Tuesday, October 14, 1952

About nine p.m. Ellie started to cry. Maggie hurried to the nursery to comfort her before Louisa woke up. In the soft glow of the night light, Ellie's cheeks looked flushed. Her blond hair was pasted against her head in sweaty curls. Even so, she didn't seem to have a fever. It must have been a bad dream.

Maggie changed Ellie's diaper, filled a bottle with cool water, and sat down in the rocking chair with the toddler snuggled in her arms.

She loved this room, the smallest room in the house, a few square feet tucked under the eaves. Maggie had sewn the curtains from fabric that Ellie had selected—pink elephants and blue whales dancing across a yellow field. The white wicker rocking chair almost scraped against the gabled ceiling, and children's books overflowed the shelves tucked under the windows.

After a few minutes, the rubber nipple slipped from Ellie's lips. Maggie rubbed her chin against her daughter's soft hair and inhaled her sweet baby smell. She stroked the small feet and smoothed Ellie's nightgown over her warm tummy

She'd do anything to keep Ellie safe and warm. Anything.

Even abandon the clinic? Maggie didn't realize she was rocking harder and faster until the floorboards creaked under the chair. What if someday Ellie was pregnant and couldn't afford a doctor? Didn't she have the obligation to give these women the same care she would want for her own daughter? It didn't matter what Bennett thought or Louisa or Grandheim . . . she had an obligation to do the right thing.

Ellie stirred restlessly as if pricked.

Maggie thought back to Sheriff Davis's questions at the hospital. She had a strong suspicion he knew the identity of the arsonist. She marched the citizens of Zillah across her mind. Who had a guilty face? Who would have cared about Jenner's accusation? Who would have turned to violence to shut down her clinic? It wasn't Peter. He had been standing next to her when the clinic burst into flames. She felt her face flush as she remembered. Not standing next to her exactly, but—

Maggie jerked her thoughts away. Sheriff Davis couldn't arrest anyone without evidence. And as far as she knew, all the evidence had been destroyed by the fire. What if the case remained unsolved? Would she spend the rest of her life under threat? Or would the hatred end with the presidential election next month, when the raucous political campaign was over?

The issue was bigger than a bunch of narrow-minded bigots in Zillah. The struggle for justice wasn't going to end tomorrow, or next month, or the month after, even if Stevenson beat Eisenhower and McCarthy lost. The people who wanted to preserve America by destroying those they didn't understand—people with a different skin color, people with different ideas—wouldn't vanish into the woodwork in November.

And Bennett would not leave Zillah. He had said so over and over. Whatever bound him to this place was too strong for her to break. She didn't want to leave either, didn't want to be scared away, didn't want to give in to fanaticism and hate. What choice did she have except to stay and fight?

She heard the telephone ring. A minute later Bennett opened the nursery door, ducking his head under the low lintel. "Maggie, it's Sadie's mother. She needs to talk to you."

"Tell her I'll call her back," Maggie said, then realized Mrs. Pierce must be using the telephone booth at the Conoco station at the junction. She motioned Bennett closer. "Take her," she whispered as she handed her baby to him.

Bennett kissed Maggie's good cheek and started singing softly to his daughter. In the doorway, Maggie paused to look back at them.

"I might have to drive out to Mrs. Pierce's house to check on Sadie."

"Be careful."

In one of those moments of marital telepathy, she realized he was reminding her to take Doc's revolver. "It's in the glove box," she said.

By the time Maggie got to the telephone, Mrs. Pierce had hung up. Maggie stretched and looked longingly at the bed, but Luther had saved her life. The least she could do was take half an hour to check on his sister. She grabbed her black bag, tiptoed downstairs, and climbed into her car. As she put her bag in the back seat, she saw Ellie's Teddy bear sitting abandoned on the floor. Maggie picked the toy up, kissed it, and set it on the seat next to her. A mascot.

It was almost ten o'clock by the time Maggie drove onto the verge of gravel and grass in front of Mrs. Pierce's two-room shack. She turned off the engine and rolled down her window. The fog drifted in, bringing with it the stench of dead fish, overflowing sewage, and autumn fires.

The door to the shack opened, and Luther's mother peered at the car through the fog. "Luther," she called. "Luther, is that you?"

Maggie opened the car door and stepped outside. The fog settled on her hair and dampened her dress against her body. Moisture slid into her shoes and up her stockings. She shivered and called back, "It's me, Mrs. Pierce, Dr. Kendall."

She pulled her black medical bag from behind the driver's seat. The leather handle felt warm in her hand, substantial, part of the real world. Maggie slogged to the doorway, missing the path, if there was one, and shuffling through the fallen leaves like an old woman who had lost her way.

She stopped two feet from Luther's mother, close enough to see that tears streaked her face. "Mrs. Pierce, what's wrong? Is Sadie worse?"

Reba shook her head. Maggie set her bag in the path and put her arms around the older woman. She smelled like wood smoke and clean laundry, like bleach and dark secrets. "What's wrong?" Maggie asked again.

"Sadie's gone."

"Gone?"

"Yes. I think she went chasing off after that white bastard." Reba shook in Maggie's arms.

"White bastard?" Maggie repeated faintly, her heart sinking.

"Peter Grandheim."

Maggie felt a rush of nausea.

Reba twisted her apron between her strong hands. "He's got that poor child all mixed up."

Of course. Maggie cursed herself for being so blind. In her struggle to save the clinic, she had closed her eyes to everything else.

"It's too soon for Sadie to go out. Her stitches might tear," Maggie said even though she knew Sadie's mother understood the danger, had understood it from the first moment she learned Sadie was gone. Maggie shivered as the cold crept into her bones. Somehow she had to stop Peter. "Where's Luther?"

"I don't know. He came home, saw Sadie was gone, and took off after her. Luther said he would kill anyone who hurt his little sister."

"I'll call the sheriff." Maggie took a step backward. "I'll call him from the gas station down the street and come back here and wait with you."

"No!" Reba grabbed her wrist. "You can't do that. I don't want the sheriff and his men messing with my son. No telling what might happen." Her hand tightened on Maggie's arm. "You go get him, Doc. He'll listen to you. You're his boss."

"What about Sadie?"

"That girl's done made her bed. I can't do no more for her. But you gotta save Luther, Doc."

Maggie's heart rebelled. She would save them both. Send Peter packing. And tomorrow she would talk to Sheriff Davis. Between them, they could save Sadie—even from Peter. She planted her feet. "Where did Luther go?"

"He went to the roadhouse between here and Kokomo. That's where that bastard takes Sadie when he wants to drink and dance with my girl. That's where Luther's headed, too."

"I know the one you mean." Maggie grabbed her bag and flung it into the seat beside the Teddy bear. She switched on her headlights, gunned the engine, and raced back to town, gritting her teeth against the potholes in the road.

A highway cut through the heart of Zillah, crossed over the river on a stone bridge built by the WPA, and snaked through the cornfields south of town. The roadhouse was on the highway about ten miles out of Zillah. Maggie had suggested stopping for a snack one Sunday afternoon when Bennett had taken them all for a drive. Louisa's lips had tightened, and Maggie had not asked again.

She thought of stopping at the gas station to call Bennett but decided no. She had a sneaking suspicion Bennett might side with Peter, his boyhood friend. Convincing Bennett that Peter had raped Sadie would take too much time. She had to catch up with Luther before he did anything stupid. Luther would make Sadie come home. She would deal with Peter tomorrow.

About twenty minutes after leaving Reba's house, Maggie drove past Luther's old Ford. She hit the brakes, backed up a hundred yards, and turned onto the grass lane between a pasture and a feedlot. Luther had driven halfway into the ditch about ten feet along the lane. The door of his car was wide open, the dome light on.

Maggie parked on the shoulder and turned off her engine. She opened the glove box and pulled out Bennett's flashlight. When she switched it on, she saw the glint of Doc's revolver and stuck it in her medical bag.

She had worn the wrong shoes for hiking down a farm road. Her ankles twisted every time her heels met a rut. She fell and was struggling to her feet when she heard a cacophony of voices, a scream, then silence.

Maggie kicked off her shoes, clutched her black bag, and ran forward into the dark. The flashlight bounced in her hand. Rocks dug into her feet.

She heard the roar of an engine and jumped sideways as a pickup slammed past her, no lights, the tires spitting gravel as they sought traction in the dirt. She heard low sobs and jogged on.

Something appeared in front of her: Sadie, her face and legs and arms invisible in the darkness. Only her white dress marked where she stood.

"Where's Luther?" Maggie put her hand on Sadie's shoulder to steady both of them.

Sadie trembled. Her eyes rolled white. Maggie shook the girl. Her dress flapped around her skinny body. Maggie pulled the keys to the Studebaker from the pocket of her trousers. "My car's at the end of the lane. Sit there. Wait for me. Lock the door." Maggie ran on without looking back.

She heard a groan and stopped. She swept her flashlight in a broad arc across the dark field. The corn had been harvested.

The broken stalks pierced the sky like rows of bayonets. In front of her was a dark mass, darker than the sky, darker than the ground. It moved. The shadow became the outline of a man. Maggie's light found his face—Luther.

She ran to him. A knife lay on the ground next to the stump of his left arm. Its polished handle glittered coldly in the moonlight. It was the knife Luther brought home from Korea. She tossed it into her black bag and knelt in the dirt. The ground felt sticky and wet under her knees. She smelled blood.

Luther's face was a gray mask streaked with red. She bent close to him and felt his breath against her cheek. She smelled the dark coppery scent of his blood and the acrid odor of his fear, smelled the damp mud under his back and the sweet oil on his hair.

"Help me, Doc," he whispered. "I want to die like a man."

She took off her jacket and pillowed his head. His short, tight curls felt soft and alive between her fingers. She took a deep breath to steady herself.

She propped the flashlight against her bag and held it in place with a rock. It cast shadows over Luther's body, tricks of light and dark indistinguishable from stains of blood. She swiftly ran her fingertips over his head and face. No soft spots in the skull, thank God. She passed over his abrasions and bruises. She shined the light in his pupils—they reacted normally. She tested his hand and feet and decided his spine wasn't damaged.

She tore open his shirt. The buttons popped off and flew onto the ground. He groaned but his chest was intact. As she felt his ribs, Luther moaned. His torso twisted. Fresh blood glistened on the front of his pants. She dragged her bag so it was close to his hips and positioned the flashlight so the circle of light was centered on his abdomen. His pants were unbuttoned and bunched around his thighs.

Luther screamed. Foam flecked his lips.

She murmured, "It'll be okay, I'll take care of you, hang on, Luther," over and over while her hands explored his abdomen, his pelvis, his groin.

"Hush, hush," she whispered even as her mind refused to acknowledge what her hands had discovered.

He had been castrated.

Could she patch him up, somehow? Drag him to her car, take him to the emergency room? Was there time? She heard a soft whimper and realized the whimpers were her own.

Luther raised his right hand. It fell across his chest. His fingers found her arm, clung to the sleeve of her dress. "Help me, Doc."

"I will." She started to pull away. She needed to find the gauze bandages in her bag, the rubbing alcohol to disinfect his wound, tape to bind him. "I'll get you fixed up. We'll go to the hospital. You'll be okay."

He stared at her. "I know what he did. You gotta shoot me, Doc. I'm a soldier. I want to die like a man."

"No, I can't. I'm a doctor. First, do no harm." She was crying. He couldn't be saved. Even if he didn't bleed to death, he would never be whole again. Never be a man again.

Luther's gaze locked on her face. "Please," he whispered. "Please shoot me."

She reached into her black bag. And found her gun.

CHAPTER THIRTY-SEVEN: MAGGIE

Maggie's ears rang with the sound of the gunshot, her hand ached from the recoil. She felt dazed and disoriented as if a bomb had exploded next to her. She crouched on the dirt road between the rows of corn and looked down at Luther. He lay beside her, his arms outstretched, his pale palm open to the sky. In the faint moonlight she watched a dark stain crawl across his chest. Blood gurgled in his throat. His head twitched. He choked and died.

Someone was screaming—shrill, ear-splitting screams. The gun dropped from her numb fingers. Maggie pressed a bloody hand to her open lips, and the screaming stopped. A sweet, metallic taste flooded her mouth. She spit and felt the artery in Luther's neck, digging her forefinger deep into his flaccid skin. Nothing. She pulled back his eyelids. His brown eyes stared back at her.

Maggie picked up the gun and hurled it as far as she could into the black field. She tugged a handkerchief from the pocket of her dress and covered the dark wound between Luther's legs. She sat cross-legged and cradled his head against her breast.

Blood soaked into her dress. She pressed him closer and stroked his head. It brushed against the bandage on her cheek. Pain rippled through her face. She began to cry but, *softly, softly, let him sleep.*

Her watch ticked remorselessly as a thousand images tumbled through her mind: Luther as he had stood in her office that first day at the clinic, at parade rest, talking in his deep voice, his eyes and voice too old for that young, proud stance. The night he carried her through the flames. She had felt like a child in his arms, pressed against his chest, his strong male smell hiding the acrid bite of smoke in her throat.

A car roared down the rutted dirt lane and bounced toward her. Its headlights blinded her. Maggie sat frozen.

A black Ford pickup stopped several yards away. The driver turned off the headlights and then the motor. He opened the door and stepped down from the cab. His moon shadow crept toward her. She heard sharp cracks as the engine cooled. The man shut the door, put his hands in his pockets, and limped closer.

"Peter?" she whispered *(softly, softly, do not wake him)*. "Is that you?"

"Maggie?" Peter stepped over Luther's legs and dropped to his knees next to her. He pushed aside her black bag. "What in God's name are you doing here?"

"Luther Pierce is dead."

"Dead?"

Something odd in his voice warned her. She turned and looked into his eyes, into the deep blue, glittering shadows of his eyes, and knew.

"Peter—" She faltered. "Why?"

He didn't bother to pretend. It was almost as if he needed to tell her. "Luther came after me." His voice was petulant. "That God-damned nigger attacked me. What else could I do?"

Maggie stroked Luther's hair, soft and crinkly, still alive under her hand.

"That boy was strong, let me tell you. Good thing I managed to grab a hold of his knife. He might of killed me." Peter's Harvard accent had slipped away.

Maggie's hand, sticky with blood, covered the bullet hole in

Luther's chest.

"But I can't believe he upped and died like that. Not from a little cut." Peter stood and stretched the muscles of his damaged leg. "Must have been softer than he looked." He nudged the stump of Luther's arm with his shoe. "I came back to take him to Indy to get him sewn up."

Maggie listened to him lie. She knew what Peter sounded like when he lied, but it didn't matter anymore. Whatever Peter had done, she had done worse—because she knew better. She had sworn to heal, to save lives. She had broken the only oath she cared about.

"Luther's dead. I shot him," Maggie said.

"What?" Peter squatted next to her. "You shot him?"

"Yes." She lifted her hand from Luther's chest and ran it through her hair. A stray curl caught on the blood drying between her fingers. "He asked me to."

"Luther wanted you to kill him?"

Maggie didn't answer. If Peter didn't understand Luther's pride, she couldn't explain it.

"Where's the gun?" Peter's voice had changed. It sounded clipped, businesslike, as if he were dictating a legal brief to his stenographer.

Maggie looked at the cornfield behind him. "I threw it away."

"I'll find it." He gave her an awkward pat and sat back on his heels, his hands dangling between his knees. "You've got to get out of here, kid. If Sheriff Davis finds you with Luther's body, he'll arrest you for murder. First degree."

Maggie looked up at him. His face shone in the moonlight. He smiled and his teeth glistened. His eyes were huge luminous circles. It was as if he stood before her naked, transformed into a beast.

"Listen, kid," he said. "You wanted to do the right thing, but you made the wrong choice." He leaned closer. "Get out of town. Disappear. Start another birthing clinic. I promise, I won't tell anyone."

"Doesn't matter. Anyone who finds Luther's body will know he's been shot."

"I've got a plan. I'll drag him to the road. It'll look like he was hit by a car."

"You're crazy, Peter. There'll be an autopsy. They'll find the bullet."

"Bennett's still the medical examiner, isn't he? I'll square it with him."

"With Bennett? He'd never cover up a murder."

"He'd cover up a murder to save you."

"But then I don't have to leave town. I can stay. If nobody knows—"

"I'll know, Maggie. Is that what you want?"

She bowed her head. "No."

Peter went back to his pickup. As he returned, he pulled on a pair of heavy leather gloves, the kind farmers used to harvest corn. He grabbed Luther's heels and dragged him from Maggie's lap. She sat there unable to resist, slumped over her stained dress and her laddered stockings.

"You're a mess." Peter held out a black trench coat. "Strip down and put this on. I won't look."

Maggie did as he said, stepping out of her dress and her stockings without caring if he watched. Dark patches covered her slip. She smoothed the nylon against her body and reached for Peter's overcoat. She pulled the coat on and buttoned it up. It hung loosely, fell almost to her bare feet. She stuffed her clothes into her black bag, seeing but not caring about the knife that lay underneath them, as bloody as a severed limb.

"You could go trick or treating, dressed like that." Peter chuckled.

A wave of nausea engulfed Maggie. The ground moved under her feet.

Peter gripped her arm and pulled a wallet from his hip pocket. "Here's a hundred bucks. It's all I've got, kid. Now promise me, you'll leave town. Right away."

Maggie closed her eyes and saw Luther's face again. When she pulled the trigger, she had destroyed her own life as surely as she had ended his. Peter was right, she had to leave. Leave now.

Peter half carried Maggie to her car and opened the front door on the driver's side. Sadie had vanished.

Maggie dropped her black bag to the floor behind the passenger's seat and slid behind the wheel.

Peter bent down. "Good-bye, kid. Remember, if you ever come back to Zillah, I'll have the gun. I'll have to turn you in, whether I want to or not. You know that."

"But—"

"Don't worry. I'll take care of everything. Go."

She gripped the steering wheel and turned on the engine. Still feeling like she was in a trance, like she had to wake up but couldn't, she slowly backed her car down the dirt lane. She reversed onto the highway and shifted into first gear.

The moon had risen above the trees. Its cold white light lit the two-lane blacktop road. Maggie stepped on the gas and pointed the car north. There was one more thing she had to do.

CHAPTER THIRTY-EIGHT

Zillah Courier. *Thursday, October 16, 1952*

Obituaries

Margaret (Mueller) Kendall, M.D., in Chicago, Illinois, after a brief illness. Dr. Kendall is survived by her husband, Dr. Bennett M. Kendall, Jr., their daughter, Eleanor, and her husband's mother, Mrs. Bennett M. Kendall, Sr., all of Zillah; and her aunt, Professor Eleanor Mueller, of Chicago. In a private service yesterday, Dr. Kendall was interred next to her parents at the Good Shepherd Cemetery in Blue Island, Illinois. The family asks that remembrances be sent to the building fund for the Kendall Surgical Pavilion at Community Memorial Hospital in Zillah.

CHAPTER THIRTY-NINE: ELLIE

Sunday, September 6, 1992

We buried my father, Bennett M. Kendall, Jr., in a cemetery tucked between two fields owned by the Amish bishop. The five-acre graveyard was no more than a dot on the landscape, a place where one could stand on a tree stump and see corn and soybeans stretching to the edge of the world.

Closely planted rows of corn murmured in the wind. They said there were no secrets here. Likewise, in Zillah there were no fences around people's yards, no plants to disguise cement block foundations, and no curtains drawn during the day.

When I was little, I spent hours trying to find a hiding place. I finally figured out how to crawl onto the kitchen roof through the window of the second story bathroom. In summer, the asphalt shingles were hot and scratchy under my bare legs; in winter they turned to ice. But on the roof I could escape Grandma Louisa's scrutiny and read in peace.

Home less than a week, I still felt naked and exposed in Zillah, and I had to strain to stay put at the farm, like a goose with its webbed feet nailed to the floor.

Like elderberry wine, rural Indiana is an acquired taste: something sweet, something sharp, something so foreign you don't have a name for it. My husband doesn't like it. Being here makes Joel uneasy, as if he could vanish and no one would notice—or care. Without saying so, he was grateful my father had the courtesy to die at the start of fall quarter when it was difficult, or so we all pretended, for Joel to leave the university. I was grateful, too. Once again, I needed time alone, sheltered from loving scrutiny.

Now I turned my attention from the horizon to the cemetery, from the rows of corn to the freshly mowed grass and the thirty people standing quietly beside my father's grave.

The oldest marker was for Amos Shrock who died in 1849. The newest was for Jonathan Troyer, age three years and seven months. His white granite stone was engraved with a brontosaurus and a little boy riding joyously on its outstretched neck. Like a superstitious fool, I stood as far from poor Jonathan's grave as I could manage, but every time the crowd shifted, the gravestone trudged back into my field of vision.

What had it been like, choosing the gravestone for this child? Could I perform that one last task for my child when the time came—if the time came—or would I cower under the table and howl, a mad dog let loose in the parlor?

I wouldn't think about that now. Tomorrow, maybe, or the day after. I had almost three weeks left to make the decision about terminating my pregnancy. I watched the minister bow his head and murmur "Amen." We murmured with him.

I dropped a handful of wild roses on my father's coffin and rode back to the farm with my stepmother, Janet. We have never been comfortable in each other's presence, and the ride in the undertaker's car was tense. She is tall, thin, well-dressed, and tightly controlled. I make her anxious, as if I might laugh or whistle at the wrong moment and she would be blamed.

I've never called her "mother."

Several years ago, flushed with the success of the first romance I published, I recklessly inscribed a copy and sent it to her. I don't know what I expected, but, like a fart in public, the ensuing silence was deafening and self-conscious.

As we drove down the long lane to the house, I saw someone

had opened the gate to the pasture. My father's Amish friends had unhitched their horses to let them graze. He would have been pleased to see the black buggies lined up across his field. After he retired, he bought this farm five miles north of Zillah. Janet bred horses, and he puttered, building strong ties to his Amish neighbors and taxiing them to town when they needed to pick up equipment or make an emergency trip to the hospital. My father admired the Amish for their work ethic, their self-reliance, their independence from what I call the social support network and he called welfare, scowling as he spit the word out.

His struggle with stomach cancer had been painful but brief. After I arrived at the farm, we managed to let go of our old battles and sit together, holding hands, peaceful at last.

With love and pity, I gave him the only gift I had: I told him I was pregnant with a son. I pressed my father's hand against my newly round stomach and said, "Bennett M. Kendall, the third."

It was a lie, of course. Or rather, the chances were fifty-fifty that I was lying. The obstetrician had said we would be better off not knowing the sex of the fetus until we made our decision, and Joel agreed.

The last night, my father and I sat in the dark and watched fireflies dance over the grass outside his window. He tugged on my hand. I bent toward him. His mouth was dry, his lips stuck together. I wiped them with a damp cloth and he whispered, his voice slow and hoarse, "Your mother . . . every night . . . I dream of her." My father's fingers tightened around my hand. "You remind me of your mother, Ellie. Beautiful. Strong." His voice faded. I leaned closer. His breath smelled chalky. "I loved her. I did everything I could . . . to save her. But the last thing she told me was, 'Forget you ever knew me.' "

He fell back against the pillow. His eyelids, blue-veined and transparent, trembled shut. His grip loosened. His hand dropped to the bed. I looked out the window. The fireflies blurred against the stars. After a moment, I went in search of Janet.

I expected to feel sad when my father died. What I hadn't expected was this stabbing sense of loss, of being alone and abandoned. And as soon as he—the person who knew her best— was gone, I wanted to learn more about my mother. Why had he tried to save her? Save her from what? Why did my mother tell him to forget her?

The only person who might know the answers to my questions was Janet. After the funeral, I would ask her.

Before the memorial service, several men from my father's church had delivered tables and chairs to the farm. I unfolded them, wiped them clean, and set them up in the shadow of the wide-spread oaks, glad for something to do.

Now their wives covered the tables with red-and-white plaid oilcloth and weighted them down with platters of fried chicken, molded Jell-O, and Thermos bottles of iced tea and Kool-Aid. There were flies everywhere, shooed away by elderly ladies whose fans were decorated with pictures of Jesus at Gethsemane, courtesy of the local funeral home.

One of the ladies separated herself from the others and came over to me. Smaller than the rest, she smelled of violets and stood so hunched over I could barely see her eyes under her straightened bangs. Hers was the only black face in the crowd.

"Maggie, dear. Is that you?" she asked with the soft hesitancy of the very old. "It's been such a long time."

"No, I'm Maggie's daughter, Eleanor."

"Oh, of course you are. I'm Reba Pierce." She stepped closer and squinted at my face. "You look exactly like your mother, dear."

"Thank you."

"Your mother is a wonderful doctor," Reba took my hand

and patted it.

Is? I must have misunderstood. I bent a little closer to hear better.

"She saved my little girl, you know, my little Sadie."

I nodded and smiled. I had no idea who she was talking about.

"But not Luther." Reba Pierce sighed heavily. "She couldn't save him."

"I'm sorry," I answered.

She peered up at me. "Why isn't your mother here, Eleanor?"

And I said, "Janet? She's talking with the minister."

And Reba said, "No, dear. Not your stepmother. I mean Maggie. Why didn't she come?"

And I said, "But she's dead."

"They still haven't told you?" Reba Pierce stroked my hand, her gnarled fingers as light as hummingbird wings. "Maggie writes to my daughter every Christmas. She always asks about you."

The hot, humid air caught in my throat. Sweat beaded my upper lip. I studied Mrs. Pierce's uncertain smile, her wistful eyes. She didn't look senile. Or confused. But—

"Reba? Reba Pierce? Is that you?" A handsome, silver-haired man smiled a quick apology to me as he took Reba's hand and buried it between his own. "After all this time! You're looking so well."

Reba giggled like a schoolgirl and patted her hair. I recognized the man. He was the lawyer who had visited my father the day before he died. He was terribly familiar—or at least his type was. He had appeared on the cover of a thousand paperbacks: the aging playboy, rich, handsome and self-assured, buffed and polished twice a week like a silver martini shaker.

"And who is this?" he asked Reba, still holding her hand but motioning to me.

"Ellie Kendall," I said in case Reba had forgotten. "Pleased to meet you."

"I'm Peter Grandheim." He ran his eyes up and down my body. At the same time, a younger man touched my elbow. He bent to whisper in my ear. "Janet would like to have the reading of the will now. In your father's study?"

"Okay, but I need to freshen up first." I made my excuses to Reba and Peter and followed the young man into the house.

Upstairs in the guest room, the atmosphere was as heavy as a steam bath. I walked to the window and yanked it up. The sweet perfume of ripe corn rolled in on the sharp edge of manure. Sunlight danced on the dense green leaves of the sugar maples. A dozen boys played baseball in the pasture, and women called greetings as they drifted between the house and the barn.

Reba Pierce hobbled to the edge of the lawn where the cars were parked. Silver-haired Peter limped beside her, leaning heavily on his black cane.

I wanted to run down and grab Reba, to make her tell me everything she knew about my mother. At the same time, I was glad to see her walk away. If Reba was right, if she wasn't delusional or demented, then something had gone terribly wrong in my family. I wanted to learn about it in private. Janet would know, I thought with tight-lipped certainty. After the will had been read, I'd make her tell me.

I stepped away from the open window and took the back stairs to the kitchen where several women in Amish dresses, aprons, and bonnets were setting out dessert. They slid thick wedges of berry and apple pie onto small paper plates, while a horde of children, some in Amish clothes, some not, rushed in and out of the room. The screen door banged and banged again. The women chattered to each other in Pennsylvania Dutch and studied me out of the corners of their eyes.

I hadn't expected to inherit anything from my father, so I was pleased he left me fifty thousand dollars. A nice round number. It came with a lecture, of course, a codicil to his will about how I had squandered my God-given talents on writing sentimental slop—which answered the question of whether he had read anything I'd written. Ironically, fifty thousand dollars, carefully managed, would be enough to finance book tours for the rest of my life.

CHAPTER FORTY:
ELLIE

A brief rainstorm ended the potluck dinner after my father's funeral. In the flurry of carrying dishes and leftovers into the kitchen, I lost track of the old woman, Reba Pierce. After stacking leftovers in the pie safe, I found her telephone number in the directory and called her home. The young man who answered mumbled, "Grandma's not here." And, no, he didn't know when she would be back. I didn't ask him if she had Alzheimer's.

Janet wanted to watch *Jeopardy!*, so I strolled down the gravel road through the orchard to the barn while I debated the best way to question Janet about my mother.

The barn was older than the farmhouse, maybe by a hundred years. It had a gable roof tiled with thick chunks of slate and plank walls that may have been sawn from the forests of cherry, walnut, and oak that covered Indiana in the pioneer days. Like everything my father owned, the structure had been well maintained. The exterior was freshly painted barn red, the tight-fitting door slid back easily, and the interior smelled of hay, not rot or mildew.

I went inside, turned on the light switch, and shut the door behind me. That's one thing you learn growing up in the country—shut the door. There's always something to be penned in or kept out.

Years of use had polished the poured concrete floor. Haylofts bracketed either end of the barn, about twenty feet off the floor, two-thirds of the way to the peak of the roof. Under the haylofts, empty horse stalls held furniture or boxes of housewares too old to use and too good to throw out. The center aisle was empty except for a tractor and a wagon, bushel baskets of apples, and a tidy stack of firewood. An open, handmade stairway led to the hayloft on the north wall.

At the top of the stairway, a good ten inches gapped between the landing and the floor of the hayloft. On the drive to the farm last week, I'd toyed with setting the first confrontation between my current hero and heroine in a barn, where they would end up rolling around half-naked in the straw. But now that idea just made me itchy.

I checked my watch. *Jeopardy!* was over by now. It was as good a time as any to tackle Janet.

I retraced my steps and shut everything up tight. As I started down the mulched path through the orchard, I saw my stepmother coming toward me. After the rain, the path was littered with earthworms, motionless and glistening. While I waited for her, I picked them up and threw them into the grass along the fence as my father had always done. A breeze blew across my face. It smelled sweet from apples blown to the ground, bruised past keeping and beginning to rot.

"Where's your book?" Janet said as soon as we were close enough to talk. "Didn't you sneak off to read? That's what you did as a kid."

"You knew about that?"

She grinned briefly at my surprise. "About your hiding place on the roof? Sure. I never said anything, but I used to envy you up there, away from your grandmother." Part of me wanted to smile back. I'd reconciled with my father, why not with my stepmother? But I didn't want to be disloyal to poor old Grandma Louisa. That's the part I hate about families: Someone's always asking you to take sides.

When I didn't respond, Janet glanced at me, her golden-brown eyes hidden in the shadow of her rain hood. Her mouth tightened. "What's on your mind, Eleanor?"

I told her what Reba Pierce had said. "Is it true?" I asked. "Is my mother alive?"

"I wouldn't pay too much attention to Reba," Janet answered without looking at me. "She hasn't been the same since Luther died."

"Luther?"

"Her son. He was killed by a hit-and-run driver."

I winced—*another dead child*—and realized I had folded my hands over my stomach.

"That's terrible," I said, knowing how inadequate the words were.

"It happened a long time ago." Janet turned as if starting back to the house.

"Wait." My throat tightened. I knew she wanted me to stop asking questions. "Do you think it's possible my mother's still alive?"

Janet rubbed her fingers as if they ached. Her hands had always been slender and clever, but now her knuckles showed signs of swelling. "She could be, I suppose. I don't know."

"You don't know? What do you mean, you don't know?"

"I don't intend to repeat myself, Eleanor."

I recognized that tone. Janet had taught fourth grade before she married my father, and she could always make me feel like I had talked out of turn or forgotten to raise my hand.

"Tell me what you do know," I persisted. "I thought she died when I was a toddler."

Janet's shoulders collapsed a little. "I read Maggie's obituary in the newspaper. It was September 1952, forty years ago. I felt like I'd been struck by lightning. It happened so suddenly. She was so young. And Bennett wouldn't discuss it. Then, six months later, he proposed. He said you needed a mother."

"Not very romantic," I said with a brief surge of pity.

"No. After we were married," Janet continued, "I discovered Louisa had no intention of letting me raise you. As far as your grandmother was concerned, I was little better than the hired help. She ordered me never to talk about Maggie. Bennett agreed. They said it would be best if you forgot about your mother."

Forget about my mother? Fat chance. "Did you know her?"

"Yes."

I waited while Janet picked an apple from the tree and took a bite. "When Maggie moved to Zillah with your father, she and I became good friends."

"Then what?"

"She left for Chicago. The newspaper said she died there."

"Come on, Janet." I gritted my teeth. "Tell me the rest."

"Are you sure you want to know?"

No, I wasn't sure at all. "Yes."

Janet stopped walking and leaned against the fence. "I saw your mother the last night she was in Zillah."

"And?"

Janet scanned the horizon as if she were watching an old movie. "I was living with my parents then and teaching school. Mother and I had been canning tomatoes all evening. She had gone up to bed, and I was cleaning the kitchen while I waited for the last dozen jars to cool." She paused. I chewed my lip while I waited.

"About midnight I heard a knock on the kitchen door. When I opened it, Maggie was leaning against the porch railing. She looked rumpled and damp. She was wearing a man's raincoat. The sleeves were too long. And she was holding your Teddy bear, clutching it to her chest."

A gust of wind blew across our faces. Janet brushed a strand of hair from her cheek. "Your mom had thrown up in the zinnias by the back stoop. I made her come in and sit down while I fixed her a cup of tea. I thought she was in shock. I wanted to call your father, but she grabbed my arm and begged me not to."

Janet twisted her fingers together and studied the outline of the barn. "I thought she had been fighting with Bennett, maybe he had hit her or something. She looked that scared."

I drew in a deep breath. My father, the man who rescued earthworms? He wouldn't have hurt his wife. Not possible. "Did she tell you what happened?"

"No."

"Why did she come to you?"

Janet drew in a long breath. "She trusted me."

"With what? Did she give you something?" I waited a second, but Janet didn't answer. "What did she give you, Janet?"

She shook her head. "Nothing."

"Did she go back to my father?"

"I don't know." Janet pressed her lips together. "After half an hour and another cup of tea, she recovered enough to leave. I assumed she drove home, but when I called the next day, your grandmother said she had gone to Chicago to visit her Aunt Vessie. A day later, I read Maggie's obituary in the newspaper."

"Two days after you saw her? That's crazy. Nobody could get sick and die that fast. Not even forty years ago."

"Well, it's possible, I suppose. Barely possible." Janet rubbed her eyes and let her hands drop to her side. "All I could think was suicide. If your mother killed herself, then it made sense that Bennett and Louisa wouldn't talk about it. It made sense that she was buried in Chicago and not in Zillah, that there was no funeral service, no good-bye."

Suicide. "Was my mother crazy?"

"Crazy? What do you mean?"

"You know, schizoid, psychotic, bi-polar, depressed." I could have reeled off a dozen more diagnoses, but the expression on Janet's face was enough. My mother hadn't been crazy.

"Why do you think she's still alive?" I asked.

"I didn't say that."

"You said it was possible."

Janet's face crumpled. She looked like an old woman. "Because your father always acted as if he expected Maggie to walk in the door. He was frozen in time, always waiting for her to come home again."

Yes, that's exactly how he was. Frozen in time. I didn't understand it then, but I always knew something was off-kilter.

"He couldn't make room in his heart for anyone but her." Janet paused. "And you."

"Oh, sure." I knew I sounded bitter. "That's not the way I remember it."

"I think you kept his pain alive. As long as you were around, Bennett couldn't forget Maggie. Neither could I."

She started walking, and I hurried to catch up.

The last rays of the setting sun pierced the clouds. I lifted my face. Janet loosened her hood, tossed it back, and shook out her short gold and silver curls. "Your mother was a good person, Eleanor. She always wanted to help people. But she didn't consider other people's feelings. Their ideas about right and wrong. She charged ahead, guns blazing. She left a trail of destruction behind her."

"What do you mean, a trail of destruction?"

"Well, take Zeke Whittaker, for example. He was a little boy in my class who wet the bed. His father tried to cure it by punishing him. He didn't know any better. But your mother—"

"Did she stop it?"

"She tried." Janet told me the whole story.

"But how's that creating a 'trail of destruction'?" I made

221

finger quotes around the words.

"She forced a confrontation with Zeke's father, made him into an enemy. He never forgave her or your father. Whittaker's land was necessary for the hospital expansion. Your father headed up the project for the hospital board. Whittaker knew he had him over a barrel, so he extracted every last penny from the deal. I thought he was going to drive Bennett into an early grave."

"But that wasn't my mother's fault."

"Everything Maggie was involved in turned out like that. Confrontation. High drama. Tears and shouting." Janet's voice sounded rough, as if she were forcing the words past a burr in her throat. "Forget your mother. For your own sake, forget her. That's all I can say."

I wiped tears from my cheeks with the back of my hand. When had I started crying? "Why did my father say she was dead?"

"I don't know. Your father was a smart man. And he loved you. He must have had a reason." Janet's eyes narrowed. "I've told you everything I know. Be satisfied with that." She turned and walked back to the house, trudging through the puddles on the path as if they didn't exist.

I stood at the edge of the orchard and let her go. I hadn't learned much about my mother, but I had discovered one fact. Janet knew something more. And she was too angry to tell me.

Or too scared.

My eyes burned. The sun went down. I crept up the back stairs of the house and into my bedroom. I wrapped myself in a quilt and stared out the window, searching the meadow for fireflies.

"I loved your mother," my father said before he died. "I did everything I could to save her."

Save her from what? A problem of her own making? Or something else?

CHAPTER FORTY-ONE:
ELLIE

9:00 a.m., Monday, September 7, 1992

The morning after the funeral, I padded across the hallway and called Reba Pierce again from the telephone in my father's bedroom. When no one answered, I decided to search through his papers for my mother's address and telephone number. I imagined them written in my father's neat script on a prescription pad. In spite of all those doctor jokes, my father's handwriting was like everything he did—precise and to the point. He put down exactly what he thought you needed to know and not one word more.

He would have been a lousy romance writer.

I walked into the kitchen. Janet was turning an omelet onto a plate. One whiff of sautéed onions and my stomach heaved. I mumbled good morning and pushed past her to the guest bathroom. When I came back, Janet was sitting at the table. She glanced at me and said in her calm way, "You're expecting, aren't you?"

"How did you know?" I took the seat opposite her and poured myself a glass of milk.

"You have that look. Glowing. Satisfied. Even after throwing up." She smiled but her eyes reddened. "I wish Bennett could have seen his grandchild."

With a twinge of guilt, I said, "Me, too. I told him about the baby. And I promised that if it's a boy, we'll name him Bennett Kendall the third."

"Thank you, dear." Janet reached across the table and squeezed my hand. "I can't wait to be a grandma. When are you due?"

"March." Maybe I was a hypocrite to let her dream about a grandchild. But I couldn't ask her to shoulder another tragedy, not so soon after my father's death. If I followed the doctor's recommendation and terminated my pregnancy, I'd tell her I'd had another miscarriage—the fourth in as many years. The fourth and last. I'd promised Joel—and the doctor—that we wouldn't try again.

But, oh dear God, I wanted to lean against Janet and sob out the truth. She must have been a rock for my father after my mother disappeared, a calm and peaceful oasis.

But instead of telling her about my amniocentesis and its ambiguous results, I talked about morning sickness, weight gain, and baby names. After a bowl of cereal, I said, "Will you show me where my father's papers are? I want to see if he had my mother's address."

Janet turned the stove on, scraped strips of bacon from the bottom of the skillet and poured the warm grease into a glass jar.

"I buried my husband yesterday, Ellie," Janet said, her back toward me. "I'm not interested in helping you find his *real* wife today." Her italics hung in the air, almost visible.

I didn't know what to say. Last night I'd thought Janet was afraid to help me. This morning I wasn't so sure. I wanted to respect her feelings, but I couldn't wait for her to finish mourning before I looked through my father's papers. I didn't have that kind of time.

After a long minute of silence, Janet turned back to me and threw up her hands. "Fine. Bennett's files are in the attic. I'll show you."

The attic was clean, light, and airy. It extended over the entire

length and width of the house. The wooden floor had been painted apple green and the plaster walls whitewashed. Bookcases were tucked into the eaves, and a tall shelf covered with a clear plastic sheet held my old toys and stuffed animals.

Janet flicked on the overhead light and waved at the filing cabinet on the east wall. "Your father's papers are over there. He planned to write a memoir about his life as a country doctor, so we organized them last winter. He had a wonderful story to tell, but no one cares about an old-fashioned doctor anymore. Medicine's become a big business like everything else."

"Why don't you write his story?" Impulsively I touched her arm. "I could help."

I thought I saw the glimmer of unshed tears, but all she said was, "Put his papers back the way you found them." Then she disappeared past the bend in the staircase.

Although it was barely ten o'clock, the attic felt warm. A dehumidifier clicked on and whirred loudly in that clean, quiet space high above the cornfields.

I opened the filing cabinet, pulled out manila folders, and set them in piles on the rag rug. Each folder was labeled and the papers inside were organized in chronological order. Something inside me relaxed. For the first time since coming to Indiana I felt completely at home. Research is the part of writing I enjoy the most.

As I sat on the rug and shuffled through my father's papers— board minutes from Community Memorial Hospital, tax returns, school records, and a sheaf of newspaper clippings—a faint odor of formaldehyde tickled my nose. That's how my father had smelled when he came home from the hospital late at night and tiptoed into my room to check on me. Now I felt as if he were close by again, hovering over my shoulder.

Among the newspaper clippings I found the announcement of my parents' engagement and a picture of their wedding, my

birth announcement, my mother's obituary, and a brief paragraph noting my father's marriage to Janet Davis in June, 1953. It was strange to see my past set in sans serif type on crumbling paper, and stranger still to know that some of it was a lie.

I found it easy to believe that the staff writer at a small town paper wouldn't question a doctor's report of his wife's death, but I wondered about the rest of the documents I'd found. Which were true? Which were fiction? And that raised the whole, ugly epistemological question—what is truth? If the whole town of Zillah, except for my father and Reba Pierce, thought my mother was dead, if everyone behaved as if she were dead, didn't they create some kind of alternative reality where the fact she was actually alive, in some other time and place, didn't matter at all?

Except to me.

I closed the last folder and leaned back, discouraged. I hadn't found an address or phone number for my mother. I glanced up at the file cabinet. The top drawer was fully extended, and a large, thin white envelope had been Scotch-taped to the bottom. I stood, clumsy, needles and pins shooting through my legs. Feeling for a free corner of the envelope, I gently pulled it away from the metal drawer. The words written on the outside stared back at me: Margaret Mueller Kendall.

My father must have hidden this envelope from Janet. I tiptoed to the stairway, locked the attic door, sat in a walnut rocking chair, and broke the seal. A handful of clippings fell into my lap.

Zillah Courier
Wednesday, October 15, 1952
Body Discovered
The body of Luther Pierce, a 22-year-old colored man, was found by George Whittaker at 7 a.m. yesterday on the

Old Burlington Highway about 1.5 miles north of town.

"He was torn up as bad as anyone I saw during the war," said Coach Whittaker, a veteran of D-Day. "He must have been run over by a couple of cars before I found him."

Sheriff Leon Davis said it appeared that Mr. Pierce had been struck and killed by a vehicle while he was walking along the highway.

Death occurred sometime after midnight, according to Dr. Bennett Kendall, Jr., coroner for Burlington County.

The sheriff asks that anyone with information pertaining to Mr. Pierce's death contact his office. He reminds pedestrians to wear light-colored clothing at night and to walk on the shoulder of the road facing oncoming traffic.

Mr. Pierce is survived by his mother, Mrs. Reba Pierce; his grandmother, Mrs. Arnold White; and his sister, Sarah Pierce, all of Zillah. Mr. Pierce served with the 8th Army in Korea and was honorably discharged.

Funeral arrangements have not yet been made.

The newspaper clipping had been taped to a piece of yellow paper. The tape had turned brown, and pieces of it flaked into my lap. Someone had drawn a line through the words "struck and killed by a vehicle" with a thick-nubbed pen. I turned the paper over, but nothing was written on the back.

I set the obituary aside and picked up an envelope addressed to Bennett Kendall. The return address was Vessie Mueller, Roosevelt University, Chicago. Vessie, my mother's scandalous aunt.

I slid my fingernail under the flap, and the old glue crumbled. Inside was another sealed envelope, this one addressed to my mother, care of Vessie Mueller. The three-cent stamp had been canceled and "Return to Sender" written on the envelope in pencil. I opened it, unfolded the letter, and recognized my father's handwriting, the uneven blue ink of his old fountain pen. A lock of hair fell from the pages into my hand.

A wave of nausea hit me, my fingers trembled. Why had my father saved these documents? Not for me, surely. Not for Janet. Had he sat up here by himself and read them over and over again? Were these thin scraps of paper his last ties to my mother?

I felt scared, nervous, like an intruder tiptoeing into a secret place, a sacred place, where I didn't belong. At the same time, I was wickedly eager to barge in and have a look around.

I sat back on my heels and took a deep breath. I couldn't stop now. I began to read.

April 10, 1953
Dear Maggie—
Of course I'll give you a divorce if that's what you want.

Mother fell and broke her clavicle last week, so I can't come to Las Vegas to sign the papers. It's just as well. I don't think I could bear to see you again.

I've hired some ladies from the church to take care of Mother during the day, and Bernadette agreed to spend the nights here. Mother is slowly getting better—her mind is as sharp as ever.

Ellie misses you terribly. I bought her a little white kitten, which she named Puff. Every morning after breakfast, Ellie and the kitten climb into Mother's lap, and they watch *Romper Room* together. I wish you could see them. Ellie is learning her ABCs, and Mother reads her to sleep every night. She's a smart little girl, but she needs a mother.

As for the other news from Zillah, Janet Davis quit teaching and I'm going to ask her to help Ellie decorate Easter eggs next week.

I ran into Reba Pierce in the hospital cafeteria yesterday. She said her daughter Sadie has moved to Chicago to live with her cousin. The day after you left, Coach Whittaker found Reba's son, Luther, on the highway north of town. Sheriff Davis called me to examine the body. I told him it looked like a case of hit and run, and Luther was buried without any fuss. No one has come forward with any information, so the sheriff closed the investigation. I'm sorry for poor Reba. She's aged twenty years in the last month.

Enclosed is a lock of Ellie's hair. It's as thick and beautiful as your own.

I love you, Maggie. I always will.

Bennett

The last piece of paper was a newspaper clipping that had been wadded into a ball and then smoothed out—a legal notice published in the *Las Vegas Sun;* a Decree of Divorce forever dissolving the bonds of matrimony between my father and Margaret Mueller Kendall upon the grounds of extreme mental cruelty. It was dated April 20, 1953.

I folded the papers back into the envelope and brushed the dust from my hands. Here was my father's secret. My mother had not died in Chicago in October 1952. With my father's connivance, she had run away and divorced him.

I still didn't know why she had disappeared—or why she had abandoned me. I clenched my teeth against angry tears and thought about what to do next. I had made a start. I had a few facts to add to my story. But the answer wasn't here in Zillah.

When I got back home, I'd call the AMA and see if they maintained a national registry of doctors. If my mother was still practicing medicine, I'd track her down.

As I made my plans, I avoided the most painful question: In all the years since she left Zillah, why hadn't my mother ever tried to find me?

CHAPTER FORTY-TWO:
ELLIE

2 a.m., Tuesday, September 8, 1992

I sat straight up in bed, wide awake. Something had awakened me, some noise. The sheer curtains swayed in the open windows of the farm's guest bedroom. A soft breeze caressed my face. I slipped out of bed, stepped to the window, and looked down at my father's fields. They slumbered peacefully under the new moon. The sky over Indiana seemed bigger than the sky at home, the stars brighter, the moon more silver.

Then I noticed a black pickup parked in the shadow of the barn.

It wasn't Janet's car, wasn't mine. And no one else belonged here.

A moment later, I heard a soft thud. Someone was downstairs in my father's library. Cold prickles danced across my scalp.

The telephone extension was in my father's bedroom across the hall. I took a step toward it and stopped. Janet had taken a sleeping pill. I couldn't wake her without creating a lot of commotion. If the intruder heard us, he might escape. I didn't want him to get away. I wanted the sheriff to catch him and recover whatever he had taken. I'd creep down the back stairs into the kitchen and call 9-1-1 from there.

As I tiptoed from the bedroom, I heard a sharp crack, as if a lock had been forced. My heart tightened. The door at the top of the stairs creaked when I opened it. I froze, one hand clutching the knob, until I was sure the intruder hadn't heard me.

I inched down the wooden steps, my bare feet icy. Down ten steps and then into the moonlight, which fell through the tall, narrow window of the landing. I wiped my sweaty palms on my pajamas and started down the last flight of stairs.

At the bottom, I glided across the polished floor of the kitchen to the telephone on my father's desk, lifted the receiver, and dialed 9-1-1. I laid the receiver down and covered it with a dishtowel to muffle the emergency operator's voice. As long as the line was open, they'd have to send someone to investigate.

The door to the library stood ajar. A flashlight beam swept the opposite wall. In the reflected light, I saw the door to the front porch was open. The house was silent except for the swish of papers in the library and the soft, almost monotonous grumble of the searcher.

Now what? Should I go outside and wait for the sheriff, or stay here where I could fend off the burglar if he headed upstairs toward Janet?

I heard a car on the gravel road in front of the farm. The sheriff! I ran to the window over the kitchen sink. My elbow hit a wooden cutting board. It fell to the floor like a mortar shell exploding. I whirled around. The flashlight beam vanished. A second later, a dark figure slipped through the front door and disappeared.

I ran to the door, slammed it shut, and locked it.

The intruder gunned his engine. I heard the pickup roar away.

I rushed into my father's office and looked outside. No sign of the sheriff's car. I picked up the telephone on my father's desk, but all I heard was a loud beeping tone. My call to 9-1-1 hadn't gone through. Damn phone company.

I squatted by the sea of papers on the floor. It would take forever to sort them out. But my father's address book had to be here somewhere. As I reached for the first pile, I heard a sharp click behind me.

A voice said, "Stand up and turn around."

I jumped and knocked the cigar box off my father's desk. The small ring of light from his desk lamp didn't reach to the doorway where a tall, thin figure stood in the shadows.

"Janet?" My voice wavered. "Is that you?"

She turned on the overhead light. I stared at her, my pulse pounding. She held a shotgun, its barrel pointed right at me.

"For God's sake, put the gun down."

Janet cracked the shotgun and cradled it in her arms, where it looked bizarre against the prim blue and green plaid of her long-sleeved nightgown. "What's going on, Ellie?"

The grandfather clock in the hallway chimed the half hour. My knees gave out. I sank into my father's chair. "Sit down," I said.

Janet stepped into the room, leaned the shotgun against the wall, and sat across the desk from me. I wiped my sweaty forehead with the back of my hand.

"I heard a noise. When I came down to investigate, I discovered a burglar in here." I surveyed my father's office again. Every drawer had been opened and dumped. All the books had been pulled from the bookcase and riffled.

"How did the burglar get in?" Janet's voice was too quiet.

"Through the front door. I saw him leave."

Janet ostentatiously turned her head and looked through the doorway into the hall. "The front door is shut and bolted. Exactly like it was when I went to bed."

I pushed a strand of hair off my face. "I closed the door and locked it after the burglar left."

"No one has a reason to search this room. No one but you."

"I didn't do it." I felt thirteen years old again, wrongly accused of some petty infraction of my father's rules—not making my bed right, not dusting the picture frames.

"Then who did?"

"I don't know. I saw a black pickup parked by the barn."

She drew in a sharp breath. "A black pickup? Are you certain?"

"Yeah. Do you know anyone with a truck like that?"

She picked angrily at the lace trim on her nightgown, but she shook her head.

"All I want is my father's address book," I continued. "I want to find out where my mother lives. Or her telephone number."

"Damn it!" Janet slammed her hand on the desk. "I raised you, Eleanor, not your mother. She abandoned you, remember? But Maggie's the one you want."

I watched her, stunned. I'd never seen Janet so angry. Or so scared.

"I took care of your grandmother even though she despised me. After her first stroke, I wiped her butt and fed her and washed her and clipped her toenails. Not one word of gratitude. I married your father, and I was a good, faithful wife to him for almost forty years, and when he died, Maggie's name was on his lips. Not mine! Maggie's.

"And now you! You sneak through my house in the middle of the night and riffle my husband's desk like you own the place." She turned away and her shoulders shook. "I want you out of here. I never want to hear about Maggie again."

I stood up, walked around the desk, and stroked her hunched back. "I'll leave if you want. Shall I help you clean up first?"

"Help me?" Janet choked back a sob. "Help me by leaving. Go now."

"Now?" I glanced at the clock. It was almost four a.m. "You can't be serious."

"Please leave." Janet sank back into the chair. The harsh overhead light turned her face into a mask of deep lines and sunken hollows, a mask of fear.

"What are you afraid of? If you tell me, maybe I can help."

"No. It has nothing to do with you. I want you to go away."

I left her sitting there while I threw my clothes into my suitcase and dragged the suitcase to my car. Just before I left, Janet came outside and stood on the front porch. She held a cardboard box in her arms. I climbed the steps to the house, and she handed the box to me. "I packed up your old books for you."

"Thanks."

I balanced the box on the porch railing and put my free arm around Janet. She stood rigid for a minute and then went limp, as if her bones had dissolved. I let her down on an old wicker rocking chair. She pulled a tissue from her sleeve and blew her nose. "I'm sorry, Ellie."

"Me, too. Will you be okay here by yourself?"

"A friend from college asked me to stay with her for a while. Her husband died last year. I'll go after breakfast."

"Good." I touched her hand, but she didn't move. I got into my car and eased it down the long gravel driveway.

Half an hour later, I pulled off the highway into the parking lot for a doughnut shop. I brought a giant cup of Indiana coffee, a couple of glazed doughnuts, and a newspaper back to the car. It was the worst breakfast in the world for a pregnant woman, but I needed comfort. I switched on the dome light and read the paper while I ate.

As I scanned the pages, I noticed a brief paragraph in the "Police Blotter" column.

A fisherman had found the body of Reba Pierce in the White River and notified police. The cause of death had not yet been determined.

Dropping the paper, I leaned against the head rest. Reba, dead? That's why no one had answered her telephone.

I checked the date of the newspaper and tried to figure out the implications. Apparently, no one had seen Reba after my father's memorial service. I was surprised the police hadn't contacted Janet. Should I postpone my trip home and talk to them?

But what could I say? I didn't want to tell the police what she had told me. Even if my mother was still alive, there was no point in digging up the scandal my father had tried so hard to hide. All I knew was that the last time I saw Reba, she was leaving the farm with that handsome old lawyer, Peter Grandheim.

I relaxed. The police didn't need a statement from me. They could ask Mr. Grandheim where Reba had gone after he talked to her.

He knew more about her than I did.

CHAPTER FORTY-THREE

ALL-POINTS BULLETIN

To: Law Enforcement Officers in Zillah, Indiana
Law Enforcement Officers in Burlington County
Indiana State Highway Patrol
From: Brady Szlovak, Zillah Police Department
Approved: Chief, Zillah Police Department
Date: September 8, 1992.
Re: Margaret (Mueller) Kendall, M.D.
The Zillah PD is requesting information leading to the discovery of the whereabouts of the aforementioned individual, Margaret (Mueller) Kendall, M.D.
Age: 66
Height: 5'3"
Hair color: Gray and brown
Birth date: April 4, 1926
Weight: 115 pounds
Eye color: Hazel
Distinguishing characteristics: Burn scar on left cheek
Last seen leaving the Twilite Motel, Zillah, shortly after noon on September 5, 1992. Dr. Kendall was wearing a black leather jacket, denim pants, a plaid shirt, black tooled-leather cowboy boots, and silver earrings.

Dr. Kendall is wanted for questioning in connection with the death of Carmen Torres at the Twilite Motel on September 5, 1992.
There are no known aliases.

Chapter Forty-Four: Maggie

6:00 p.m., Tuesday, September 8, 1992

The elevator inched silently to the top floor of the main building of Community Memorial Hospital. The same butterflies that had danced in Maggie's stomach forty years ago when she rode the elevator to meet the hospital trustees were churning now.

Much had changed, of course. That building had been renovated into a nursing home for elderly patients with dementia and enough money to finance twenty-four-hour care. The Bennett M. Kendall, Sr. Memorial Pavilion was now a clinic for day surgery, but the hospital was still a beacon of hope—and the source of immense personal wealth.

She could only guess how much of that money had flowed into Peter Grandheim's open hands.

She checked her reflection in the elaborate filigree of the brass doors. Her severely tailored dress of pale coral silk gave the illusion of a trim waist and full breasts. Her only jewelry was a plain watch and simple silver earrings that sparkled when she swept the brown-and-gray curls from her shoulders. Even her fingers with their short nails were bare of rings and polish. Her high heels and tiny clutch bag matched her dress in a deeper shade of coral.

When she bought the purse, she'd realized it was big enough to carry the gun Doc had bought for her. Talking to Peter had disturbed a lot of memories she'd buried a long time ago. The gun was one of them.

The elevator door opened. She stepped onto the royal-blue carpet. Peter's secretary had given her clear instructions: "Turn right from the elevator and go to the foyer off the boardroom, which can be reached through the door numbered 1001-A. Mr. Grandheim will meet you at six p.m. sharp. He has another appointment at six-fifteen, so don't be late."

Maggie checked her watch. Ten minutes early, exactly as she had planned, enough time to scope out the situation before she confronted Peter. She needed every advantage she could muster.

She walked slowly down the corridor, her footsteps muffled by the thick carpet. According to the secretary, Peter was hosting a political fund-raiser. Maggie assumed the event was as much to help Peter in his upcoming confirmation hearings before the Senate Judicial Committee as to benefit local candidates.

She had planned to slip past the open door to the boardroom, but was distracted by the sound of a string quartet playing chamber music. Mendelssohn? The tinkle of ice cubes and alcohol-fueled roars of laugher almost obscured the delicate notes. As she glanced into the room, she remembered the cocktail reception at Community Memorial Hospital the night she had met Peter. Nothing important had changed. The power brokers were still old, white men in tailored suits with monogrammed cuffs.

Between the bottles standing on glass shelves, the mirrored bar cast splintered reflections of the room. She had a confused impression of a score of men, almost as many bejeweled women hanging on their arms, and then Peter, unmistakable, talking with a man whom Maggie recognized as a Senatorial candidate.

Peter was taller than she remembered, his hair a silver mane, his tan as deep as ever. He leaned on an ebony cane, but casually, as if it were a fashion statement and not a necessity. Maggie bit her lip. She had underestimated Peter before. She wouldn't do it again.

He turned toward her as if he heard her thoughts, then brushed the candidate aside and hurried toward her, expertly wielding his cane to clear a path through the crowded room.

"Maggie, you came!" He grasped her hands and pulled her close enough to brush his lips against her cheek. He smelled like rum and cigarettes. Maggie felt dizzy, lost in the past. Why couldn't she stay focused around this man? She knew he was responsible for the death of the motel maid, had to be, and yet here he was, holding her as if he had a right to, as if they belonged together.

He stepped back and held her at arm's length. "You haven't changed a bit." His deep blue eyes glittered behind his wire-rimmed glasses.

She laughed as she pushed her hair from her shoulders. "Neither have you. Always the consummate politician."

"No, I mean it. You're as gorgeous as ever. And still making a difference. I understand your clinic in Chicago is a model for delivering obstetrical services in impoverished communities. Have you heard from the Department of Health and Human Services about your plans to expand?"

Maggie rocked back on her heels. "No. How do you know about my grant application?"

Peter winked. "I keep track of my protégés."

"Protégé? You've got to be kidding." Maggie shook herself. He was doing it again, binding them together. She glanced up and saw a couple of well-dressed men walking toward them. She tugged on his arm. "Peter, we have to talk. Not here. Somewhere quiet."

"Of course." He took her elbow with his left hand. "I reserved the room next door."

He opened the connecting door and led Maggie to a tiny

wrought-iron balcony with only enough space for the two of them. A breeze lifted Maggie's hair, but not Peter's mane, which sat as motionless as polished silver.

She grasped the wrought-iron railing. The gritty metal bit into her palms. "Peter, you have to withdraw your name from consideration for the Appeals Court."

He lifted an eyebrow.

"I know you were responsible for the death of that maid. Why did you have to kill her? Because she walked in while you were searching my room for the knife?"

"I was halfway across the continent when she died, making the rounds on Capitol Hill."

He hadn't bothered to ask which maid she was talking about.

She leaned closer. "Peter, I insist."

"You insist? My dear, you, of all people, are in no position to insist."

"If you're talking about Luther's death, you're wrong. I'm perfectly willing to go public with what I did that night, if that's what it takes."

"Why now?"

"I didn't care when you were elected attorney general. I figured the good people of Indiana would kick you out when they learned what they got. But a lifetime appointment to a Federal court? No! That's a whole new ballgame. I won't let it happen."

Peter's eyes were shadowed. "You'd risk losing your daughter?"

"Ellie?" Maggie knew he heard the pain in her voice. "I lost her forty years ago."

"But she's alive and well, married. She looks like you. She may even be happy, in spite of what you did to her. Do you want to risk that?" Peter spoke so softly that she had to lean close to hear him over the noise of the bus that rumbled past on

242

the street below.

"How do you know about Ellie? What do you know?"

Before he could answer, the door to the room crashed open. A cold light flooded the balcony. "Peter? What's going on?"

A tall, blond woman stood in the doorway. Diamonds gleamed at her throat and wrists, but her carefully styled hair, floor-length black gown, and elaborate makeup couldn't hide the extra thirty pounds she carried on her stomach and hips.

Smoothly, Peter turned to Maggie. "Dr. Kendall, may I introduce my wife, Amber Veldyke Grandheim?" He glanced at his wife. "Darling, this is Dr. Margaret Kendall."

"Another one of your *friends,* Peter? I can't believe you'd have the temerity to smuggle her into the hospital. Isn't a two-bit room on the bypass more your style?"

"She's a friend, darling. An old friend and nothing more. And she's leaving. Aren't you, Maggie?" He gave her a discreet push in the small of her back.

"No." Maggie stepped between Peter and his wife, trapping him on the balcony. She edged closer, and he retreated until he was backed against the dusty railing. "What did you mean, I could lose Ellie?"

Peter smiled and grasped his cane. "Get me that knife, Maggie," he said too softly for his wife to hear. "The one I used on Luther. My confirmation hearing starts Wednesday morning. You've got seventy-two hours if you want your girl to live."

He lifted the cane and pushed Maggie aside. Halfway across the room, he reached out to his wife. "Amber, darling, isn't it time we returned to our guests?"

Leaden with fear, Maggie let him go.

CHAPTER FORTY-FIVE:
ELLIE

Wednesday, September 9, 1992

The parking ticket was the last straw.

After Janet had thrown me out of her house at four in the morning, after I had eaten too many doughnuts and drunk too much coffee, after I read about Reba Pierce's death in the *Zillah Courier*, I headed into town, trying to figure out what to do next. In the past few days I had conjured a lot of interesting stories about my mother, but I still didn't know if she was alive or dead.

Time was running out. I had three weeks before my appointment with my obstetrician. I would need a week to drive back to Seattle. Once home, I wanted some quiet time with Joel before we made the decision to end my pregnancy, if that's what we decided to do. End it and tie my tubes. I was too old and too tired to try for a baby again.

Joel would say I couldn't afford to waste any more time chasing my mother's ghost.

I tucked that thought in the back of my mind and decided to make good use of my last hours in Zillah. Before I drove to Chicago, I'd stop by the bookstore. It didn't open until 10:00 a.m., so I parked at a meter on Main Street, the only parked car in the whole darn block, and wandered away looking for a cup of decaffeinated tea. Which I didn't find.

When I returned at 9:45, my car was still the only parked car, but a white ticket waved from my windshield wiper.

Damn. One last middle finger from my good old hometown. Buzzed on sugar, with pregnancy hormones seasoning the stew, I didn't know whether to laugh or cry.

The police station was across the street. I had plenty of time to walk over and save a stamp before the bookstore opened. And time to give someone a piece of my mind.

Stepping inside the Zillah Police Station was like walking into a meat locker. The air conditioner must have been set at 65 degrees. The round-cheeked woman behind the reception desk wore a fluffy pink sweater around her shoulders. She patted her blond perm and adjusted her glasses. "Can I help you, dear?" Midwest friendly, totally disarming.

I couldn't argue with a grandmother about something as dumb as a parking ticket, so I wrote a check for my fine and slid it across her desk.

"We don't take out-of-state checks, hon," she said.

I dug through my wallet. "But I don't have enough cash. What about a credit card?"

"Sorry. Do you know anyone in town who'll cash a check for you?"

"Maybe one of my father's friends. Or his widow. But I don't want to drive all the way back to the farm."

The clerk glanced at my check with the imprinted name. "Dr. Kendall was your father?"

"Yes, ma'am. I came home for his funeral."

"Okay. I think I can make an exception. I'll have you sign a receipt, and then you can leave."

While she searched her desk for the form, I glanced around the ice-cold station, rubbing my bare arms to keep my circulation going. To my right, small windows framed the courthouse square. On my left, a bulletin board held the usual clutter of official notices and "WANTED" posters. I peered more closely at a sheet of paper pinned at eye level and saw—my mother's name. My knees wobbled. I braced my hip against the clerk's desk.

"Miss?" she said. "I found the receipt. You can sign right here."

"Wait a minute. I need to talk to—" I turned and checked the notice again, "—Brady Szlovak about Margaret Kendall."

"Oh, so Mrs. Kendall is one of your people?"

"Yes, ma'am. That's my mother's name. I'm sure there's been some mistake. She passed on a long time ago."

"Let me call Detective Szlovak, hon. You sit down and wait right there."

I perched on a wooden bench against the wall opposite the clerk's desk. She picked up the telephone, had a brief conversation, then busied herself with filing, all the while sending sympathetic glances my way.

Good news and bad news bubbled in my stomach like toads' feet and eye of newt. I didn't need sympathy. I needed answers. The good news? If the cops were searching for my mother, then Reba Pierce was right. My mother was alive.

The bad news? I didn't see how being involved in a murder could be anything but bad news. If my mother had witnessed a murder, why didn't she come forward? Maybe she didn't know what she'd seen. Maybe she was scared.

Maybe she was involved.

No, not possible. I refused to give myself permission to write that story.

"Miss Kendall?" The clerk knuckled her desk to get my attention. "Miss Kendall, Officer Jeswine will escort you to Detective Szlovak's office."

I stood as Jeswine entered the foyer. I may have been forty-two, pregnant, and worried to death, but I wasn't blind—or dead. Jeswine was as cute as they made them with that wholesome, country-boy, tossing-around-bales-of-hay physique that I remembered from high school. He smiled at me and I couldn't help smiling back.

"Follow me, ma'am." He opened a door that led to a wide hallway with a scarred, but newly waxed, linoleum floor.

"Here you go." He opened a door and motioned me into a small office. "Have a seat. Detective Szlovak should be back in just a minute."

Szlovak's office inspired confidence. Every piece of furniture was utilitarian, government-issued, and set exactly square with the corners of the room. Every surface gleamed as if recently dusted, even the top shelf of the bookcase. His desk was bare except for an inbox/outbox combo, a blotter, and his telephone. The window behind his desk was open exactly three inches. Fresh air drifted in and kept the room at a balmy seventy degrees.

I sat in one of the two visitor chairs in front of Szlovak's desk and wondered how to persuade him to tell me what he knew about my mother.

"So, you're Eleanor Roosevelt Kendall."

The voice came from behind me. I pushed myself up from the chair and held out my hand, but by that time Detective Szlovak stood behind his desk.

"Have a seat." Szlovak was every bit as neat, clean, and self-contained as his office. He was about my age, dressed casually in khakis and a blue, short-sleeved shirt, unbuttoned at the neck. I studied his blond buzz cut while he opened a folder on his desk and paged through it.

"When did you last see your mother, Margaret Mueller Kendall?" Szlovak asked, still flipping papers.

I cleared my throat. "About forty years ago."

That got his attention. He shot a steely glance at me. "A murder is not a joking matter, ma'am. Not here in Zillah."

"Not back home in Seattle, either. I wasn't trying to make a joke. I'm searching for my mother. I hoped you could help me find her."

He shut the folder and folded his hands on top. "What's the story?"

"She died in Chicago in 1952. Supposedly. When I was eighteen months old. Last week I found a copy of her obituary in the *Zillah Courier.*"

Szlovak raised his eyebrows but didn't say a word.

"Then, yesterday, at my father's funeral, someone told me she was still alive."

"Who was your informant, ma'am?"

"An old woman, Reba Pierce. I couldn't tell if she was, you know, mentally competent. And then this morning I read in the paper that Reba drowned. On her way home from the funeral. So now I don't know what to do. That's why I wanted to talk to you."

"Did Ms. Pierce say when she'd last seen your mother?"

"No. She said she got Christmas cards from her. That's all."

Szlovak rubbed his chin and made a considering noise. "Well, we have located a Margaret Mueller Kendall who runs an obstetrical clinic in South Chicago under the name of Dr. Mueller. Folks there think she walks on water. She wasn't available for questioning when we contacted the clinic. She hasn't been at work for the last week."

"That's got to be my mother. She worked in a birthing clinic in Chicago before she and my father moved to Zillah. What's wrong with her?"

"Wrong?" Szlovak queried with an eyebrow.

What could I say? Clearly, my mother hadn't been held captive in a dark basement for the last forty years, she wasn't paralyzed or in a mental hospital. Presumably the clinic had a telephone. She could have called Janet for my address any time. Nothing was wrong with her—except she didn't care about me.

When Szlovak figured out I wasn't going to answer, he said, "Your mother is a person of interest in a murder, ma'am. Do you have photo ID?"

"An out-of-state driver's license. Is that good enough?"

"It'll do." He opened a desk drawer and pulled out a tape recorder. "I'd like to interview you about your mother and about your interaction with Reba Pierce. I'll need to make a record of the interview. Is that okay with you?"

"No."

I wanted him to shut up so I could think. My mother, alive, hadn't tried to find me, hadn't come to my father's funeral, hadn't done anything except get herself mixed up in a murder.

In that moment, my whole understanding of the world shifted. I had spent my whole life yearning for my mother. And now, when I found out she was still alive, I discovered that she didn't want to be found. Not by me.

And my father?

Maybe I had misjudged him. True, he'd been cold, self-absorbed, critical. But he hadn't abandoned me.

Suddenly I didn't want to find my mother anymore. I wanted to apologize to my father. I wanted to tell him I loved him. I wanted to turn the clock back exactly five days.

Szlovak leaned forward in his seat. "Do I have your permission to tape record our discussion?" he asked again.

"No. I don't want to get mixed up in your murder investigation. I need to get back to Seattle. And I don't know anything anyway." I stood up. "Sorry to have wasted your time."

Before Szlovak could answer, I barreled out of his office. I race-walked through the lobby and out the door with only a brief glance at the clerk. I needed to go home. My father said he'd spent his life protecting my mother. And what had it gotten him? As far as I could see, nothing but grief.

249

I had enough grief of my own. I didn't need to borrow any more.

Especially not from a ghost.

CHAPTER FORTY-SIX:
PETER

Peter sat on the dust-covered chicken crate in the hayloft of Bennett Kendall's barn and nudged Maggie's leg with the toe of his shoe. She still wasn't moving.

Shit. If he'd had more time with her, it could have been different—more talk, less violence. There was a certain irony in bringing her to Bennett's barn. They had both struggled so hard to leave haylofts and barns and Zillah behind. He'd been much more successful, although sometimes he wondered if he'd paid too high a price.

Amber, for example. Marrying her had been a sacrifice to the gods of career. She'd delayed him today, calling his Zillah headquarters, shrieking about some damn thing. He'd finally hung up on her, never a good move. She'd call Daddy next and then he'd have to deal with the both of them and he was so damn tired of all their crap.

Because of Amber, he'd gotten to the barn late. When he stepped off the stairway into the hayloft, the boys had Maggie trussed up like a goddamn chicken. They weren't used to dealing with a woman like Maggie, a woman who would sacrifice anything for her principles.

The boys. An Amish kid who'd discovered heroin during rumspringa, and a wetback Mexican. What a pair of losers.

He had made the boys untie Maggie. He'd given her water. He'd let her pee in private behind an armoire with a cracked mirror. Then he'd asked her a simple question: "Where is the knife?"

She wouldn't answer.

The boys wanted to rough her up, so he let them play around a little. He was pretty sure nothing had been broken. When she passed out, he'd sent them after Ellie.

Not that he minded sitting here, waiting for stage two. It was satisfying, almost restful to relax in this dim light, surrounded by boxes, broken furniture, shelves of canned fruit, and listen to Maggie breathe while he decided what to do with her. Sort of like listening to the radio at night before his father finally bought a television.

Sort of like being God.

Peter snorted. Television! The old man had made such a fuss about television. Called it an invention of the devil. And now Peter had a TV in every room of his house, bathrooms included. One more thing Josef Grandheim had been wrong about. Like all his fussing and fuming about that goddamn hospital, about keeping the blacks out.

Of course, the colored cook had been okay with Josef. And black help around the house.

Maggie's fingers twitched.

Now there were as many black families in Zillah as anywhere else, and the whole town was united, up in arms about the Mexicans.

Same song, different verse.

It wasn't Peter's style, fussing and fuming about things that didn't matter. He spent his energy on the important stuff. That's why he was in line for the Federal Appeals Court. Because he kept his eye on the ball. Only one thing stood between him and his goal: Maggie, a sixty-five-year-old woman with a forty-year-old grudge.

He would have to use a knife on Maggie. After that night

with Luther, it had taken him a long time to get used to the feel of a knife again, to hold one without feeling shaky, without smelling phantom blood.

Post-traumatic stress was his guess. He'd cured it his own way, no psychiatrist involved. The party bosses might pay lip service to men who achieved great things despite a physical handicap, but they didn't want their Federal judges twitching on the bench. Peter had made himself into exactly what they wanted.

Maggie stirred again. Her eyes were closed, but she might be trying to fake him out. It didn't matter. He was willing to sit here, anticipating, until the boys brought Ellie.

Then the fun would really begin.

How could he get the maximum value out of Ellie? He didn't want her to see Maggie right away. No fun there.

He studied the hayloft and spotted a nice little dark corner. It had possibilities. Maggie tied and gagged in that corner would see everything he did to Ellie. Everything.

He stood up and rubbed his arms and shoulders, enjoying the feel of his well-defined muscles. Years of working out had given him tremendous strength in his upper torso. Despite his bad leg, he could do almost everything he wanted. It was merely a question of applying the proper leverage.

He allowed himself a small smile. The proper leverage. He loved that term. He'd spent a long time perfecting his levers, had built a whole series of them, enough levers to lift himself onto the Federal bench and from there, if his luck held, onto the Supreme Court.

Too bad Maggie wouldn't see it happen. What an asset she would have been. He remembered her standing next to Amber in the boardroom at Community Memorial. Maggie—slim and elegant, still utterly desirable. And his wife? She might be twenty years younger, she might spend a fortune on upkeep, but she had a sour soul. And it showed. Amber had been a good enough lever in her time. She'd brought him Daddy's money, his status, and his connections.

Should he dump Amber? A sweet fantasy, but he pushed it aside. Right now he had only one thing on his mind. Burying all traces of the murder, of his tie to Luther's death, of his boys' visit to Maggie's motel room. Incompetents. Killing the maid, shooting that damn dog, but not coming back with the knife.

Leaving it up to Peter to bury everything that might interfere with the smooth operation of his final set of levers.

The final lever, his nomination to the Federal Appeals Court, had been announced at a fund-raising dinner in Indianapolis. If only his old nemeses from Harvard had still been alive to see it. Professor Lawson, who had tried to make a fool of him in constitutional law, and Professor Jacobson, ditto for torts.

He'd gotten even with them, better than even. It hadn't been only Harvard. It had been all the little moments: shoved on the playground, ridiculed because of his limp, scorned by the returning GI Joes, pushed so far down the totem pole that even a scumbag like Luther Pierce—

Luther had known about Sadie.

He had to silence Luther before Senator Jenner found out, before Peter's only chance to grab the brass ring, to become a power broker in the great state of Indiana, was blown to hell.

A car squealed to a stop beside the barn.

Ellie.

Time to make things happen.

Peter grabbed Maggie by the arms and dragged her to the dark corner. He sat her up, her back braced against the wall. She'd see everything if she opened her eyes. She'd hear everything no matter what.

The moveable stairway creaked. The boys were bringing Ellie

othing much." Peter tightened his grip on my arm.

ntie her this minute."

studied me. "Don't be stupid."

hat do you want?" My voice wavered. I clamped my low
etween my teeth. I had to stay calm. I had to work o
ructing a scene where a happily-ever-after ending was sti
le, where my mother and I could walk away from the
flag down a passing buggy, and drive into the sunset. "I'll
atever you say."

at's better." Peter glanced at the stairway. A short, stocky
with brown skin had joined the Amish guy at the top of
airs. They shifted their weight restlessly as if they itched to
me against the wall. Like comic burglars in a French farce,
lasped miniature penlights in their huge hands.
ir guns were real though.

downstairs and watch the doors." Peter jerked his head
stairway. "Get going. And remember, no overhead lights."
uld have told him my father's barn was so tightly caulked
othing less than a mercury vapor lamp would be visible
he outside. But I didn't. I preferred the image of those
rks stumbling around in the dark.

that a good idea? You might need some help." The short,
lar guy leaned over the thin railing and shot a wad of
o to the cement below. It landed with a wet smack.
ching me, Peter said, "I've got an old lady and a pregnant
think I can manage."

he men banged down the moveable stairway, the platform
top bounced against the floor of the hayloft. I steadied
by holding one of the wooden roof supports and peered
e edge. Below me, the men were barely visible, outlined
beams from their small flashlights.
n't shoot the snakes," I called down. "My father keeps

up. She was arriving right on time, a lamb ready for slaughter.

He stepped to the edge of the hayloft, ready to start the show.

Really, does it get any better than this?

CHAPTER FORTY-SEVEN:
ELLIE

Still stewing about my mother, I got into my car and fastened my seatbelt. I glanced into the rear-view mirror and saw a tall man with a clean-shaven face and straw hat pointing his gun at the back of my head.

"Let's go," he said. "Drive to Kendall's farm."

"Who are you? What's going on? Why go there?"

I looked around for help, but the street was still deserted. The police station slumbered in the sunshine like a fat white cat.

The man yanked on the seatbelt until it tightened against my throat. "Drive. Don't talk." He moved the gun so the barrel pressed against the right side of my stomach. So it pointed at my baby.

My baby. In that instant I made the decision I'd come to Indiana to think about.

No one was going to kill my baby. Not the guy with the gun, not my obstetrician, not Joel, not me.

And that decision meant I would follow the gunman's instructions to the letter. I started the car and pulled away from the curb, thinking furiously.

I had seen him before. He had been one of the Amish bachelors who'd loaded their plates with fried chicken and apple pie at my father's funeral.

Knowing he was Amish didn't help.

Whoever told him to kidnap me had a hold on him more

important than God.

He told me to stop the car next to my father['s]
me into the barn and up the moveable stair[way]
pushed me off the platform before I could
jumped the narrow gap and stumbled on t[he]
the loft. The smell of dry hay rose up and em[...]

Peter Grandheim waited in the middle of t[he]
it hadn't been for his mane of silver hair [and]
glasses, in the dim light he could have been [...]
half his age. His tight-fitting tracksuit show[ed]
torso, but his steel-toed, shit-kicker boots hin[...]
purpose. He tapped a Maglite against his thi[gh]

"I heard you were hunting for your moth[er]."
flashlight, Peter motioned toward a shad[ow]
against the north wall. "There she is."

"Oh my God." I took a step toward her.

My mother? Here? Alive?

The figure stirred and suddenly I was t[...]
crying with a two-year-old's voice. "Momm[y, is it]
you?"

She whimpered. A hand clamped on my [...]
I clawed at Peter's fingers. He held me tig[ht]
the shadow in the dark. "Let me go," I crie[d]

"We've got business first."

"I want to see her."

Peter let the flashlight beam wash into t[he]
you want."

Tiny, fragile, old. That was my first impr[ession]
next, a dirty white rag stuffed into her mo[uth ...]
her head. And her eyes, deep brown pools [...]
fitted dress. Then I realized her hands w[ere]
back and her ankles bound with ropes.

"What have you done to her?"

them in the barn to hunt for rats."

"Mierda." One of the men stumbled against the tractor.

I caught Peter's eye and grinned as if we shared a joke. I figured a smile would unnerve him more than snakes.

"How did you find out I'm pregnant?" I asked, as if we were making small talk at a cocktail party.

"Reba Pierce."

"Oh." We listened to his men get into position, one near the east door and one near the west. I considered my options. Even if I overpowered Peter, I still had to get past the guards.

The beam of Peter's Maglite bounced off his glasses and turned his eyes into blank, motionless pools. Shoving me forward, he aimed the flashlight beam at my mother.

"I want that knife now. Luther's knife."

Her eyes rolled wildly in her pale face. She shook her head.

"I don't know anything about a knife." I stepped between them. "But she can't talk with a gag in her mouth."

My mother banged her shoes on the floor. Her sheer stockings were full of snags and runs as if she'd been chased through a cornfield.

Maybe she had.

When Peter looked at her, she made emphatic, meaningless sounds.

"She can't talk unless you take off the gag," I said again.

"Don't move or I'll shoot you." Peter stuck the flashlight into a joint in the rafters and positioned it so the beam lit the loft like a small, cold moon. Then he reached into his jacket and pulled out a Swiss Army knife.

My blood froze.

He opened the knife and walked to my mother, limping noticeably.

Where was his cane? He had it at the funeral. Could I use it to club him? I scanned the hayloft but didn't see it.

He lifted Maggie into a standing position and squeezed her chin between his fingers. He pressed the blade of the pocketknife flat against her cheek. Her face turned white. He pulled the blade away. It left a red dent in her skin. He leaned closer and examined her intently, like a lover trying to memorize her features.

"Don't make me hurt you again," he said.

She cowered against the wall. My breath caught in my throat.

With the point of the blade, as thin and sharp as any scalpel, he carved a shallow X below her eye across the red scar on her cheekbone. She flinched. A scream gurgled in her throat. He held her fast. Blood oozed from the cut.

Peter licked the point and moved the pocketknife toward her again.

I lunged. He whirled and kicked me with his boot.

I hit the floor. He kicked my face. My nose cracked. Blood spurted. Pain shot through my skull. I covered my face with my hands and tried to stand. My knees buckled.

Peter hauled me to my feet. He shoved me against the wall next to my mother, then slipped the pocketknife between her cheek and the gag. He sliced the fabric. She shook her head, spit, and the gag fell to the floor. It was the size and shape of a dead rat. She bent over and gasped for breath—long, wheezing, shuddering gasps.

"Hold her up, Ellie." Peter jerked his head. "Now."

I put my arm around her waist. She leaned against me. I don't know what I expected to feel. A rag doll? A broken toy? But her body was a coiled spring. She smelled of fear and wild roses. Her hands were still behind her back, but she stroked my forearm with cool fingers. She'd managed to work the knot loose. I kept my face blank despite the fierce drumbeat of adrenaline that rocked my body.

"So you're going to be a grandmother, Maggie." Peter

smirked. He stepped closer and waved his pocketknife in my face.

Without releasing my mother, I knocked his hand away. He grabbed my wrist and clamped my arm against the wall. He ran the knife blade down my cotton shirt from the hollow of my throat to the waistband of my jeans. The fabric fell open, leaving a gap of bare skin and a long red cut that burned like crazy.

I tried to wrench my arm away, but it was impossible. I couldn't escape Peter without abandoning my mother.

"Little Ellie's going to have a baby," Peter said. "It's right about here."

He held the point of the knife below my sternum. I screamed. I felt a pinprick and then a warm trickle of blood. Maggie whimpered, but her body coiled more tightly than ever. Her fingers squeezed my wrist.

She was trying to tell me something.

"Now that I have your full and undivided attention, Maggie, where is it? Where's the knife I used on Luther?"

He twisted his wrist. The blade dug deeper into my skin. I sucked in a shot of fear. The whole world collapsed into that small sharp point which I imagined, suddenly and clearly, poised above my baby's throat.

"Tell me. Or I'll carve her into little pieces starting here." He jabbed again. The barn wavered around me. Blood pulsed down my jeans.

"Don't hurt her," Maggie said, her voice low and throaty. "Please, Peter. I don't know where Luther's knife is."

She kept talking softly, begging, acting scared to death. But her coiled-spring body told me something else. I felt her brace her foot against the wall.

What did she want from me?

I glanced at her. Her eyes flicked downward for an instant. I looked back at Peter and finally understood. He was turned on by her helplessness. As a romance writer, that was my field of expertise.

I pulled the pieces of my shirt away from my breasts and shook my shoulders. I hadn't bought any maternity bras yet. My breasts spilled over the cups of my bra and shimmered in the cold light.

"See something you like?" I whispered to Peter, trying to sound like a woman who'd do anything to stay alive. I yanked my bra down. My nipples were rigid with fear.

A self-satisfied smile played across his mouth. The knife wavered.

Maggie slammed her head into his face.

He grunted and fell backward. His open pocketknife skittered into a dark corner.

Ankles still roped together, hands free, Maggie dove onto Peter's chest and pounded his face with her fists. His glasses shattered. His lip split and splattered his face with blood. I hunted furiously for his cane. I wanted to beat him to death.

"What the fuck's going on up there?" It was the short guy, the Mexican. I ran to the edge of the loft and kicked the stairs away.

They rolled less than a foot. The Mexican bounded up the steps, leaped across the gap, and tackled me. I went down and hit the back of my head. When I came up for air, he was standing over me, his gun pointed at my face. I choked on the blood running from my nose into my throat. I turned my head and spat.

A thud, then someone moaned. I turned over and pushed myself onto all fours. My mother was on the floor, curled into a tight ball. Peter kicked her again. "Where is it? Where's the fucking knife?"

"I have it."

The voice came from behind a stack of hay bales against the

wall. Startled, I looked up and saw a mass of gold and silver curls.

Peter wheeled around and grabbed the gun from the Mexican. I crawled across the floor to my mother and crouched beside her, panting.

"Who's there?" Peter said. "Come out with your hands up."

"Calm down." Janet sounded as sedate as if she were sitting at her desk in the fourth-grade classroom.

Why, in God's name, hadn't she spoken sooner?

I watched Janet slowly walk towards Peter. Pain bit into my abdomen. I cradled my stomach with blood-drenched hands. My placenta might still be intact.

My mother moaned. I pulled her head into my lap and stroked her hair. Sweat and tears flooded her face. I wiped them away with the tail of my shirt, smearing blood across her skin like war paint.

Janet stopped several feet in front of Peter.

"What the fuck are you doing here?" he asked.

"I know where Luther's knife is. I came back to get it, to throw it in the river. When you hauled Maggie up here, I hid behind the hay."

"Where is it?"

Janet pointed to the metal shelves that lined the east wall of the loft and held row upon row of home-canned fruit. "It's in one of those Mason jars. I sealed it up the night Maggie gave it to me. The jar was sterile, so all the evidence should be intact— blood, fingerprints, DNA, everything."

"Get it." Peter's voice cracked.

"I'll need some help." Janet looked around, upended a crate, and sat down gracefully. "There's a lot of jars on those shelves. Also, some more light would be nice."

"For Christ's sake!" Peter jerked his head at the Amish guy

who stood on the platform guarding the stairway. "Find the knife."

"What about them?" he said.

Peter waved his gun in our direction. "They're not going anyplace."

The Amish guy danced across the uneven planks. He grabbed the jars, one by one, and threw them against the wall. They shattered, releasing the smells of summer—sun-ripe tomatoes, cinnamon-spiced applesauce, grape juice as sweet and heavy as a baby's blanket.

Underneath my circling arm, my mother's thin shoulders shook as she wept silently. Her tears soaked into my jeans. My broken nose throbbed, but the bleeding had stopped. I breathed hoarsely though my mouth, gagging on the coppery taste of blood.

A new sound caught my attention, a metallic *thunk*. I looked up.

"Got it!" the Amish guy shouted.

Peter aimed the flashlight where the man pointed. In the middle of it all—pieces of fruit, creeping fingers of purple juice, broken glass that glittered like newly fallen snow—lay a knife, its blade stained black with dried blood.

"Good." Peter stepped back. With the barrel of his gun, he drew a wide circle in the air around Janet, Maggie, and me. "I don't need them anymore. Take care of it."

Chapter Forty-Eight:
Ellie

"Hey, man. You ain't gonna kill her?" The Mexican wasn't asking a question.

With a hoarse chuckle, Peter tossed him the gun. "No way, Jose. You are."

The man caught the gun. He spit noisily and took a step back. The floor boards creaked under his weight.

"Okay, Jose?" Peter wasn't asking a question either.

The man folded his arms over his chest. "My name's not Jose."

"I don't care what you call yourself. I gave you a job. Now do it." Peter turned on his heel and limped toward the moveable stairway.

Janet rose from her overturned crate, shuffled to the wall, touched a beam, and flicked a switch. Light flooded the hayloft.

Peter wheeled around. He shaded his eyes. "What the fuck?"

Janet leaned against the beam.

She's got balls, I thought. The Amish man pointed his gun at her.

My mother shook off my arm and pulled herself into a sitting position.

"You're doing it again, Peter." Janet sounded as if she might waggle a reproving finger under his nose. "Overlooking the obvious."

"The obvious?"

Peter smiled at Janet and sketched a mocking bow. "Madam

teacher, you have the floor."

"It's obvious that your helper here, Mr. I'm-Not-Jose, isn't a killer. I wonder why." She fixed Peter with her steady golden eyes. "You should wonder, too."

We all turned to Not-Jose. A dark flush covered his cheeks.

He pointed at Maggie. "You tell me she has something that belongs to you. Something important. So I say, okay, I help you get your belongings back. You say nothing about killing her."

He waved the gun at Janet and then at me. "Them I don't care about."

I pressed my palms against my stomach as he wrote us off. If he shot me but didn't hit the baby, and they found me in time, Joel could make them keep me alive long enough for my baby to be born. Five months, that's all it would take.

"You know who she is?" Not-Jose jerked his chin toward Maggie. "That's Doc Kendall."

Beside me, Maggie stirred. She wiped her eyes with her fingers. "Isadore, is that you?"

"A reunion. How sweet." Peter slammed his fist against a beam. "So what, amigo?"

"Last winter Doc Kendall delivered my sister's baby back in Chicago. He's my godson. I was there. Man, what a mess. The baby, he's not in the right place. Blood everywhere. The priest comes. He wants to give my sister last rites, but Doc says no. She takes care of everything."

"Oh, for Christ's sake." Peter glanced at his watch. "I don't have time to argue with you, Jose. If you don't have the *cojones* to do your job, give me the gun and get out of here." He dug in his pocket and threw a set of keys to the Amish boy. "You, too. Go downstairs and start the car. And take that goddamn knife with you. I don't want to lose it again."

The Amish boy picked his way through the field of broken glass while Isadore studied Maggie and me.

"It's okay, Isadore," Maggie said. "Peter can't kill me. *Estare bien. Vaya con Dios.*"

I grabbed her shoulder. What was she thinking? He was our only hope. She brushed my hand away.

Isadore hitched up his pants. "Whatever you say, Doc."

He tossed his gun to Peter and walked to the stairway.

Peter fired. One shot. He caught the kid square in the back of his head. It exploded in a fountain of blood and brains.

Isadore fell forward over the edge of the hayloft and hit the floor below like a sack of wet cement.

I screamed and choked on the blood in my throat.

Peter turned and pointed the gun at us. My heart thudded in my chest.

Behind Peter's back, the Amish kid dropped his gun. He sprinted toward the stairway. He kicked the gun he'd dropped, sending it spinning into the center of the loft. He banged down the stairs. Seconds later a car coughed into life.

Over the sound of approaching sirens, I heard something new: a dog yapping.

The car roared away.

Peter swore under his breath.

"Your helper just left," Janet said. "With the knife you used on Luther. The game's over." She held out her hand. "Give me your gun."

Without a word, Peter lifted the barrel and shot her in the face. She fell backwards over the crate. Her eyes were still open and staring, but she was dead.

Bile filled my mouth. I bent over and vomited. Blood and doughnuts spewed across the floor. I lifted my head and wiped my face. My mother started to rise.

"No. Don't move." I held her down.

Peter had nothing left to lose.

But I did. Everything I cared about was still on the table.

"Eat the gun, Peter," I said. "You have only one way out. Take it."

He froze.

Below us, outside the barn, the dog barked again. Someone whistled and the barking ceased. So did the sirens. Another car ground to a stop on the gravel next to the barn.

Peter took two steps toward me. He grabbed my hair and yanked me to my feet. He jabbed the barrel against my stomach. His hand was caked with blood. His body smelled hot with fear. "Get going." He shoved me toward the ladder. "You're my ticket out."

"Peter. Don't!" I heard Maggie stumble and fall.

Peter didn't even glance back. One hand tangled in my hair, the other holding the gun against my stomach, he pushed me forward to the edge of the hayloft.

Below us, the barn door opened. Dawn rolled in. A small black and white dog dragged itself up the ladder.

Maggie cried, "Freckles, stay!"

The dog stopped on the landing and stood there panting. It had one of those ridiculous plastic cones around its head and shaved patches all over its body, highlighted with fine black stitches—funny and horrible, like a circus dog from hell.

"Come out with your hands up." The voice was deep and official. The speaker stood next to the tractor below us.

I couldn't see him, but I heard another car screech to a halt.

Peter jabbed me. "Tell them to call off the damned dog. I want a car." He jabbed me again. "Tell them I have hostages. And two bullets left."

"Tell them yourself, Judge." I spit out the last word.

He lifted the gun and slammed the barrel against my temple. "Don't fuck with me, Ellie. I don't need you. Maggie will do just fine."

Something kicked inside me. My baby? Oh dear God.

"Okay." I took a breath and shouted, "He's got a gun. He'll kill us."

Freckles barked frantically, teeth bared. But he didn't move from the landing.

Voices muttered below us. Someone called through a bullhorn, "Come on down, nice and easy. Hands in the air where I can see them."

Peter growled. He poked me with the gun.

"He'll kill us," I said. "He's going to kill us."

"Tell them I need a car."

I nodded. Leaned forward to peer over the edge of the hayloft. Heard a sound behind me.

Peter's head exploded. Chunks of wet red gelatin showered my body.

The dog went wild.

CHAPTER FORTY-NINE:
ELLIE

After bits of Peter Grandheim rained down on me, I collapsed. The medics took me to the hospital in Zillah where I spent two weeks on bed rest. My husband, the professor, flew in from Seattle. He sat by my bed and read his students' essays to me, grading and correcting as he went along. So typically Joel. His bald head shining under the hospital lights seemed very dear.

"You're going to be a great father," I said. "And you get to be the parent who helps with homework."

He pressed his lips to my hand. "You've got a deal."

By the time I was well enough to give a statement to Detective Szlovak, Peter's family lawyer had concocted a story in which Peter died defending Maggie, Janet, and me from a crazed Mexican, the same Mexican who had killed the motel maid. The ballistics and fingerprint evidence didn't rule out that story. My mother didn't dispute it either, probably because the prosecutor decided Peter's death was an unfortunate consequence of his brave actions rather than a homicide that needed to be prosecuted.

The whole town, maybe the whole state, was busy celebrating the myth of Peter's heroism, and I decided to fall in line. Fortunately, I hadn't mentioned Peter by name during hostage negotiations, if that's what you'd call the ten-minute standoff that ended with Maggie shooting him.

The day Peter was buried, the editor of the *Zillah Courier* wrote a self-righteous opinion piece about America's lax immigration policies, and my mother headed back to her clinic on the south side of Chicago.

None of the local Amish families admitted knowing the boy who had kidnapped me. I assume he disappeared into one of their far-flung communities, taking with him the knife Peter had used to butcher Luther.

What did I learn? I learned a story doesn't have to be true, factually true, to change the course of the world, at least my small portion of the world. I learned that Justice doesn't need Truth either. Peter paid for his crimes with his life. That was justice enough for me.

When I was discharged from the hospital, Joel and I went to Chicago. I dropped him and the last of his students' essays at a coffee shop, drove to my mother's clinic, and parked across the street. I studied the building, a two-story, wood-frame duplex with starched white curtains in the windows. A wrought-iron fence enclosed a small yard, which exploded in a glorious display of zinnias, marigolds, and bachelor buttons. The "Roseland Clinic" sign was small and neatly lettered.

This was the life she had chosen over me.

Four black teenage boys stood on the street corner in baggy jeans and do-rags. Each one wore earphones. They bounced carelessly to the music. I settled into my seat.

At four forty-five, a teenage black girl pushed through the doors of the clinic. She was hugely pregnant. She paused outside the gate and shouted at the boys. One of them detached himself from the group and followed her down the street, moving awkwardly in her wake. I decided he was the baby's father.

At six-thirty, the boys drifted away and the streetlights flickered on. Many of them were broken, but the one outside the birthing clinic cast a bright yellow circle on the sidewalk. A few minutes later, my mother walked out of the clinic. She shut the door behind her and passed through the iron gate. She paused under the light.

Her gray hair was caught in an untidy roll at the top of her head. She wore a white lab coat with a stain across the front and sensible shoes. She glanced at me and raised her eyebrows.

I opened my car door and climbed out.

Stepping into the street, I saw my eyes in her face, my nose, my mouth.

"Ellie," she said. "Come inside. Let's see how that baby's doing."

"He's fine," I answered. "And his name is Bennett."

ABOUT THE AUTHOR

Award-winning author **Judy Dailey** grew up on an 80-acre organic farm in Indiana. Now she lives on a 1,200-square-foot urban farm in Seattle, Washington, with four chickens, a dog, and her husband, the writer Tom Argentina. A graduate of Bryn Mawr College, Judy earned an MBA from the University of Washington and a certificate in compost management. She has been a pilot, skydiver, spelunker, bicyclist, skier, and night-time sailor. She managed a multi-million-dollar grant fund for affordable housing. She handcrafts artisan salami, beer, and ricotta cheese. Her first mystery in the Urban Farm Series, *Animal, Vegetable, Murder,* was published in 2013. Her second book, *Forget You Ever Knew Me,* is a suspense novel set in 1952. Follow Judy at http://www.judydailey.com.